Also by Robert N. Chan
From Indigo Sea Press

girl

No Such Agency

indigoseapress.com

BASED ON A FALSE STORY

BY

ROBERT N. CHAN

Deep Indigo Books
Published by Indigo Sea Press
Winston-Salem

Deep Indigo Books
Indigo Sea Press
PO Box 26701
Winston-Salem, NC 27114

For information regarding bulk purchases of this book, digital purchase and special discounts, please contact the publisher at indigoseapress@gmail.com

Cover design by Pan Morelli
Manufactured in the United States of America
ISBN 978-1-63066-474-9

To all those who want Trump to resign
so he can spend less time with his family.

I
The Blood-Dimmed Tide is Loosed

When Mexico sends its people, they're not sending their best.... They're sending people that have lots of problems, and they're bringing those problems...They're bringing drugs. They're bringing crime. They're rapists. Donald J. Trump June 16, 2015

I had a bigger problem than the longshot possibility that a hate-mongering former client would become a major party's presidential candidate. I was bored. People weren't crawling all over each other to be represented by a sixty-eight-year-old lawyer. Clients and referral sources had retired or worse. Undoubtedly, the writing was on the wall, but with my failing eyesight I couldn't see it.

My wife, Lauren, claimed I was dangerous when bored. I hoped she was right; at least that would be interesting.

Unable to come up with anything dangerous that I could do without hurting myself, I contacted former clients, acquaintances and adversaries, with whom I hadn't communicated in over a year—generally for a good reason. I hoped that if I implicitly reminded them that I was still practicing law with undimmed brilliance, my name would pop into their heads when someone asked if they knew of a good litigator or if they themselves had such a need. In the past I'd noticed a positive correlation between looking for business and getting it. However, that correlation seemed merely coincidental, as cases rarely came from where I'd directed my efforts, and I hated that, after all these years of practicing law, I still had to market myself.

"Hi, Madelyn, it's Matt Bloom." I tried to infuse my voice with a happy lilt. "We haven't spoken for a while, so I'm calling to touch base, see how you're doing and see if there's anything I can help you with."

The lilt failed to materialize. Maybe my chilly tone was okay, though. Clients didn't want a happy litigator; they wanted a psychopath, who billed with a light hand. Even the light hand part wasn't necessary; they loved to brag about how their lawyers were ripping them off.

"Oh, hi," she sounded as unenthusiastic as I felt, and while vaguely familiar, her voice rang no Madelyn bells. No surprise. I hadn't spoken to her in five years, and our conversations then had been neither exciting nor memorable.

I wanted to hang up, but I rarely did what I wanted and wouldn't have gotten to where I was if I had. Perhaps that meant I should've changed my ways, but I also rarely did what I should have.

"Recent cases having concluded, and with no one looking to embark on new ventures until after the election, I'm using my free time reconnecting with old friends, remind them that I'm still alive."

I'd tried to make the last phrase sound like lighthearted banter, but at my age there was a statistically significant probability that I'd have gone gently into that good night, or at least retired, which for me would have been like being dead.

"Yeah, the election," Madelyn said. "'The blood-dimmed tide is loosed, and everywhere the ceremony of innocence is drowned.'"

I knew times were bad, but I had no idea they'd become so desperate that Madelyn would be driven to quoting W. B. Yeats. When I represented her and the petrochemical company she'd inherited from her father, *Fifty Shades of Gray* had been the furthest she'd ventured into the world of literature, and she'd barely made it through the first five shades.

"'The best lack all conviction, while the worst are full of passionate intensity,'" I said, never one to miss an opportunity for gratuitous pedantry.

Her modest chuckle sent a shaft of sunlight through the dark clouds of my mood, even as it illuminated how desperate I'd become for even a few watts of approval.

"So, Matt Bloom, I've seen from the occasional pieces in the *Wall Street Journal* and *Bloomberg News* that you've notched some impressive wins. You've become a veritable giant killer. Big step up from your days representing Hair Hitler."

How had she known I'd represented Trump? Viewing it as a shameful blot on my otherwise stain-free integrity and being subject to a non-disparagement/non-disclosure agreement, I'd avoided discussing the experience. Also, it was strange that she'd bothered to follow my career.

Based on a False Story

"I've been fortunate to win cases on slow business news days," I said. "How have you been?"

"Succeeding beyond my wildest dreams. If the trend continues, I'll be greater than Dangerously Deranged Donald thinks he is."

I'd googled her company's annual report before calling. A thirty percent drop-off in sales and an eight-figure loss didn't seem to be steps down the road to greatness. Perhaps she'd changed her medication.

"That's wonderful."

I'd run out of things to say and was concerned that the conversation, like most I'd been recently involved in, would degenerate into tiresome handwringing about the election.

I was about to sign off, when she asked, "How are Jason and Lauren?"

"Doing well. Jason's going into his sophomore year at Stanford. He's in China for the summer, studying Mandarin and Asian girls. Lauren's a docent at the Met. They're both busy, healthy and happy."

My turn to ask about her family, but I knew next to nothing about her personal life. Indeed, I was surprised she even knew I was married and had a child. I didn't discuss non-legal matters with clients unless they'd invited the conversation, and Madelyn had treated me like an over-paid servant, nowhere near her social equal.

Lauren claimed that my reluctance to engage in small talk was but one of many indications of my presence on the Asperger's spectrum. I suspected that most wives believed that of their husbands. Maybe, if I'd had more empathy, though, I'd have been better at judging the extent to which I lacked empathy.

"Last we spoke you'd just been through a thermonuclear divorce," I said.

"Well, I'm no longer radioactive."

I chuckled.

"So, Matt, any new fun cases?"

Fun cases, there was an oxymoron. But I'd just had one that, while not all that fun and not even quite a case, qualified as amusing.

"A few weeks ago, an inmate telephoned me from the Manhattan Psychiatric Center, claiming to have been sent back in time to kill the *orange horror clown*. She called me because, in her time, I was one of the *Twelve Revered Martyrs*."

"And?" she asked, sounding fascinated. I'd never heard Madelyn sound fascinated by anything she hadn't herself said.

"I got her released due to a defect in the medical certification that had led to her involuntary confinement."

"We can only hope she succeeds in her mission."

"I wouldn't go that far."

"The time may come when it's him or us," she said, with stunning vehemence. Before I could respond, she changed the subject. "Did this visionary potential mercy killer pay you?"

"She promised to pay me in Federation Bitcoins once she returned to the time from which she'd traveled and received her fee for the successful completion of her assignment."

"If you need help monetizing that promise, I know people who know people."

"Thanks, but I probably blew it by notifying the Secret Service. The agent, though, seemed unconcerned. She told me the mental hospitals have been filling up with such self-styled time-travelers."

Madelyn's full-throated laugh brought a smile to my face, even as I realized my comment hadn't been all that funny. One of my main criteria for choosing friends, and for that matter my wife, was that they got my sense of humor and enjoyed my stories.

"In all the time I represented you, I don't recall you ever laughing. I'm delighted you sound so happy. It's turned out to be quite nice talking to you, Madelyn."

"My sense of fair play requires that I disclose to you that I'm not Madelyn. You dialed the wrong number."

"Oh, I'm sorry." The number shown on the screen on my phone bore little relation to the one I'd intended to dial. "But how did you know—"

"About your litigation wins and the name of your wife and son? I could have called upon my psychic powers, but instead I used Google."

I couldn't have found all that information on Google while talking on the phone—I wasn't even the only New York attorney named Matthew Bloom—but as computers are programed to malfunction when operated by people over sixty-five, perhaps someone younger could have.

"But if you knew that I had the wrong number, why—"

"I'm a professional tease."

4

"I wouldn't have thought there'd be much of a market for people in that line of work."

"You'd be surprised. Look how well Agent Orange is doing," she said.

"His success proves the old adage that no one ever went broke underestimating the taste of the American public." These days all conversations turned to Trump if allowed to continue long enough. "No other election has affected me so emotionally."

"True for all of us, and we're barely beyond the Beer Hall Putsch stage." I grimaced at her gratuitous Hitler analogy. "In any event, I enjoyed talking to you. I hope you have at least as good a conversation with the real Madelyn."

"What's your name, by the way?" I asked, but she'd hung up.

Just as well.

I was about to call the real Madelyn, but my heart wasn't in it. I checked a variety of Internet news sites and found them all dispiriting.

I hit redial.

"Matt, you did it again."

"This time on purpose. Since my son left for college, I've been on a campaign to expand my circle of friends and business contacts. And…well, I enjoyed our conversation and you said you did as well so…." My voice rose an octave like it used to when I'd ask a girl out in high school. "Maybe we could meet for coffee. I'm not coming on to you. As you know I'm married but—"

"You're speaking very quickly, as if you're nervous." She ran her words together in exaggerated imitation of what I sounded like. At least I hoped it was exaggerated.

"Thank…you…for…pointing…that…out," I said.

"How's that campaign going? Better than Hillary's, I hope."

"Humiliating and frustrating, but when I embark on a project, I stick with it."

"They say insanity is doing the same thing over and over again and expecting different results."

"Einstein said that, but he devoted the better part of his life to seeking the Grand Unified Theory without success."

"Nice idea getting together, but I don't drink coffee."

I felt as if I'd been punched in the solar plexus—an uncharacteristic overreaction that harkened back, again, to how I'd felt when shot down by a girl in high school. *Does anyone recover from high school?*

"What do you drink?"

"Alone."

"Well, okay then," I said.

"Matt, come on, I'm a professional tease. We take a hypocritical oath, 'First do some harm'."

No clever come-back occurred to me, although I knew it would after I hung up.

"I very much look forward to meeting you," she said, then hung up.

I look forward to meeting you? WTF, you turned me down.

I pushed through my calls to old acquaintances. To my surprise, I enjoyed a number of the conversations and made several follow-up lunch or drink appointments.

I replayed in my mind my telephone conversations with the professional tease and still didn't understand why they'd so unsettled me. I'd felt almost as if I'd been flirting with her. Of course, I hadn't been, but if my intentions had been innocent why had I been so nervous when I'd asked her for coffee and so upset when she'd turned me down?

Perhaps I'd call her again and find out.

Bad idea.

When I got home, I found Lauren's friend, *Huffington Post* senior reporter Emily Bouvant, lurking in the foyer.

"Hey, Matt, I'm delighted I got a chance to see you," she said. "I was afraid I'd miss you."

I kissed Lauren hello and hung up my hat in the hall closet.

"Good to see you, too, Emily," I lied. "Sorry it has to be so brief, but I need a shower."

I stepped toward the hallway that led to the bedroom.

"Emily has a favor to ask you," Lauren said, stating the obvious. Then turning so Emily wouldn't see her face, she mouthed something I couldn't fully make out but understood to be along the lines of, "Sorry, Honey. I didn't mean to sandbag you but…you know."

Yes, I did know.

"Well, I'll leave the two of you alone," Lauren said, as she walked toward the bedroom. "I need to call Jason. With the time difference, he's just getting up and I want to catch him before he starts his day."

She closed the door behind her.

I neither led Emily into the living room nor offered her a drink. Since Trump announced his candidacy, I'd been stalked by reporters seeking dirt on my former client, and some took my "no comment" with more grace than others. The only grace Emily had any familiarity with had married a prince and gone to live in Monaco.

"Matt, why have I recently gotten the feeling that you're avoiding me?" she said.

"I assume that's a rhetorical question."

"You have to tell me something about your representation of Trump. You owe me big time. It's time to pay up," she said. "Knowing you, you must have some priceless anecdotes." Emily had a good basis to believe that I owed her a favor. Early in my career, when I was a senior associate at a large law firm with little prospect of being elevated to partnership, I'd won a series of interlinked cases in which I'd represented investors against major financial institutions. Emily, then a junior reporter for *Bloomberg News*, had reported on my victories and written a laudatory story about me. That was before the age of the Internet, but the wire services picked it up. On the strength of that good publicity, I started my own law firm. Not only that, but a few years after that, she'd fixed up Lauren and me on a blind date.

As far as I was concerned, though, my debt to her had been extinguished a decade later, when she'd breached my confidence. I'd given her an off-the-record, deep-background statement in connection with a class action I was handling against a Fortune 500 company that had been polluting the Hudson River. She published what I'd told her, attributing it to *an unnamed litigator*, but in the context of her story I was easily identified as the speaker. As if that wouldn't have been bad enough, she'd edited my comment so it appeared that I'd disclosed a major weakness in my case. I lost my position as lead lawyer for the class and became the subject of an ethical complaint—ultimately dismissed but a blot on my otherwise spotless record. Emily won some sort of award for her story, and that became the stepping stone to her current position. Always intensely loyal to me, Lauren cut her off.

Lately though, Emily had been reaching out to her, and I'd been encouraging her to bury the hatchet. Lauren had given up her high-powered consulting career to be a stay-at-home mom, and Jason's going off to college in California left a big hole in her life—even if by becoming a docent leading tours at the Metropolitan Museum of Art, she'd adjusted much better than I had. These days we all needed all the friends we could get.

"You know how much I want to help," I said, sure that she knew exactly how much. "I can't though. It's not just attorney/client privilege, but also I signed a non-disclosure agreement."

"That's got to be unusual," Emily said.

"I don't know what's usual," I said, meaning yes. "Trump and I mutually agreed to part ways, and that's how we decided to do it."

"Did he pay you? Some attorneys I've been speaking to have told me they'd had trouble collecting from him, problems preparing him to testify due to his lack of focus and concerns about him lying under oath. The piece I'm writing will give them valuable publicity. You could use some good press. Indeed, any press."

"He and I resolved the loose ends of our affiliation in a mutually satisfactory manner," I said parroting what the agreement permitted me to say.

Having neglected to pay my bills, he'd owed me a great deal of money, and his dishonesty was threatening to damage my reputation. I couldn't just dump him, though, because I had an ethical duty to put my clients' interests ahead of my own. So, he and I had a difficult negotiation—made easier by his susceptibility to flattery and his delusion that he was the world's greatest negotiator—while I simultaneously negotiated with his adversaries to settle his cases. Ultimately, we reached an agreement, and I intended to honor it in thought and deed.

"So there were loose ends?" Her smile reminded me that when chimpanzees, our closest genetic relatives, bare their teeth it's a sign of aggression.

"Every relationship has them. Maybe one day you and I will tie up ours," I said. "Emily, I don't mean to be off-putting, but I just got home and I'd like to take my suit off, shower and then relax with my wife. Sorry I couldn't be more helpful."

In case my brush-off had been too subtle for her, I opened the front door, and called out, "Lauren, Emily's leaving. Anything you need to say to her before she goes?"

"You must've met some interesting people in his circle," Emily said feet firmly planted in the foyer, while I looked longingly at the bedroom door. "Surely there's no reason you can't talk about *them*."

"The non-disclosure agreement was very broad." Not so broad, though, that I couldn't talk about Trump associates.

"Please, Matt. I know I overstepped, but that was a long time ago."

"Okay, fine." The woman was harder to get rid of than herpes. "As a gesture of good faith, I'll tell you one thing. I once had lunch with, Jared, his then son-in-law to be. He was a nice fellow, laughed at my jokes, didn't say much."

"That's all?" She raised her meticulously trimmed, tweezed and tinted eyebrows.

"That was a huge deal, as far as I was concerned. My sense of humor is my favorite quality."

"There's got to be something else you can tell me. Deep background, off the record, I promise."

"I've heard that before."

"Come on, Matt. I've explained that over and over. That was my editor's mistake."

I rolled my eyes, and we settled into a staring contest.

Their recovering friendship was good for Lauren, and I didn't want to antagonize Emily by tossing her out.

"Here's something that might be helpful, Trump had a very attractive receptionist/assistant, Margarette, some name like that. I'm not so good with names or faces," Odd that she'd popped into my head; I hadn't thought of her in years. "I heard she was going to appear in *Penthouse,* but I never knew if she actually did. If you find her and get her to talk, she'll have some good stories. She managed his calendar, did a variety of other things for him as well, some of which might have been in the legal gray area. He referred to her as his *girl Friday, Saturday, too.* It was a small office, people didn't have precisely defined tasks. I've no doubt that she saw a lot, much of which skirted the law. She seemed to know everything that was going on in the office."

"Interesting. You have anything more than a first name?"

"I'm not even positive of that, could've been Margorie, Maryanne. I'm pretty sure, though, that it started with an M."

Her turn for an eye-roll.

"Describe her, at least."

"I only actually met her twice and didn't look all that closely out of concern that my glance would degenerate into an inappropriate gaze. First time I saw her, she had long black hair worn in a French twist. The next time, her hair was red and worn down, and she looked like a different person. Her eerie violet eyes didn't change, though. Under other circumstances her surgical enhancements would have caught my attention."

"Perhaps, they're the reason you don't remember her face so well."

"I'm not good with faces," I repeated, which was true, but, as loath as I was to admit it, Emily might've had a point—those enhancements would have been attention drawing even without the inappropriate *décolletage*.

"And Trump was doing her?" Emily leaned forward, eyes wide, encouraging.

"Not in my presence." I smiled. "And not to my knowledge."

He'd hinted broadly that there was a sexual side to their relationship—"She'd do anything for me, and I do mean anything"—but he could have been talking about something other than sex or implying something that wasn't true.

"You may not remember names or faces but your recollection of conversations is fucking lapidary. Tell me about one conversation you had with her, and I'll let you go. I promise I won't quote you."

"Deal. I'd said something along the lines of 'Hi, it's Matt, Bloom. Is he there?' And she replied, perhaps not in these exact words, 'Tied up, but I'll leave him a message.'"

"Matt, it comes so naturally that you really don't have to *try* to be an asshole."

I again looked longingly toward the bedroom. Why hadn't Lauren come to my rescue?

"Okay, one real conversation, but that's all." I underlined my statement with a horizontal swipe of my hand. "Indeed, it's the only actual conversation I recall, and I'm surprised I remember that one. On the way out of Trump's office, I mock congratulated her on her upcoming magazine appearance, and she pouted rather fetchingly and said something along the lines of 'Just part of the job, but what he has me doing with my clothes off is less disgusting than what he has me doing with them on. Still, I take comfort from the fact that I'm not as big a whore as you are, and I have far better future prospects.'"

"So he *was* boffing her?"

"I thought she was talking about the photo shoot, but maybe if you track her down, she'll tell you something different."

Stupid mistake mentioning her. All I needed was for Emily to think I hinted that the woman had a possible sexual harassment claim, even if the statute of limitations had run.

"Thank you." She smiled. "Just one more thing, and I promise—"

"Emily, that's all I'm going to say. I'm tired. It's been a hard day, and I want to spend time with my wife."

"You're no fun." She pouted in a cute way, even if it wasn't age-appropriate.

"That's the majority opinion. Strange, since I think of myself as endlessly entertaining."

Holding her phone, Lauren emerged from the bedroom—finally.

"Really great of you to stop by, nice surprise," she said to Emily, in a tone that her friend might have found convincing. "Let me know when you and Jim"—her real estate mogul husband who was never free for a meal or anything else and, according to a running joke between Lauren and me, might not have actually existed—"are available for dinner." She handed me the phone. "Jason wants to speak to you."

On my way into the bedroom with the phone, I heard Lauren say to Emily, "Matt and Jason may be on of a while, then we've got to rush out to meet some people for dinner."

"So what's doing Jason?" I said, after shutting the bedroom door.

"The usual."

"Well, that's quite informative."

He'd spent a mere three days at home between the end of his school year and the start of his Mandarin study program in Beijing. In our call the previous week, he'd reported, sort of, on his room, *good,* his roommate, *fine, same as he was a few weeks ago in school,* his courses *good,* the food, *okay, what you'd expect.* Although I'd have liked more details, he sounded upbeat and happy, which was all I really cared about.

We often had exhilarating conversations. This one, though,

wasn't going to be one of them. When he wasn't in a communicative mood, there was nothing I could do to draw him out.

Still, I was about to make an effort when he said, "I don't have time to talk. I need to go out for a run before it gets too hot and the air gets too brown. Mommy said you needed rescuing from a vicious reporter, so I'm rescuing you."

An only child, he shared everything with Lauren. I was his pal, we tweeted about current events and spoke on the phone once a week, but he rarely confided in me or asked my advice.

"Just how are you? How are you classes? The other students? Your roommate?"

"Great. Everything's great, really." He sounded happy, which made me happy. "I'm glad I decided to do this, rather than an internship."

"Well, okay, thanks for the rescuing. I love you. Talk over the weekend?"

"Sure."

Even when our conversations failed to get off the ground, they improved my mood and this chat had been no exception.

"Sorry about that, Honey," Lauren said, after seeing Emily out. "But you know how aggressive she can be."

"I'm sorry I couldn't have been more helpful, but—"

"Emily understood. She respects your integrity."

"Working with Trump wasn't an experience I like to dwell on."

"You've made that clear."

"Actually, I might have slipped, told her more than I should have, mentioning Trump's receptionist-slash-assistant."

I'll talk to Emily, make sure she keeps any clue or hint that you spoke to her out of her story and doesn't tell the receptionist how she heard of her."

Over dinner—we'd had no plans to meet people or go out—Lauren reported on her unsuccessful efforts to get rid of Emily before I came home and on Jason's moaning, on the phone with her, about his course of study, his roommate and his housing situation. According to her, he was miserable and wanted to drop out and come home. While I didn't know how to square her report with Jason's upbeat tone on the phone with me, she'd succeeded in negating the emotional uplift I'd gotten from hearing his voice.

She'd often reported that he was failing a course, ill, or

depressed, when he ended up getting A's and, at least by the time I'd speak to him, was healthy and happy. Perhaps, I'd hear what I wanted when I spoke to him, but also, Lauren was a worrier and tended to hear what she feared. She believed she had an obligation to solve every problem. I considered it a fact of life that children have to work things out on their own and parents can only help within a limited range. I hoped he was happy and healthy.

As I finished clearing the table and loaded the dishwasher, she asked about my day. Burying the lead, I told her about the increasing frequency with which I'd been dialing wrong numbers and my worry that that was an initial step down the road to dementia. I concluded, "I always had the tendency to misdial. So, maybe I'm not actually doing it more often."

"It's been a long time since we actually *dialed* telephone numbers," she said. "Now we *enter* or *punch in* the numbers."

With that, she repaired to the bedroom and turned on the TV news.

I showered, then joined her in the bedroom, intending to tell her about my conversations with Non-Madelyn and the weird feelings they'd evoked. The television, however, flashed *Breaking News.*

Trump's helicopter was about to land in Youngstown, or maybe Toledo or Akron, and the camera was trained on the empty sky.

That's breaking news? Why the hell are they always giving him free publicity?

Angry, I switched to CNN, then MSNBC, same damn thing.

When I represented him, Trump couldn't handle testifying at a deposition without coming off as a lying, self-promoting jackass. So, I figured that his overwhelming assholishness would come through at the debates. No way he'd win the nomination, let alone the presidency. But just the same, I was concerned. I wondered why Non-Madelyn's puerile Hitler analogy had so resonated with me?

"They know not what they do," I said. "They might get him elected."

"You can't be serious," Lauren said.

She ran a hand through her long beautiful black hair. Although she was approaching sixty, age had yet to lay a finger on her.

"How could I not be serious, I just quoted scripture?"

The helicopter came into view.

Annoyed by the free publicity being lavished on Trump, I

13

wasn't in the mood to discuss Non-Madelyn, or much of anything else. Lauren would either not understand why the calls had bothered me so or more likely would understand all too well.

"Let's watch *House of Cards*," I said. "It has a better class of politicians."

At Jason's suggestion, we'd begun streaming television, and it had quickly become a centerpiece of our evenings.

I fumbled with the Roku and the remote. Losing patience, Lauren took both from me.

"Kevin Spacey would destroy Trump," I said, "but then again so should Hillary

I woke with Lauren holding me.

"You were thrashing and moaning," she said. "You must've been having a nightmare."

My pillow was wet, and I felt fearful but didn't remember my dream.

Lauren continued to hold me, and I fell back asleep, only to wake later feeling guilty about not telling her about Non-Madelyn. Maybe I had no reason to feel that way but I didn't need a reason.

As I was about to slide out of bed in the morning, she gave me a lovely good morning kiss, and I didn't want to ruin the mood.

II.
By the Pricking of My Thumbs

Look at his wife, she was standing there... Maybe she wasn't allowed to have anything to say. Donald J. Trump, speaking about Ghazak Kahn, a gold-star mother, July 30, 2015

I received an email from a former litigation adversary, whom I'd emailed the previous day. While former adversaries had historically been among my best sources of business—which I took as the supreme compliment—he'd been one of the people I'd emailed because I couldn't bring myself to call.

Good to hear from you after all these years. I don't know if this is a favor or payback for your kicking my ass in court, but my wife's niece's husband, Jonathan Walker, was just fired from his position as an SVP of a Fortune 500 company. I don't know if he has a case (I try to avoid entanglement with my wife's nutsy relatives, I've got enough trouble with my own), but it's probably worth a meeting. He'll be calling you shortly.

Walker called before I even had the chance to move the email to my recycle bin, and we made an appointment for that afternoon. Perhaps my contacting people hadn't been such a bad idea after all.

Tall, thin and swarthy, Walker wore a blue suit, with an upside-down American flag pin on his right lapel, white shirt, red tie and matching turban.

"May I trouble you for a glass of water?" he asked with the Received Pronunciation of an upper-class Oxbridge educated Englishman.

"Yes, of course." I unfurled my arm, bidding him to take a seat mid-conference table. "My apologies. I should have offered."

"Do you have Islandic Glacial or Volvic Natural Spring Water?" He eased into the seat keeping his head erect and back straight, then positioned his right calf over his left, maintaining a straight line with both legs, very proper and ladylike. "I'm quite particular about what I put into my body."

Islandic Glacial or Volvic Natural Spring Water, give me a fucking break.

"Which would you prefer?" I asked.

"If you have both, you're are very sophisticated…for a lawyer." He'd perfected an arrogant, condescending tone that complemented and enhanced his Imperialist accent. "I prefer Islandic Glacial."

"I don't have it refrigerated. Some say that affects the taste. Would it be OK if I pour you a glass with three cubes of ice, made from the same water, of course?"

"Brilliant." He flashed a winning smile, showing off perfectly aligned white teeth.

I left the conference room by the side door that led to our small kitchen, where I poured tap water into a tumbler and plopped in three ice cubes. Whether Islandic Glacial or New York City, both were H_2O and therefore interchangeable. Whatever slight difference in mineral content, the power of suggestion would trump the subtle taste difference—even to the highly-evolved taste buds of a former senior executive.

Returning, I placed the glass on a coaster with a picture of the Parthenon that a former partner of mine had brought back from a vacation as a present for the office. That, in his mind, allowed him to write off the cost of the trip as a business expense, and that ethical squishiness was why he was a *former* partner.

He took a sip.

In the ensuing silence, I feared I'd miscalculated and he'd spit the peasant libation all over the table's cherry wood veneer.

"That hit the spot." He wiped his thick lips, the kind described as *sensual* in bad novels. "Most people don't appreciate the huge difference between waters"—disparaging snort in case I wouldn't otherwise pick up on the vast gulf that separated him from *most people*—"and can't even tell one from the other."

"That's true." I smiled, showing off my coffee-yellowed, bicycle-accident-chipped teeth. "Please tell me the basic facts, just enough so I can form a preliminary opinion of the case. If you decide to retain me, we'll get into the details."

He'd been the subject of three sexual harassment complaints—

all of which human resources had declined to act on after investigations, seemingly for good reasons. In one, he'd told an account executive to go home and change because her outfit would offend a Christian Fundamentalist customer with whom they were scheduled to meet. The customer had communicated his no-cleavage or visible knee policy in an email prior to the meeting. My prospective client had forwarded the email to an account executive, suggesting that she exercise her own judgment. In another, an administrative assistant had sent him a series of amorous emails, to which he'd responded, "Nothing personal, but I have an adamantine rule against personal relationships with co-workers." She'd filed a complaint after she'd been fired for erratic attendance. In the third, he'd told an intern to "bend your knees and blow." According to him the boy had been lifting a heavy box and he'd said that so the kid wouldn't get a hernia.

He handed me the company's employee handbook, with a Post-it sticker marking the sexual harassment policy. The policy included an unusual *three strikes and you're out* provision, even if the complaints were judged to be unfounded. And that had been the reason the company gave him for terminating his employment and withholding the million-dollar bonus to which he'd otherwise have been entitled.

"It's all bollocks," Walker said. "The president of the company is a big Republican muckety-muck, and I haven't been quiet about my political leanings."

"I gather from your turban, you're a Sikh?"

He nodded.

"Born in India?"

"Yes, the Punjab. Last name originally Singh, but my father, who was big on assimilation, thought it too ethnic."

"Have you ever been the butt of disparaging comments at work based on your religion or national origin?"

"Just ignorant attempts at humor."

"Tell me about them."

His frown communicated displeasure over my time-wasting question.

"Please," I said. I'd have asked him to humor me, but humor and he appeared to have an antagonistic relationship.

"The COO asked me if I was going to be around for an

upcoming meeting or if I'd have joined ISIS by then. Once when we were to be going through security on the way to a sales meeting, a VP *jokingly* suggested that they search my briefcase, then stepped back with an exaggerated fearful look on his face as if he expected a bomb to explode."

"Perhaps the reason they gave for firing you was a pretext for—"

"My religion and background are personal matters." He enunciated each syllable with precision. "I don't want to bring them into this."

"You were entitled to significant bonus money, and it sounds like you may have been subjected to organized and persistent harassment. So, if I can get you a recovery based on religion or national origin, and it compensates you for the loss of your deserved bonus, why not? Money is fungible, one dollar is the same as another."

"I said, 'No'."

He took several sips of water, bending his head down to the glass like a drinking bird.

"Are you sure your termination had nothing to do with your religion or your background?"

"I'm quite certain it had a great deal to do with both, but the genesis of the problem was that I referred to Trump as an 'ignorant demagogue' at a meeting of people with a different view of the matter."

"Well, then—"

"If we don't claim that I was harassed, do I have a case? I reiterate that there's nothing to any of these trumped-up sexual harassment claims."

I pointed to his empty glass, quizzical expression on my face.

He held out his glass, and I went took it into the kitchen and refilled it.

"Perhaps if I looked deeper into these complaints against you…" I said, pursuing a hunch on my return from the kitchen. "Starting with the third. Does the intern still work for the company?"

"I told you!" he shouted, then composed himself and continued in a raspy whisper, "I don't want…" He gritted his teeth.

"Right, you don't want to claim against the company for harassment or discrimination on ethnic, religious or sexual orientation—"

"SEXUAL ORIENTATION?!"

He got out of his chair and leaned forward as if he intended to bite my nose off.

Seems I touched a nerve.

"A lawsuit would be a public record, so that's out of the question, but I can write a letter in the hope of initiating a settlement discussion," I said.

"Why would they settle if we don't mention harassment?"

"Typically when terminating a senior executive, employers hold something back in case the employee hires a lawyer, and if the lawyer seems to know what he's doing, they offer yet more. Large corporations tend to be afraid of litigation, and given the cost and uncertainty, they should be. Even bogus claims can run up big fees and bad publicity."

He took a dainty sip of water, then wiped his lips with a napkin.

"What will all this cost me?" he asked.

"A five-thousand-dollar retainer, against which I'll bill for my time," I said. "Then I'll draft a demand letter, which we'll discuss. Once we're both satisfied with it, I'll send it. Hopefully, that'll lead to a settlement discussion."

"You expect me to pay five K on a hope?"

What did I do to deserve such a hostile tone? Nothing but be a lawyer, which in the minds of many was plenty.

"In my experience, there's a good chance of getting you enough money to make the endeavor worthwhile, but—"

"But a great chance of you walking off with my five K."

"It was very nice meeting you." I stood, causing my arthritic knees to register their usual protest. "Give my regards to...your wife's aunt's husband." I'd already forgotten my former adversary's name. Darrell? No, Dave.

"What about a contingency, where you get a percentage of what I get?" he asked, remaining seated. "I'm told that's the way you work and the best way for both of us."

"It's not," I corrected, remaining standing. "I'd be surprised if Dave told you that."

Rather than answer, he drained his glass in three gulps, taking longer than necessary between each.

"On a twenty-percent contingency, if I were to recover for you even one tenth of your million-dollar anticipated bonus. I'd get a

19

multiple of my hourly rate," I said. "You'd be much better off on an hourly basis, particularly as we're not contemplating actually getting into litigation."

He tented his fingers.

"What about a ten-percent contingency?"

"I'd still do far better than on an hourly basis." A fearful look, crossed his face. What was I missing? But, if he wanted to pay me more than I deserved, so be it. "Okay, fine, I'll email you a retainer letter. When I get back a signed copy, I'll draft a demand letter."

He exhaled, then stood.

"Deal."

We shook hands.

"Why did you take the case of an unpleasant serial-sexual harasser, who was righty fired for violating company policy?" Lauren asked, after I told her about my day.

"He himself was harassed."

I glanced at the television which was turned to mute. I'd already had more than enough doubts about my having taken the case, without Lauren helping me to get in touch with my feelings about it.

"Your client's subordinates don't deserve to be harassed." Although she wouldn't admit it, Lauren considered any claim of harassment, if the alleged victim was a woman, to be true until proven false.

"He himself was harassed."

"I don't mean to be hard on you." Her softer tone caused me to reestablish eye contact. "But listening to the way you describe your meeting with him, it's obvious you don't want to represent him."

"Maybe one day I'll start doing what I want to."

She shook her head. I hated it when I disappointed her.

"If you're so dissatisfied with what you're doing, do something else."

I could have said I was too old and didn't know how to do anything else, but Lauren would have shredded those excuses. In truth, I liked practicing law when I was busy and had likable clients and interesting cases, an increasingly uncommon trifecta. Twelve-hour days without a lunch break was my sweet spot, any less and my nemesis, boredom, lurked.

Based on a False Story

With Jason away and my work slow, I'd have preferred it if we went out more, rather than eating at home and watching TV on most nights. When Jason was living at home, Lauren wanted to be around in case he needed help—or, in my view, needless interference—with his homework, and I liked to be available to chat with him when he wanted to take a break. He'd now been gone over a year, but Lauren was set in her ways and happy to spend our evenings at home.

My cell phone quacked. For reasons I couldn't recall, I'd set my ringtone to duck-quack when I got my phone and never bothered to change it. Perhaps on a psychological level I wanted to duck my calls or maybe I thought that anyone who'd call me must be a quack. Possibly, though, I just wanted a distinctive tone. The display said *unknown caller*. I had a premonition that Non-Madelyn was calling.

Although it was drizzling and chilly, I stepped out to the terrace. So as not to disturb Lauren, I told myself.

"Hello, Mr. Bloom, you have been selected for a very special offer," a computer-synthesized voice said.

I disconnected and went back inside.

"Everything alright, honey?" Lauren asked.

"Just a telemarketer. I thought it would be someone else. So much for the do-not-call registry."

I winced and wiggled my fingers.

"What's wrong?" Lauren asked.

"I just had a weird feeling. Like a prickling in my thumbs."

"How Shakespearian. Perhaps something wicked this way comes." One thing I loved about Lauren was that she got all my jokes and allusions, even those, like that one, that I didn't intend.

21

III
Sikh and Ye Shall Find

You could see there was blood coming out of her eyes. Blood Coming out of her—wherever. Donald J. Trump, August 7, 2015

I sat down to draft a demand letter on behalf of Walker. After the form opening paragraph, I realized I had nothing to say. The man had no case, or rather no case that he'd permit me to allege.

I stared at the framed photos on my bookcase: Lauren, at our wedding, and Jason, ranging from infancy to high school graduation.

In the hope that inspiration would arise from my sub-conscious—it sometimes happened that way—I forced myself to type:

After twenty-three years of loyal, superlative service, during which he consistently out-performed his peers, bulls-eyed each and every one of his sales targets, and received reviews bordering on the ecstatic; Mr. Walker had every reason to expect a solid seven-figure bonus.

The bullshit then flowed freely on a stream of content-light run-on sentences until I reached my desired two-page length—long enough to show I was serious but not so long that no one would bother to wade through it. My style was to write quickly, sloppily and floridly, then improve it over successive drafts. In love with my own words, I enjoyed writing even when I didn't have much to say. Still, if I'd received such a flaccid letter, I'd have consigned it to my junk file without bothering to respond.

I emailed the draft to Walker, along with a cover email begging him to let me raise the issue of discrimination on grounds of religion and ethnic background. Maybe, when he saw how vapid the case was without this angle, he'd permit me to cast aside the restrictions he'd imposed on me. Then, perhaps I could convince him to also let me reference discrimination on grounds of sexual orientation.

He responded, *You're a talented writer. Go with what we have—then negotiate as if you were Trump.*

In spite of his suggestion, I didn't think that lying, then caving in and blaming someone else for my failure would be an efficacious strategy. How had even Trump's opponents been deceived into believing that he was a great negotiator? Putting aside his one great success—being born with a filthy rich father—he'd made some good deals and some bad ones, but nothing he'd done had displayed outstanding negotiating skills or business acumen. His portrayal of a successful businessman on *The Apprentice* had been compelling, but by that standard we should elect Martin Sheen of *West Wing* fame or Harrison Ford of *Air Force One*. Or, if voters wanted the country to be run by a fake businessman, what about Jesse Eisenberg of *The Social Network*? Or, if searching for an agent of real change who'd shake things up, it would be hard to find a better candidate than Al Pacino from *Scarface* and *The Godfather*.

In my letter, I'd given the company five business days to respond—a deadline without teeth, as I had no intention of suing if they failed to respond.

Having no work to do yet again, I straightened the already-straight artwork on my walls, all picked out by Lauren, who had excellent taste.

I was bored, but in spite of Lauren's dictum, not yet dangerous. A big new case, for a client I liked who had a viable claim, would capture my excitement, but where would that come from? When? Were clients looking for a lawyer who was approaching seventy? Curiously, though, both presidential candidates were older than me, as was Hillary's prime primary opponent. On the other hand, not many people were excited about giving them the job.

I found myself punching in Non-Madelyn's number. Why the fuck was I doing that?

That question didn't need answering, because I reached a recording informing me that the number had been disconnected with no further information.

I called Lauren to tell her I loved her, but she was about to lead a tour of a new exhibit of Egyptian art, so she only had a few minutes for me. Then I read the most recent issue of *The Economist* and did the stretching my orthopedist had recommended but which I generally didn't get around to doing.

When I arrived at the office the next day, an email from an in-house lawyer for Walker's prior employer was waiting for me:

Your baseless letter has been referred to me for response. If you'd bothered to Google us, you'd have learned that the company has an immutable policy of not settling strike suits such as the one you threaten to bring. Please be advised that if you follow through on your implicit threat to bring a frivolous lawsuit, we will seek sanctions not only against your client but also against you personally.

I forwarded it to Walker, along with a cover email, *I'm heartened by the swift response, seems we struck a nerve. I'll call her tomorrow afternoon.*

I went to the gym on my way to work. I lifted weights, longer and harder than usual, then did ten thousand meters on the rowing machine.

I got myself settled behind my desk and put on Miles Davis's *Seven Steps to Heaven*. Regretting that I'd told Walker I wouldn't call back his former employer's lawyer until the afternoon, I read *The New York Times* and *The Wall Street Journal*, responded to emails, then checked my newsfeed. A black man had been coldcocked by a septuagenarian at a Trump rally. Rather than outrage, my first response was to wonder if I could knock someone out with one surprise punch. There had been reports of increased anti-Muslim hate crimes, including the fatal beating of a cab driver, who in spite of the turban and brown skin, wasn't Muslim but rather Sikh.

Finally, 12:01 arrived. Probably I should have spent some of my downtime preparing for the call to the company's lawyer but having been forbidden to use my only effective arguments, what was there to say? My morning news read had inspired a strategy of sorts. Although feeble, I didn't think I'd be able to come up with better.

"Hey, it's Matt Bloom," I said, smiling to impart a friendly lilt. "Just calling to thank you for your thoughtful note and to confirm that you'll accept service of our summons and complaint."

"I look forward to reading it, then filing a complaint against you with the First Judicial Department Attorney Grievance Committee."

"That no-settlement policy you mentioned is similar to that of a certain presidential candidate who's been involved in over twenty-five hundred lawsuits—more than every episode of *Law and Order* and every other lawyer TV show combined—and he's settled almost all of them."

"Except that he's a liar and a con-man." She sounded as if she was about to spit. Apparently she didn't have the same politics as her CEO.

My adversary had taken the bait that I'd cast out. Now, all I had to do was reel her in. Not that that would be so easy when using two-pound test line on a human-sized specimen.

"I like the way you do righteous anger, you put real feeling into it."

"I assume you've seen our three-strikes-and-you're-out policy with respect to sexual harassment that is incorporated in Walker's employment agreement." Her tone conveyed that she was not amused by my banter, but how could she not have been? "With Walker, though, that was only the tip of the iceberg."

"That's cold," I said—not all my lines could be great, or even middling, but just the same I loved them all. "H.R. investigated each claim like the congressional committee investigating Benghazi, and Mr. Walker turned out to be as innocent as a newborn."

"Not quite true." Her gotcha tone stimulated the flow of my competitive juices. "I assume he told you in detail about the intern."

"That caused me to read the company's strict policy against discrimination on the basis of sexual orientation," I said. "Some might say the company had violated it."

"The kid was at work maybe five days before Walker hit on him," my adversary said. "His company mentor happened to overhear and filed the complaint on the boy's behalf, he having been too intimidated to do so himself. And that story about the boy lifting something was horseshit. Walker was flirting with someone who reported to him, plain and simple."

"Do you have the intern's contact information?" I asked, deadpan. "Perhaps if I talk to him directly—"

"Didn't your client tell you anything?"

"My clients think I'm such a great lawyer that it wouldn't be fair to the other side if I don't operate with a handicap. So out of a sense of fair play, they never tell me the full story and often dispense with the truth entirely."

"In violation of our rules about relationships between employees and their superiors, your client had been paying Hakan's rent."

"Whose?"

"Hakan Yaldiz, the intern. Walker had the gall to put the expense through on his company credit card, claiming he used the apartment for business entertaining." She punctuated her statement with a mirthless snicker.

"The boy's still an intern?" I tried to sound shocked.

"Yes, until about a month ago."

"Wow! That's…. Is it possible he was actually using the boy and apartment for business entertaining?"

"He claimed he *entertained* the number two person in Sberbank, the largest Russian bank, Michael Flynn, a former Director of the United States Defense Intelligence Agency, and an intimate of Erdogan, and that the young Mr. Yaldiz was part of the package. The story was so revolting that no one questioned it, and we did get moderately lucrative deals involving Russian magnesium and Turkish soft-goods."

"So while this boy was working for the company, Walker wasn't just using him for his own pleasure but also to bribe customers affiliated with foreign governments and maybe our own as well? Of course, to be the number two person at a large Russian bank one has to be hooked in to the FSB, formerly known as the KGB." Was I overdoing the outrage?

"Now you're getting the idea of the kind of person you're representing and why we had every reason to fire him."

"I'm amazed you didn't give him the ole heave-ho earlier."

What a great case this would've been if I'd had permission to use any of what she was telling me. As it was, I had to let the fish tire herself out without snapping the line or tearing out the hook.

"If it had been up to me, we would have, but we were about to sign a big deal with the Russians, via Sberbank, and the powers that be didn't want to rock the boat." Adversaries say the darndest things. "He pleaded, said his wife would divorce him, claimed he felt sorry for the kid…an intern having to deal with sky-high New York rents. Also, the Russian deal was *sensitive*."

"Some would say that the three harassment complaints was a pretext, a"—I snapped my fingers as if I were having a problem coming up with the right words—"cover-up for worse?"

"We struggled to come up with the most anodyne grounds for termination. That's one of the reasons why we're so outraged that he dug up a bottom-feeding lawyer to pursue his frivolous claim." I could practically hear her smirk over the phone.

"Guilty as charged."

I hung my head. Not that she could tell over the phone, but I try for verisimilitude.

"This isn't our first rodeo," she said.

"Then you know that bull riding is full of unexpected twists and turns and bone-crushing falls."

"Somehow I'm not concerned."

"You're made of sterner stuff than me. I'd be afraid that this cover-up and the multiple violations of Federal anti-bribery statutes, particularly as they all took place on U.S. soil, if made public, would spread through social media like the black plague."

"You better not be threatening—"

"I'd never.... But, hey, we all have to understand the world we're living in. The vultures from the press hang out at the courthouse and read every filed complaint. And, of course, everything said in a legal pleading is privileged and the press is also protected from libel if the story is newsworthy or involves a public figure, like a New York Stock Exchange listed company, such as your employer."

"Your client would never let you—"

"*Au contraire, mon ami.*" There are few more effective ways to get under someone's skin than the gratuitous use of French idioms. "He recognizes that the system needs to change, and it's his civic duty to drain the swamp."

"That's how you rationalize your attempt to shake us down for money?"

"I'm just representing a client. To him this is a crusade, a matter of principle. But practically speaking, as a whistleblower, he stands to do just fine financially."

I was softening her up for the *coup de grace*, or rather an argument that might pass the red-face test. Walker wouldn't permit me to pursue any of the issues I'd raised so far, but he hadn't told me not to play with my food before eating it.

"WHISTLEBLOWER? The only thing he's blown is…"

"You seem to have stopped mid-sentence." I paused but she chose not to complete her thought. "Just curious, how many homosexuals has the company fired recently? One class action against you was unfortunate, two might…. Probably it wouldn't lead to a boycott but hard to say—"

"You are without a doubt the most loathsome…."

"Years of practice, it didn't come naturally," I said. "By the way, your real outrage is much quieter than the put-on version. That tremolo in your voice…very effective."

"You have anything else to say before I hang up on you?"

"I'd like to apologize for my role in us getting off on the wrong foot."

"Apology accepted," she said, her tone communicating that she'd take her anger to the grave.

"It seems that unlike your CEO, you and I, at least, are on the same page politically," I said, hoping my change of tack wasn't so abrupt as to capsize my boat.

"Perhaps." Her tone softened just a bit.

"Did you see the news today?" I asked. "The articles about increased Trump-inspired anti-Muslim hate crimes, including the fatal beating of a Sikh cab driver who, in spite of the turban, wasn't Muslim. To quote Ramsay Bolton, 'If you think this has a happy ending, you haven't been paying attention.'"

"We're going through terrible times," she said, "and they can only get worse."

"I shouldn't have mentioned discrimination on grounds of sexual orientation," I said. "My client probably wouldn't even let me assert it."

"I'm sure not." It sounded like she'd intended to come off as bored, but the temptation to gloat had been too much for her.

"In any event your company is on the right side of history. When in doubt, beat the crap out of the turban-wearing Sikh, even if he isn't a terrorist or even a Muslim. Or in this case, even if he met every criterion there was to be entitled to a bonus."

"I hope you're not imply—"

"The damage from the publicity, combined with the legal fees would dwarf the million dollar bonus Walker's entitled to."

"For a minute there, you almost sounded like a reasonable human being."

"If we do go before a jury, and the company realizes that you blew the chance for a confidential settlement.... We live in trying times, and we all have to cover our rear ends."

"You can't help yourself, can you?"

"At my age the need to give avuncular advice to younger, up and coming professionals can be overwhelming. It's too bad that they rarely take it before it's too late."

"Is that your final pitch?"

"No, this is: the company has to decide how much it fears the truth. It knows what actually happened, I don't," I said. "It's admirable that you put the company's interests ahead of your own, which clearly call out for settlement."

"Your point?"

"The company will avoid a lawsuit if it wires one million dollars to my escrow account by the close of business tomorrow." It would also avoid a lawsuit if it did nothing. "I'll email you the wire information. Once I receive the money, we can work out the terms of a settlement agreement, including non-disclosure, confidentiality, etc."

"You're bluffing."

"I can see why you might think that, but you can't afford to call the bluff. The risk to you personally of being wrong is too great. An adverse decision after seven figures in legal fees would be devastating to your career."

"My job's to take small risks like that," she said, but all confidence had drained from her voice.

"One million is not outrageous severance. It's approximately two weeks of Walker's most recent compensation for every year of service."

"He was vastly overpaid, due in part to—"

"His success in generating business for the company, via bribing foreign governments and working with their spies, with the company's knowledge and deliberate disregard—"

"You can't prove—"

"This conversation started with my claim being frivolous and sanctionable. Now it comes down to a question of proof. Next it'll depend on what the jury believes. The trend's not your friend."

She attempted a disparaging sigh but couldn't pull it off.

"We're headed for a time of unprecedented political polarization. Public companies are desperate to avoid controversy," I said. "Sikhs are being beaten to death because they look like Muslims. The optics for a company that appears to be on that bandwagon... A million bucks is a bargain."

I didn't know if I was making sense, but having a narcissistic, hate-spewing, pathological liar as the candidate of a major party had shaken many people's basic assumptions about the nature of our society and the level of gullibility of the masses—the sort that sat on juries. When my adversary had vehemently, and gratuitously, described Trump as *a liar and a con-man* I knew she was one of those people with shaken assumptions.

She said, "Humpf" or something similar.

"Your employer needs to stay out of the fray. You need to cover your butt," I said, on a roll and enjoying the sound of my own voice. "Also, in your heart you know that at least some part of Walker's problems stem from him being a closeted gay Sikh and that he earned his bonus by doing exactly what the company expected him to do. They saw a dark-skinned Indian and they thought, 'Coming from his culture, bribery is in his blood, we'll just turn our backs and take in the profits'."

"No way you can prove—"

"Paying him the bonus he earned, as severance, is the right thing to do."

After a hard exhale communicating frustration, she said, "I'll talk to the company, maybe some sort of *de minimis* nuisance settlement could be in order."

When a lawyer stoops to using stock Latin phrases, it's a sign of desperation.

"Non-negotiable. One mil, barely covers the nuisance I can cause."

"I suppose I have an obligation to advise the company of your demand. I'll be back to you but don't hold your breath."

"My bank will advise me when the money hits my account. No need for us to talk until that happens," I said, voice raspy from holding my breath like a pothead trying to keep the smoke in his lungs.

I called Walker to report on the conversation.

"YOU'RE CRAZY!"

Ouch! I pulled the handset away from my ear. Lucky for my eardrums that I'd given him the sanitized version.

He ranted on, and with the telephone handset on my desk it sounded like he was speaking at normal volume.

"I'd never let any of that go public," he concluded.

"Neither would they, and not to worry, settlement conversations are off-the-record, can't be used by anyone in litigation."

"I hope you know what the fuck you're doing," he said.

Not being so cruel as to take away another man's hopes, I didn't respond.

"You actually think they'll counteroffer?" he asked in a quiet enough voice for me to pick up the handset.

"If they do, I'll reject it."

"YOU'LL WHAT?"

"Please, Jonathan, in spite of my age, my hearing's not as compromised as you seem to believe."

"I know these guys; they'll never pay anything like that." The strain of speaking at normal volume imparted the gravely texture of a heavy smoker's morning voice.

"That's what their lawyer said."

"So they call our bluff, and we walk away with nothing?"

"Could happen."

"You're awfully casual about this."

"The first rule of negotiation is always be ready to walk away from the table."

Easy enough here, as I didn't give a shit. Perhaps that was a symptom of my growing alienation or perhaps there really wasn't much there worth caring about. Walker was an overpaid sexual harasser, and he and his company seemed to have been involved in bribery and might have crossed the line separating the unethical from the criminal. On the other hand, he seemed to have been a victim of discrimination on grounds of sexual preference and subjected to a pattern of harassment. Used to be I felt for my clients, or if not, I at least had an almost desperate desire to win, which amounted to the same thing.

"I'm not quite ready," he said.

"That's why you have me." I paused for a three-count. "Sorry,

Jonathan. I need to go. Emergency call."

Just a white lie, I told myself.

My desk-side manner left something to be desired, but unreasonable though it might have been, I expected my clients to have confidence in me. If a certain candidate could *stand in the middle of Fifth Avenue and shoot somebody* and not *lose any voters*, why couldn't I be the beneficiary of a similar unthinking loyalty?

When I told Lauren about my day, she asked, "Don't you have an obligation to follow your client's instructions?"

"What would you like to watch tonight? How 'bout *Black Mirror*?" I said, drawing a bemused smile, quite a beautiful one in fact.

The next day, the settlement money hit my account.

I called Walker.

"That's incredible, you actually know what you're doing," he said.

"That's one of the only things I find credible these days," I said. "After we have a signed agreement with the company, should I take my ten percent out and send you the balance?"

"Yeah, sure," he said, apparently not realizing that I'd intended my question to be rhetorical. "You made out pretty well. What's that, like thirty K an hour?"

"Probably more like fifteen K, once we get done with the settlement agreement. I told you, you'd be better off doing it by the hour."

I called Lauren to tell her the news.

"That's great!" she said, with heart-warming sincerity, but then she dropped her voice. "How do you feel about it?"

"Dirty, but it's always better to win than to lose," I said. "I'm going to give most of it away. Too bad I've already given the legal maximum to Hillary's campaign."

"She doesn't need your money."

"If she loses to that clown, I'll feel better having done my part."

I called Dave to thank him for the referral and to tell him about the great result.

The number I had for him had been disconnected. No surprise, as it had been years since I'd spoken to him. So I replied to his email.

A message came back. *This address has been hacked and is no longer in use.*

Odd.

I googled him. He'd died two years earlier.

I called Walker.

"I tried to contact Dave to thank him for referring you and—"

"Dave?"

"Didn't you tell me your brother-in-law had referred you to me?"

"My brother-in-law's a moron. I wouldn't take his advice on where to have lunch."

"But you said..." I didn't remember exactly what he'd said to me. "Maybe I'm not remembering clearly. How did you come to me?"

After a long pause, he said, "Hakan raved about you, via someone he knew."

"I got an email from Dave, telling me you'd call."

"My brother-in-law's name's Peter," he said. "I don't know what else to say."

"Me neither."

I told myself that, given how well the Walker case turned out, I had no reason to worry about how it had come to me. That damn thumb-prickling feeling, however, belied my attempt at self-reassurance.

IV
Something Wicked This Way Comes

*I watched when the World Trade Center came tumbling down.
And I watched in Jersey City, New Jersey, where thousands and
thousands of people were cheering as that building was
coming down.* Donald J. Trump, November 21, 2015

I ran across the subway platform to squeeze into the express.
That way I'd have an additional three minutes to sit at my desk
waiting for an email or phone call regarding a new case. Wiggling,
squirming and shoving, I made enough room to put down my
briefcase. But the train didn't move. The local that I'd gotten off of
pulled out of the station. I endured several announcements warning
that the train wouldn't move until the passengers cleared the doors.
Finally, it started to screech and jolt toward Times Square. Bent on
retaking the precious inches I'd misappropriated for my briefcase,
passengers pressed in from all sides. What an unpleasant way to
start the day—my own fault, as I'd had a comfortable seat on the
local, but why blame myself when I could blame the people
crowding me?

Having wrestled my phone from my pocket, I checked the news
feeds from the *Economist* and *Seeking Alpha*.

The subway stopped short, sending me and my fellow sardines
careening forward. Lucky none of us had room to fall.

An announcement, "We are being held up due to train traffic
ahead." The lights flickered. Odors of the unwashed and the too-
washed—shampoo, aftershave, skin creams—combined into a
sickening stench. A second local sped past us. My knees begin to
stiffen and ache, my lower back joining the chorus of pain. Maybe
when I turn seventy, I'll treat myself to a more civilized way to get
to work.

Arms circled my chest.

I spun out of their grip, drawing hostile shoves from those I bumped into. I turned toward my attacker.

I found myself face to face with a stunning, young, blonde with intense gray gold-flecked eyes. She was so ethereal that she could have materialized out of a handful of fairy dust. The crowd parted, leaving a few feet free around her. I'd never know whether someone who invaded that space would dematerialize or pass right through her ghostly presence, as no one seemed willing to attempt it.

"You're a hard man to get ahold of."

I had the feeling I'd met her before, but I couldn't place her. That could have been due to my chronic problem recognizing faces. Lauren contended that I didn't suffer from prosopagnosia, the fancy term for the problem, but rather that I didn't care enough about people to remember what they looked like. Perhaps I'd known the woman in a former life.

The lights stopped flickering, and I realized that actually she was neither stunning, young, nor blond but rather reasonably attractive and middle-aged with long gray hair. Her eyes continued to be gray and gold-flecked but seemed somehow otherworldly.

The train began to move, then stopped short, sending her careening into me and us into others.

"You had my phone number and my email," I said, finally recognizing her voice, although she'd disguised it somewhat on the phone or was doing so now.

"I don't use any of those things. Not with the FBI compromised and the Russian hackers reading everything I send."

"Does your paranoia interfere with your work as a professional tease?"

"Face-to-face communication is so much nicer," she said, mouth so close to my face that I could almost make out her words by the pattern of her hot wet breath on my cheek. "And far more intimate."

Her slim, hard, no-longer-ethereal body pressed against me. She smelled of rosemary and basil, like gourmet pasta sauce.

"I'm flattered that you've been stalking me," I said, more curious than concerned. "All in a day's tease, I guess."

She rubbed her body against mine, in a way I'd have found erotic if it hadn't been so weird—and if I'd been more honest with myself.

"You're easy to stalk," she said, her voice a breathy whisper, sex flavored with paranoia. "Too, easy. We've got to train you to avoid surveillance."

I pushed back the couple of feet that the crowd permitted me.

Her eyes scanned the car.

"Afraid of being overheard?" I asked.

"Just being careful. One of us needs to be."

In my single days, I'd noticed a positive correlation between sexy and crazy, but those days were long over. I now understood that crazy was an unalloyed negative. Well, I was pretty sure that I understood that.

"Thank you for referring Jonathan Walker to me," I said, testing a sudden hypothesis.

"You did a fabulous job," she said, no hint of surprise over my deduction. "Did your representation of him make you feel dirty or had you been looking for an opportunity to make quixotic charitable contributions?"

Deciding not to ask how she knew about my recent contributions to various congressional candidates and funds that opposed global warming, I said, in an angry harsh whisper, "I'm not as flattered as you seem to think I should be by your having paid such close attention to me and my doings."

"I pay very close attention to those I care about," she said. "It's one of my biggest flaws."

"I gather you're referring to Walker."

"No, silly, both of you."

She touched her finger to my nose, and I felt an electronic jolt down my back and to my fingertips.

The train jerked forward, again throwing me into her and us into a mass of passengers.

"On the phone you told me you're on a campaign to expand your circle of friends and business contacts," she said. "I have a sort of salon of interesting and influential people. You'd be welcome to attend our next soirée."

"May I bring my wife?" It was time to cut short any further flirtation—if that was even what had been going on.

"You know you hurt my feelings?"

Her eyes looked sad, but I didn't know what to make of her lopsided suggestive smile. Perhaps her feelings had been hurt, maybe she was flirting with me, or she could have been an alien teleported from another galaxy trying out facial expressions. A breeze I didn't feel appeared to ruffle her hair that now looked to be not gray but platinum blonde.

"Sorry, but it certainly wasn't on purpose."

"You didn't mean it when you accused me of being paranoid?"

"Your mention of the FBI being compromised and Russian hackers reading everything…"

"Oh, you meant *prescient*." The train pulled into Times Square. "On second thought, our salon might be too paranoid for your taste. Certainly it would be for Lauren's."

I found her petulance as annoying as I believed she'd intended me to.

"Well, it was nice to meet you," I said, tone communicating the opposite, even though I already knew that it would be the high point of my day.

"Nice? Not fascinating, stimulating, terrifyingly erotic, otherworldly?"

Her smile seemed to cover every corner of her face, and light glinted off her gold-flecked eyes.

"All that and more." I punctuated my statement with an insincere smile, but something electric passed between us, and my thumbs prickled. "By the way, what's your name?"

The train's doors opened.

"I change it all the time. I've transcended the need for identities and electronic footprints." She handed me a small box, resembling a child's birthday present—wrapping paper a mélange of clowns, balloons and cakes with candles—tied with a neat red bow. "A memento of our encounter."

I shoved it into the outer pocket of my briefcase and bulled my way through the horde of in-coming passengers, barely making it out of the train before the doors closed.

I hurried through the Times Square station. The doors were about to close on the shuttle to Grand Central, and a lost step would consign me to the next train which wouldn't come for another two, maybe even three, minutes. So I sardined into the shuttle.

After the short, crowded ride, I entered my office building directly from the Grand Central subway station. It being only 8:30 A.M., the staff wasn't in yet, and the door to my offices was locked. I reached into my pocket.

Damn it! I'd forgotten my keys. I feared that incidents of absentmindedness were becoming more common and were a sign of approaching dementia. My memory, however, wasn't clear enough for me to recall one way or the other. Regardless of whether or not that concern was justified, though, not having my keys was a damn inconvenience.

I reached into my briefcase for my phone in order to call the building management office.

No phone either. What the hell? I'd just had it in the subway. What did I do with it? Being without a phone was like being transported back to the 1980's.

Fuck! My wallet and credit card case were missing as well.

Despair clenched my stomach.

Now what?

I sat on the floor, waiting for someone from my office to arrive.

Finally, a paralegal showed up, greeted me with an irritatingly pleasant "Good morning!" and unlocked the door.

Before using my Find iPhone app, I called my phone from my office, hoping a Good Samaritan had picked it up and would answer.

I heard a quacking from my briefcase.

I ripped apart the package Non-Madelyn had given me. It contained not just my phone, but also my wallet, keys and credit card case, but also a note on insubstantial salmon-colored paper, written in elaborate calligraphy: *Matt, you'll need to be a lot more careful. Only a fragile blue wall separates The Abominable Showman from the presidency and disaster.*

The paper crumbled into dust like a time-lapse film of a decaying leaf.

At dinner that night my shoulder muscles felt tight, an invisible vise squeezed the sides and back of my head, and my gut cramped. I attributed those symptoms to a conflict between my unaccountable reluctance to tell Lauren about my encounter with Non-Madelyn and my feeling that I should tell her. After I cleaned up and loaded the dishwasher, though, I finally came clean.

"And you didn't think to tell me about her earlier?" Lauren's scorching tone.

"I'd intended to tell you over dinner that night, but when I got home that evening, Emily was there, then I talked to Jason. I'd mentioned calling the wrong number, but then Trump was on the news, we mutually bitched about it, or maybe I did and you listened, then we started watching TV. By then, I guess, it slipped my mind."

"Her stealing your phone and wallet this morning was hardly a non-event, yet it took until now for you to finally mention it."

Her laser stare intensified. If I hadn't looked away, it might've burned my corneas. One advantage of Lauren's Asperger's spectrum diagnosis of me was that I wasn't required to make eye contact.

"By the time I finally got into my office and calmed down, I had calls and emails to respond to, so I figured I'd wait until tonight to tell you about it."

"I thought you had no work to do."

"Doing nothing turns out to be very time-consuming," I said, which was true although I didn't know why.

"This nutcase has been hacking into your computer.... You're not concerned?"

"Our IT guy found no evidence of an intrusion."

"All that means is that she's very good at it. Should've concerned you more." Tone having gone from angry to worried, she rested a hand on mine.

"Maybe she found some other way to keep tabs on me. Surely, Jonathan Walker reported back to—"

"Did it even occur to you that that Johnny Walker was a suspicious name?"

"I used to play tennis with a Jack Daniels, once had a case against a Jim Beam, and I even knew a Bud Weiser." I stared longingly at the TV remote—so near yet so...remote. "The company's settlement money was real enough."

"Did you tell Walker that you intended to contribute the settlement money—"

"I'm not sure."

"That's a no?"

I could have learned a lot about cross-examination from Lauren.

"Non-Madelyn didn't mention the specific charities and candidates, only referred to them as *quixotic*, which was meaningless in context, so I—"

"Really?" She raised her neatly trimmed, jet black eyebrows.

"Campaigns have to post their contributions. So mine to the

various democratic congressmen would've been available online."

"It didn't raise any red flags that she'd been checking so closely?"

"No more than at a typical Stalin-era May Day Parade." Lauren's tight lipped facial expression communicated that she didn't appreciate my clever rejoinder. I rejected out of hand the possibility that it hadn't been all that clever. "She described herself as a professional tease. I've got no reason to believe she's anything other than a harmless prankster—one that sent me a very lucrative matter."

"Maybe this *harmless prankster* is about to clean out our bank accounts."

"So far the only financial consequences have been a case that earned me a hundred K fee for less than ten hours of work."

"Sounds too good to be true," she said.

I shrugged.

"From now on you'll tell me about any further communications from her or strange occurrences that might be attributable to her?" Although she'd raised her tone at the end of her statement to make it sound like a question, I knew it was a command.

"Of course."

"And you're not going to this supposed salon?" Another verbal question mark to be disregarded.

"She killed any interest I might have had in going by declining to invite you," I said, which wasn't as true as it should've been. I needed new business, was intrigued by Non-Madelyn, and curious about her salon.

Were there grades of truth? It used to be binary, something was either true or not true. Then Trump ran for president.

A human lie detector, she shot me an incredulous look. She knew me too well.

"Also, she disinvited me because I'm not sufficiently paranoid. Fine with me. I have more than enough trouble without looking for it."

"Everyone on the planet, has more than enough trouble, but unlike most of us, that never stopped you from looking for it and finding it. That's why I worry about you when you're bored."

V
The Hardest Thing to Predict is the Future

I know where she went. It's disgusting, I don't want to talk about it. No, it's too disgusting. Don't say it, it's disgusting, Donald J. Trump, December 22, 2015

Everyone who claimed to know anything said a Trump victory would result in a catastrophic stock market crash and a Hillary victory, already priced in, would be a non-event for the market. Therefore, I considered liquidating my stock portfolio. But when everyone agreed about the stock market they were always wrong. So I threw all my available cash into stocks of pharmaceuticals, U.S. international banks and investment banks. Drug stocks would shoot up on a Trump victory, as investors believed that he'd repeal ObamaCare and related regulations, giving the big drug companies leave to charge what the market would bear. Financials would also boom, on the belief that he'd repeal Dodd-Frank and other the post-2008 recession regulations, giving the banks a free hand to bring on another, even worse recession. As no one in their right mind predicted a Trump victory, those stocks had been hammered in anticipation of Hillary's triumph. So it seemed that they didn't have much downside risk if Hillary won and had big potential upside in the event of a Trump victory.

Did my seeking to make money on human misery make me as bad as Trump, who'd sought to make money from the 2008 financial crisis? No. First, what good were financial crises if you couldn't make money from them? Second, unlike him, I actually did make money in 2008 by buying stocks on the cheap and selling as they rebounded. He lost money by starting a mortgage company that, like most of his business ventures, failed.

Since we'd both had disastrous first marriages, Lauren and I maintained separate accounts. We lived off the income from my law

41

practice. We tended not to discuss our investments, because when we did, she'd accuse me of having an *erratic, bordering on irresponsibl*e investment style. Still, I intended to tell her when I got home that night.

Excited about relating how well her new tour had gone, Lauren went first. Then, due to our hectic television-watching schedule, and my having burned the broccoli, setting off the smoke alarm, it slipped my mind. Curious, how excellent my memory was vis-a-vis work-related matters, and how poor in other areas, such as subjects I was ambivalent about discussing with Lauren. Was early-stage dementia that selective?

I texted Lauren, *leaving the office soon, should I pick up anything for dinner on the way home?*

For decades, I'd put in twelve-hour work days. Now, I was struggling to keep busy until 5:00. Lauren seemed pleased having me around more, but I feared I'd wear out my welcome.

Got dinner covered, looking forward to seeing you ♥. Let's start Season 6 and see if Jon Snow really is dead.

I had mixed feelings about Jon Snow. Like most *Game of Thrones* fans, I was upset when he died, but I didn't like people coming back from the dead. The supernatural wasn't my thing, since I had so much trouble dealing with the natural.

At 5:38 it was already dark. The temperature hovered in the mid-fifties. The climate deniers, however, probably believed it to be in the low-thirties. No real American would trust those darn socialist, globalist thermometers, undoubtedly made in China. Not like the good old days when American workers were free to expose themselves to mercury poisoning.

To take advantage of the clement weather, I decided to walk home. The fifty-five blocks would take me about fifty minutes, less if I caught the traffic lights right. I had to tell Lauren about my stock market gamble, or rather *investment*, and by cogitating on the walk home, I hoped to come up with a positive spin.

I took my phone from the outside pocket of my briefcase to text Lauren that I'd be home later than I'd thought.

A size extra-large man appeared at on my right, a second one on my left.

One snatched my phone.

Steps came from behind.

Something hard and gun-like was jammed into my lower back, presumably from a third thug.

My stomach clenched.

"Walk slowly into that limousine," the man behind me said, referring to the dove gray Mercedes straight ahead. "Running, shouting, turning to look at our faces or in any way drawing attention to yourself would be a serious error of judgment."

"Sounds like fun, but I need a rain check. I'm expected home for dinner."

"We'll let Lauren know you're going to be detained, so she doesn't worry."

His mention of her name felt like a punch in the solar plexus.

"If there's something you'd like to talk about, here is fine, or there's a Starbucks—"

"Speaking of coffee, Jason had coffee this afternoon with a nice girl," he said, tone casual, gossipy. "She's on the crew team, an A-minus student, still scarred by her parents' divorce."

Fury rose from my gut.

"You better not—"

"No one means to do you or your family any harm."

I tried to catch the eyes of passing pedestrians. Some looked at the sidewalk in front of them, others across the street—not that there was much to look at, just a wooden wall surrounding a construction site for a huge office building slated to be the new Morgan Stanley headquarters. All, however, avoided my stare, like waiters in a mediocre restaurant.

"Into the car, please."

While the first rule of negotiation is *always be ready to walk away from the deal*, the second is *you need to pick the right time and place to walk*, and this wasn't either.

The man on my right—top coat with lapels turned up, ski hat, leather gloves, large dark glasses—sprinted three steps to the car, opened the door after some clumsy fumbling, and climbed into the back seat.

The similarly dressed man on my left cut in front of me. Bent at the waist like an obsequious chauffer, he unfurled his arm, bidding me to get into the back seat.

I hesitated but, when the gunman behind me nudged me

forward, I followed. The second thug climbed in next to me. The one who'd been behind me got into the driver's seat. I didn't get a look at him. Due to the opaque partition between the back and front seats, I wouldn't until we reached our destination, and it would likely be too late to matter. The thugs on either side of me unbuttoned their coats, revealing tuxedoes underneath. They left their masks in place.

"I never imagined I'd be underdressed for my own murder," I said, hoping they'd deny the murder part.

They didn't, and the car pulled out, heading east.

The man on my left—the one on my right had yet to make a sound—dictated into my phone, "Sorry, honey, something came up. I'll probably be home late. Don't wait up."

He showed me the screen, so I could see it was a text to Lauren. Then he hit send, turned off the phone and stuck it into his pocket.

"You'll get it back later."

"Where are you taking me?"

"Something to drink?"

He pulled out the panel in front of me, revealing a full bar.

"No thanks," I said. "I asked you—"

"You sure we can't tempt you with a stiff Jameson and ice?" he asked, a gracious host, under the circumstances.

"Just tell me where we're going and why you've abducted me," I said, keeping my tone as neutral as I could manage. I didn't want to acknowledge my discomfort over his knowing what I'd have requested had I been inclined to drink—not that the rest of what was happening hadn't pushed my discomfort to its maximum level.

How was I going to explain my death to Lauren?

"I'm instructed not to ruin the surprise."

"A hint about where we're going and why I'm here would enhance the surprise, whet my appetite." Getting no response, I said, "Given all your research, you must know that I'm hardly worth the effort."

"I couldn't agree more." He paused like someone who'd lost his train of thought. "Preparation is the key to spontaneous success."

As I'd often uttered the same sentence, it appeared he wanted to drive home the fact that he'd been monitoring my communications.

My shoulders were so tight, it hurt to shrug. My wince undercut my effort to appear unafraid.

He took a blindfold and headphones from under the seat.

I didn't resist when he put them on me. If I could neither see nor hear what was happening, perhaps it wasn't actually happening.

Lucinda Williams's, *World Without Tears,* began playing through the headphones, a choice that only someone familiar with my taste in music would make.

I made a mental note to get myself a good pair of noise-canceling headphones, if I survived. I could wear them through the election, and worst case, for the following four years.

"So who's calling the shots?" I asked, pulling aside the headphones.

"Is the music selection satisfactory?"

"Under the circumstances."

He readjusted my headphones, and Lucinda kept playing and we drove on.

My stomach churned like a washing machine at its highest setting.

Half way through *Righteously,* the second cut on the CD, he put his hands on my shoulders and squeezed.

"Ouch!"

He put the music on pause.

"You're awfully tight there. I'm a licensed physical therapist, mind if I give you a message? It'll help you to relax."

"Better idea: drop me off at home and I'll take a hot bath."

"So that's how you got to be so clever," he said, "you're always practicing."

"Yeah, it's gotten me where I am today. If only I knew where that was."

"Practice doesn't make perfect, you know. Only perfect practice makes perfect."

My head began to throb. My jaw hurt. I must have been clenching my teeth. I had to be calm; I'd need a clear head. I pulled aside one of the headphones.

"May I have my phone, if I turn off the GPS? Your text assuredly worried my wife, and I've no doubt she responded with questions."

"Most likely, you'll get it back when you leave."

"Most likely?"

"As Yogi Berra said, 'The hardest thing to predict is the future.'"

As I was sure he knew, I'd quoted that frequently.

"Less so for those who control the future," I said by rote; I had no reason to verbally spar with the man—or for that matter not to.

He slid the headphone back over my ear and continued to knead my shoulder. It annoyed me that it felt good.

Three tracks later, I turned toward the smell of marihuana. The man pulled away my left headphone.

"Would you like a hit?" His raspy voice indicated that he was holding his breath to keep in the smoke.

"No, thanks," I said. "By the way, cannabis is absorbed in the first couple of seconds, so holding your breath is as pointless as kidnapping me. Although it exposes you to far less severe criminal penalties than does kidnapping."

"Sobriety won't be a plus where we're going."

"Oh, really. Where *are* we going?"

"Sit back, relax, enjoy the music. We'll be there soon."

"Relax? You've got to be kidding."

"You sure you don't want anything to drink or smoke?"

"Positive."

He slid the left headphone back.

At the conclusion of *Bleeding Fingers and Broken Guitar Strings*, I said, "I'm about to vomit."

He rolled down the window and helped me stick my head out. I did my business. He handed me a towel. I wiped my face. Then he gave me a bottle of water.

"Icelandic Glacial," he said.

That I had a pretty good idea who was behind this gave me little comfort. I doubted that I was about to be killed, but whether I'd be subject to worse was an open question. Also annoying, albeit less so, was that, as usual, Lauren had been right.

I took a sip and swirled it around my mouth.

The car started up again.

"Here, spit into this."

He put a large paper cup into my other hand. I did as told. It sounded like he tossed it out the window. I had some more water from the bottle.

Words Fail, the last track to the CD, started just as the limo stopped. Knowing the approximate length of the CD, I figured we'd been driving for a little more than fifty minutes, although it had felt like that many hours. The door opened, and we got out. I staggered, knees having locked from sitting. I brought my hand up to remove the blindfold.

One of them pulled my hand away. "Not yet."

A heavy metal door scratched a flat note. They nudged me up a narrow, rickety flight of stairs toward a noise that sounded like a flock of squawking geese.

Will I be pecked to death? If only I could get access to my phone, I could put in an emergency call to PETA. No, they'd take care of the geese and leave me to my fate.

Stop, I told myself, *direct your mind to something useful.*

At the top of the stairs, another door squeaked open and the sound from inside became louder. I was nudged forward. I tripped on the threshold, and a pair of large hands stopped me from falling. Someone took off my blindfold.

47

VI
Fools Russian Where Angels Fear to Tread

I would bring back a hell of a lot worse than waterboarding.
Donald J. Trump, February 6, 2016

I found myself in a large, black-enamel-walled, elliptically shaped loft, where approximately sixty prosperous-looking, well-dressed people were arranged in tight scrums and engaged in animated conversation. A bartender, in white tie and dark glasses, manned a well-supplied bar at one of the foci of the room. A circular table stocked with a stunning variety of food occupied the other focus. Tuxedoed waiters, also wearing dark glasses, circulated with trays. The windows were painted over with colorful harlequins—homages to Picasso presumably—against a blood-red background. Day-Glo gargoyles and other phantasmagorical figures hung from the ceiling, some individually, others in Calder-style mobiles. A chamber orchestra, musicians in black tie and wearing dark glasses, played Franz Schubert's "Death and the Maiden" with rare feeling and subtlety.

More than half of the attendees wore masks as if attending a *bal masqué*, white tie for the men, full-length designer dresses for the women. The rest wore cocktail dresses or business suits, depending on gender, and went without disguise. Several women were half the age of their partners and achingly beautiful. Most, though, appeared to be appropriate matches for their mates, in age, sophistication and self-satisfied look of prosperity. The sulfurous odor was probably a product of my imagination and not the stench of ill-gotten big money. If Bob Dylan had been correct that *money doesn't talk it swears*, then no minor should have been permitted to listen.

Non-Madelyn, in a long clingy red dress—calling to my mind Melisandre, the witchy Red Priestess of *Game of Thrones*—ran up to me.

"Matt, delighted you could make it." Her radiant smile was illuminated by a shaft of light from a hidden source. "Come let me introduce you around."

She leaned forward to plant a kiss on my cheek.

I hopped back.

"Give me my phone. I'm leaving."

She pouted, fetchingly. I'd seen that same pout somewhere before in a different context. She was the type of person who gave *déjà vous* a bad name.

"I'm sorry, Matt. I'm afraid I can't do that," she said, perfectly aping the tone of HAL in *2001: A Space Odyssey.* "The GPS will reveal your location That's why we have a no-phones-on rule."

No one was talking on or looking at their phones, unusual for these days.

"Please stay," she said. "Have a few drinks, something to eat, meet some people. It's a very interesting crowd. Even as judgmental as you are, I'm sure you'll like several of them. Others could become major clients, if you employ even a modicum of your monumental charm. Unless, that is, you're too busy to take on new work. Once you're physically and spiritually satiated, we'll run you home."

She took my hand. I again yanked it away.

"I don't like being kidnapped, having my son threatened or my wife worried."

"Threatened?" she actually sounded incredulous. "My man simply told you about Jason's coffee date. We thought you'd be interested. And I'm sure Lauren's tickled pink about the flowers you sent her along with the note, 'Boy, do I have a story to tell you?' Not to worry, Matt, I'll help you make one up."

"I don't tell my wife *stories.*"

A waiter came up to us bearing a glass of whiskey on a silver tray.

"Jameson with ice," he said.

"No, thank you."

"Please, for me," Non-Madelyn said.

"Well, in that case, definitely not."

"Matt, be reasonable. Can you blame us for subjecting our potential members to extreme vetting in these troubled times?"

"Members in what?"

"You passed with flying colors. Lauren and Jason, too."

Guests were piling their plates high with delicacies. As I hadn't had lunch and had emptied my stomach on the way over, the food table called to me like a Siren luring sailors to their destruction.

"By the way, you don't have to worry about being recognized. Our members are way out of your league. If your paths crossed, it was when you were standing at a crosswalk as their limos breezed by."

"Then why am I here?"

"You told me you were on a campaign to expand your circle of friends and business contacts. I wanted to help. Blame it on my bird-with-a-broken-wing complex," she said. "By the way, the waiters are blind, as are the men who brought you."

I doubted that they'd have been able to have coordinated grabbing me if they were blind.

"Hope the driver wasn't."

"Newest Google self-driving vehicle."

She took the glass from the tray and held it out to me. The waiter bowed and wandered off. I did want a drink.

"I don't believe—"

"Everyone here had a similar initiation. Now, they come enthusiastically. Ask around, if you don't believe me, not that I've ever given you the slightest cause to doubt my veracity."

"Did you intend that to be comic or ironic?"

From the animated conversation and peals of laughter, it appeared that my fellow attendees were enjoying themselves…and others. Additional people filed in, seemingly under no compulsion and happy to be there. A tuxedoed man accompanied each group, then joined the waitstaff.

She flashed a yet more brilliant smile, blinding like the searchlight poachers use to freeze a deer in place before they shoot.

"Would it really hurt you to stay awhile, talk to some people, decide if you like us?" she asked. "If you can't land a client here or meet a potential friend, you might as well go off to a monastery and contemplate your navel."

"I've already decided."

"The food and drink is on a par with that of a Michelin three-star restaurant. You're already here. You might as well make the best of it." She smiled again. "Put another way, take the fat, studded dildo out of your ass and allow yourself to have a good time. Your whiney-little-bitch persona is not your most attractive—too reminiscent of The Bouffant Buffoon."

A waiter came by with blinis, topped with sour cream and caviar that did look good enough to qualify for three-star status.

Fuck it. I took one. Delicious.

"You'll like my friends but it's not all fun," she said. "We're here for a serious purpose. One I'm sure you'll agree with."

I took a proffered small barbequed lamb chop, encrusted with macadamia nuts. The server waited for me to deposit the bone back on the tray. I regretted not taking the Jameson, which would have been the ideal accompaniment. When in Rome take in a gladiatorial game and have your way with multiple slaves of various genders, unless you're a slave yourself in which case you're fucked.

"And that purpose is?" I asked, considering it unlikely that I'd hear the truth.

"I'm laying the groundwork for an anti-Trump coalition," she whispered, mouth so close that her tongue flicked my ear and a sickly sweet funereal smell wafted into my nostrils. "So we'll be prepared to take extreme action if he wins. And as you hate the man—"

"While I believe he's supremely unqualified, I don't *hate* him."

Her Mona Lisa smile communicated her understanding that it wouldn't do to publicly admit our loathing for the man if extreme action were to be required in the future.

"Always the careful lawyer, Matt Bloom. You wouldn't even commit to today being Monday."

"It's Tuesday, and there's no way I'd be involved in—"

She put a finger to her lips.

"Of course, I'm not contemplating doing anything illegal."

She winked, or maybe it was just a one-eyed blink.

"Of course not. You limit yourself to pickpocketing, theft, kidnapping, assault and related felonies."

"Our initiation ceremony might be a trifle over-the-top. But I promise you won't regret being here and throwing your lot in with us."

It did look like an interesting group.

"Give it an hour. You must be curious, at least," she said. "And truth be told, this isn't the easiest place to get home from, no public transportation, no Uber. Then there's the Vietnamese-style mantraps, hidden electrified fence and *Schrapnellmines*, bouncing betties that, when triggered, launch into the air and detonate at castration level."

"Have you ever tried trademarking your brand of hyperbolic bullshit?"

"You found me out." Shamefaced, she looked at her Christian Louboutins. "Have a stroll outside and check for yourself. Take a bunch of those lamb chops to distract the hungry pit bulls and give yourself a fighting chance."

My stomach rumbled. The food table shimmered. The bar murmured seductively. The image of castrating landmines lodged in my mind. Her eerie gray gold-flecked eyes twinkled.

"If I want to leave in an hour, you'll return my phone and have a car drive me home?"

She put her hand over where her heart would've been, if she'd had one.

A pixyish man bounded up to us. His bald head and Van Dyck beard gave him a passing resemblance to Vladimir Lenin. He'd have been out of place in this crowd even if he had been appropriately dressed, but in his professorial tweed jacket with worn leather elbow patches, brown corduroys and scuffed desert boots he stood out even more than I did. He smelled of old leather, cheap pipe tobacco and an Eastern European aversion to personal cleanliness.

"You are lawyer we hear so much about?" He grabbed my hand and gave it a hearty shake. "Welcome."

Hand on my back, he nudged me toward the food table. I didn't resist.

"Something I have you need see and listen but first...," he said, while cutting several slices off a leg of ham, putting them on a plate with a dab of fancy mustard. "This you have to try. Iberico ham, most expensive in entire world, in London sells for eighteen hundred pounds for fifteen-pound leg joint. Raised in western Spain, acorns and roots the pigs are fed to give meat flavor with distinction." His accent made him sound like a B-movie Soviet spy.

He handed me the plate. I had a piece.

"Wow, it's quite good. Hardly worth the price but—"

"A lot of money in this room, so much that it is of no object. If I were lawyer hoping for new business, a better gathering I could not imagine."

He took my plate and cut a slice off of a large pastry thing.

"Beef Wellington, made with Wagyu Kobe Strip steak. It's—"

I held up a hand.

"Don't tell me the price, just let me enjoy if for what it is."

"Quite right. This gathering…it is so intoxicating, my manners and any trace of grace I have lost."

"Don't be silly. Thank you for introducing me to—"

A waiter brought over two more glasses of whiskey on a silver tray.

"Glenfiddich 40-Year-Old Single Malt Scotch. You join me, yes?"

"It would be rude not to."

"Absolutely. An offense that cannot be forgiven. A duel we would have to fight. Like your current national favorite Alexander Hamilton."

He smiled, showing off a set of teeth that called to mind an accident in a graveyard.

I had a sip.

"Nice. No worse than whiskey a tenth the price."

He had an endearing, genuine laugh

"Myself, I neglected to introduce. Lev Georgorovich Zhukov at your service." He bowed.

"You said you had something to show me?" I asked, well aware that I was getting sucked into something that I should avoid, but my curiosity, like my hunger and thirst, overpowered my good sense.

"Our hostess says you are man that can be trusted, a person of very highest integrity, judgment and discernment."

"I doubt that she knows one way or the other."

"Oh, she knows, of that you can be most sure, like tomorrow's rising of the sun."

"Much of what she says is simply untrue."

"It is not what she says that's important. It is what is in her heart."

I considered that unworthy of response, but I followed him anyway to the least crowded part of the room.

"I suspect this isn't as strange a question as it sounds, but what's her name?" I asked.

"A girl has no name."

"I get the *Game of Thrones* reference but…," I said, not

bothering to conceal my annoyance but I did note that the referenced character, Arya Stark, had started to work down her kill list. "Let's start with another question, why does she go to such great lengths to—"

"She must be riddle wrapped in mystery inside enigma, like your Roosevelt the Second said. A most dangerous game she is playing."

"That was Churchill describing Russia. In any event, games of this sort—and I say this even without knowing what sort—are most dangerous for us pawns."

"End of day, pawns and kings go into same box." He shrugged. "But a good person she is. Saint disguised in clothes of courtesan. The future she sees clear and its bleakness she feels."

Refraining from rolling my eyes, I asked, "What are the rules of this *dangerous game,* and what does one have to do to win? Or more importantly, to lose?"

He led me away from the food table, but I intended to return in short order.

He took his phone from an inside jacket pocket and started playing a recording. I couldn't understand a word of it, except perhaps a name.

"Sorry, I don't speak gibberish."

"It is Russian but, how you say, grainy."

"All the same to me," I said. "I thought I heard a name, sounded like Rex Tillerson maybe? Means nothing to me."

"President of Exxon and Putin good friend. Putin wants Secretary of State him to be. Part of deal."

"You're saying that this tape—"

"A recording of meeting between Trump and Putin henchmen. Putin's man agrees emails damaging to Hillary Clinton to release, documents damaging to Trump to withhold, and false stories to spread throughout Internet, using battalions of bots, all to hurt Mrs. Clinton and get elected Trump."

"If this tape is what you claim it is—"

"Sanctions lifted and massive investment to modernize its oil production Russia needs. Exxon best to do that. Then money Russia will have to upgrade military. Re-establish Soviet Union Putin's goal"

"That's what this tape is saying?" I asked, wondering why he expected me to believe this or why it mattered to him what I believed.

"You hear of *Federal'naya sluzhba bezopasnosti Rossiyskoy Federatsii*. FSB for initials? Same as mafia but with all power of state behind it. When U.S. and European banks realize loans he does not honor and refuse to lend more, Trump desperate, in danger of losing everything, to Russian banks he goes. They answer only to FSB. And Putin, very smart, says Trump would be good person to own."

I considered this moderately interesting cocktail party chatter, not to be taken seriously. As alcohol spread through my bloodstream and my hunger dissipated, I compartmentalized my fury with Non-Madelyn over my kidnapping. Zhukov's credibility didn't particularly matter as, even if I believed him, there was nothing I could do with his information.

I stepped back toward the food. He stepped in front of me. I sidestepped. He mirrored me. From a distance it might have looked as if we were dancing.

"Trump surrogates: Sessions, Kushner, Manafort, Flynn, and Page all here"—he tapped his phone—"meeting with the FSB."

"Wow, Jimmy Page of Led Zeppelin is working for Trump? That's huge. So much for *Stairway to Heaven* and on to *Dazed and Confused*."

"No," he said as if he took my comment seriously. "*Carter Page*, of Trump foreign policy team. They all with Sergey Kislyak met, the Russian ambassador to United States of America and head spymaster."

"If you have actual evidence of that, there are far better people to tell about it than me," I said, desirous of returning to the real world and more importantly the food table.

"I just got final piece. Now, it is complete. The only copy right here." He again tapped his phone. "Hostess said to come right away. ASAP. Do not even change clothes."

He handed me his phone so I could see a video. It was hard to tell for sure, but it appeared to be two attractive naked women and a well-built black man urinating on a Trump look-alike, who was sitting on a bed, stupid grin on his face.

"That is the bed when he was in Moscow Obama slept on," Zhukov said. "A germaphobe Trump is and urine is sterile, so...

FSB know he is into this. Not just grabbing the genitals of woman. That is his cover story. Impotent he is, from drug he takes for hair to grow."

I took a long sip of scotch. Oh how I wanted his story to be true.

"Why are you showing me?"

"Our hostess told me to. You know how confidences to keep, attorney/client privilege. And if something were to happen to me or the video—"

"You're not a client."

"Here is dollar." He held out the money. "I give it to you and then we have relationship between lawyer and client. This is correct, right?"

"Doesn't work that way." I left the bill flapping in the air. "And whatever legal issues are involved, they are way beyond my ken. Even if I were to testify that I saw the tape, which I wouldn't because I am not sure what I really saw or if it was authentic, my testimony would be hearsay, not admissible evidence," I said. "Why are there no other copies of the video?"

"Two hours ago, I just got this, the last piece. Everything now in one place together. She somehow heard about it. She hears all, sees all. She whisked me over here, so her people can watch over me until we devise a secure way to send it." He held his phone out to me. "You take phone. Hold in escrow. Just for day or two. You are respected and neutral. Not a suspect."

"No. I know nothing about espionage and don't want to learn."

I'd heard rumors about a Trump/Russian connection, and the candidate's repeatedly expressed admiration for the Russian tyrant had struck a strange discordant note. Just the same, I gave little credence to what Zhukov showed me. Even if I'd believed that the tape was authentic, however, my answer would have been no different.

"You think I am not legitimate?"

"I have no way to know, but I know I don't want to be involved." I made a chopping motion to emphasize my resolve. "That you'd ask me to take the only copy…why me? Never mind. On so many levels it's too absurd to even discuss further."

"A former high-level MI 6 operative I work with. When information we have is verified, so cannot be questioned, into the right hands we will get it put. She will help. She told me to ask you as lawyer, totally neutral person."

56

"Best of luck with that."

Resolute, I strode back to the food. He followed.

"Involved you do not want to be. That I understand. But you are. All humanity involved. You know that famous poem, 'First they came for the communists, and I did not speak out - because I was not a communist; Then they came for the socialists, and I did not speak out - because I was not a socialist; Then'—"

"Excuse me." I made an open sandwich with Iberico ham, truffle mousse pâté, and quail egg, then heaped Beluga caviar on my plate. "I enjoyed talking to you, but my stomach insists that I devote the entirety of my attention to savoring and devouring the food."

His forced smile melted on itself like a burned-out candle, replaced by a fearful look, eyebrows drawn together, lips stretched horizontally and eyes wide. Then, he shuffled toward our hostess bent under the weight of the bad news he had to convey. Hard to imagine that Non-Madelyn would believe I'd take his phone to hold in escrow. So, why had she sicced him on me? If she had wanted me to become a member of her *coalition*, she'd made a lousy start, and she didn't seem like the lousy start kind. I reminded myself of the old adage about the effect of curiosity on felines and that unlike them I had only one life.

Thirty-one minutes until my hour was up.

I looked for a place to sit and enjoy my food, sans conspiracy theorists.

In an effort to avoid a tipsy woman, who staggered doggedly toward nowhere in particular, I brushed into a tall, thin man, who looked elegant in white tie.

"Excuse me," I said, choosing to follow established conventions rather than display my creativity.

"No problem." He smiled, and why not? He had good teeth, bright white against his acorn-colored skin and a trimmed black moustache. He had a passing resemblance to a middle-aged Omar Sharif and could have been Indian, Turkish, Arabic or Jewish. "I don't believe I've seen you here before. What brings you to this gathering?"

"I was kidnapped at gunpoint. You?"

He responded with an elegant little snicker.

"For one thing, I'm here for the food and drink." He extended his hand. "Jerome Curtis."

I shook it.

"Matt Bloom." I pointed at the clip on his plate that held his glass of red wine. "Clever. I never quite figured out how to eat and drink at the same time at cocktail parties. Always seemed like I needed an extra arm."

Squinting, he turned his head left then right, as if scanning the room for eavesdroppers or terrorists. I hoped that, if he was going to show me another salacious video, it wouldn't involve excretion or anything else that would interfere with my appetite.

"Tell no one where this came from," he whispered, then reached into his pocket, and with a quick surreptitious motion, pulled out a clip and affixed it on my plate. "Now, you need a drink."

He snapped his fingers, as making eye contact with a blind man would've been pointless.

A waiter strode over to us.

"What would you like, sir?"

"I'll have what he's having," I replied sensing that *red wine* would be an inadequate response. I wondered, though, how he'd known I was a sir rather than a madam. Perhaps by sense of smell. More likely, though, he could see just fine.

"Chateau Margaux 2009," Curtis said.

The waiter nodded, then toddled off to do my bidding.

"The other reason I'm here," he said, "is I'm flattered by Erinye's erotically tinged attention."

"Is that our hostess's first name?" I asked, suspecting that I'd misheard him.

Appearing by Curtis' side, as if conjured up from the netherworld by the mention of her name, Non-Madelyn got up on tip-toes and kissed him on the cheek.

"Matt's one of the few people here who will get your references to Greek mythology," she said, then unfurled her arm in my direction.

Not one to miss out on an opportunity for pedantry, I replied, "Otherwise known as the Furies, the Erinyes were three goddesses, seeking vengeance against anyone who'd sworn a false oath or done an evil act."

"Quite apt, don't you think?" Curtis said.

"I hope not," I said. "Since she's right here, though, I'm sure she'd like to tell us her given name, so we don't have to fall back on pretentious, precious pseudonyms."

"So glad you two met," she said. "Jerome's a serial entrepreneur about to embark on an exciting new venture. He needs a lawyer, or rather a whole... Lions come in prides, geese in gaggles, sheep in flocks. What's the word for a group of lawyers?"

"A quarrel," I said.

"Matt's one of the city's finest attorneys. He's forgotten more about the law than most lawyers know."

"Is that a good thing? I mean wouldn't it be better if he remembered—"

"I can't recommend him more highly."

"That's good enough for me," he said. "Matt, do you know much about non-profits?"

"No, but I have a partner who's something of an expert," I said. "Tell me about this venture of yours."

"Our mission is to provide low cost drugs, particularly in the Rust Belt, circumventing the cabal of big pharma and insurance companies and the cumbersome, unnecessary regulations designed to maintain their monopoly power. If ObamaCare is repealed, there'll be a whole lot of hurting people."

"Interesting."

"It's far more than *interesting*," the Woman-Who-Has-No-Name said. "It's potentially transformative, revolutionary."

"I'm sure Jerome's as interested as I am in hearing your real name and learning more about what you're really up to," I said.

"Not to worry, Jerome, he doesn't bill for his attempts at humor." She flashed her disorientating smile. "Jerome's planning on doing to the drug industry what Uber did to the taxi business."

My wine came.

"Join us in some wine?" Curtis asked her.

"Matt's leaving soon, and I want to give you boys the chance to discuss business without the distraction I provide."

She drifted off, seemingly light as dandelion fluff, feet barely grazing the parquet floor. Just the same I wouldn't have been surprised if the wood had buckled and turned black from the proximity of her footsteps.

Curtis raised his glass. I touched mine to his.

"To doing well by doing good," he said.

I swirled the wine around in my glass, smelled it, took a large sip, swirled it around in my mouth and swallowed.

"Pure lush, sensual sexy textures," I said. "Powerful, yet light on its feet, everything is in balance and harmony. Layers of opulent, silky, perfectly ripe fruits."

"Wow, you know your wine."

"No, I have a facility for bullshit. I can tell it's expensive but beyond that... I'm not big on connoisseurship."

"Don't we members of the East Coast elite have a responsibility to preserve and perfect effete snobbishness?"

I had some caviar and a bite of my Iberico ham, truffle mousse pâté, and quail egg sandwich.

"Does being hauled out here against my will in a limo qualify me as a limousine liberal?"

"Some of us paid five-grand."

I couldn't tell if he was bragging, complaining or chiding me for being ungrateful.

"It sounds like you need FDA counsel."

"I'm looking for an outside general counsel, a sort of *consigliere*," he said. "Do you have any thoughts on what I told you so far?"

"Free, off-the-cuff legal opinions are worth less than they cost." I handed him my card. "I'd be delighted to talk to you in a more professional atmosphere."

He put it in his pocket.

"I'll call," he said, which I interpreted as the equivalent of the check is in the mail or we've got to have lunch sometime.

"You seem to be something of a regular at these get-togethers, I'm curious—"

Non-Madelyn reappeared. A statuesque woman, whose permatanned face had been stretched tight by a surgeon's knife, followed as if dragged along in our hostess' slipstream. The woman's long dress whispered *haute couture*.

"Curt, meet Heidi, formerly marketing director of Pfizer, now a member of the President's Counsel."

Heidi extended a bejeweled hand, and he shook it.

"Lovely to meet you," she said. "I hear you're a pharmaceutical visionary."

"Heidi, this is Matt Bloom, lawyer extraordinaire," our hostess said, "Panicked that he'd fall victim to my charms, he ill-advisedly committed to staying but a single hour."

"What a shame. He'll miss the big reveal," Heidi said. "Matt, I find it hard to believe you haven't already fallen victim to her charms."

"I'm hoping that by successive small exposures I can build up a tolerance."

Arm around my waist, Non-Madelyn, led me away before I'd had the chance to find out more about her background or these get togethers.

"I've been getting good preliminary reports on you."

"From the nutcase who believes the president of Exxon will be Secretary of State if Trump's elected?"

"Zev was at one time part of Putin's inner circle," she said. "The FBI and the CIA are covering up the facts surrounding Dangerously Deranged Donald working with Putin."

"Probably because these *facts* lack credibility," I said.

She plucked a tempting hors d'oeuvre of indeterminate content off a passing tray and tried to stick it in my mouth.

I turned my head away.

"Your loss," she said, plopping it into hers.

She rubbed her stomach, indicating that it was delicious. I had no doubt that it was.

"Lev gave you his phone, right? You'll guard it as you do the most sensitive client information?"

"As I believe he told you, I didn't take it. Surprising as it might be, I'm not a safe-deposit box for dubious and dangerous information."

"You think it's fair that the FBI is investigating Trump's Russia contacts, and while they prepare to trash Hillary based on nothing, they keep their investigation under seal?" she asked.

"I don't know enough of the facts, but if that's your concern, post all the information publicly or give it to the DNC. You know that old saw about sunlight being the best disinfectant?"

"It's too late now for the news cycle, and I can't both run this soirée and devise the best strategy to break the news for maximum effect. That's why I wanted you to keep it under wraps, so we can maintain a credible chain of custody, in case something were to happen to Lev. You have to know he's putting his life on the line to—"

"I have no idea, but I'd have thought that, if his tradecraft was up to snuff, he'd have an impenetrable legend and be holed up in a safe house," I said. "Also, if possessing this tape puts one in mortal danger… Lauren doesn't like me risking my life for people I meet at cocktail parties, one of her silly little quirks."

"I get it. Don't worry about it. My fault. I expected too much of you, too soon."

Had she actually thought that she could make me feel guilty about not wanting to involve myself in something that was either a total scam or a partial scam with potentially fatal consequences? Preposterous. What the hell was she up to?

"Much too much and way too soon."

She shrugged her well-defined, creamy white shoulders, and the sickly sweet smell of death returned—surely an olfactory hallucination grounded in my overactive imagination.

A waiter came by with a tray of what appeared to be chicken on skewers—but was likely an exotic creature on the endangered species list that just tasted like chicken—with peanut sauce. To demonstrate what a good sport I was, I took one. Under her gaze, I ate it and nodded my approval.

"Stay another hour." Her gray gold-flecked eyes glittered. "I don't yet have enough feedback to decide if you'll be invited back."

"No need. I've already decided." A waiter had refilled my wine glass without my noticing—good trick for a blind man, but a blunder for someone pretending to be blind. I took a sip. "Good food and drink notwithstanding, I haven't changed my mind about being kidnapped or having my communications listened in on. I particularly detest having my son and wife—"

"Surely you don't think we were the only ones listening in."

"What is it about me that has attracted your unwanted interest?"

A woman in a Hillary-like pant suit came charging up to us, like an angry rhinoceros. Concerned that she might not swerve in time, I stepped out of harm's way.

"Freya, you've really out done yourself! The food the drink the people, magnificent."

She hugged our hostess.

"*Freya?*" I rolled my eyes. "Is it the wine, or are the pseudonyms becoming even more ridiculous?"

"Freya was, or rather is…" Non-Madelyn, a/k/a Freya, etc., unfurled her arm

"Norse goddess of sex, beauty, fertility, war, and death," I said.

"Fitting, don't you think?" the new woman said.

"Like O. J. Simpson's glove," I said. "Am I the only one who thinks our hostess' efforts to be mysterious are excessive and irritating and that her goddess complex borders on the insane?"

"As a matter of fact, yes, you are," the new woman said. "Maybe you should lighten up. Nothing succeeds like excess."

"Or fails like it," I said.

"You don't believe that goddesses still walk among us?"

"Or that they ever have," I said.

"I pity your impoverished soul."

"I devote some time each day to doing that."

"Matt, Leslie," our hostess said. "Leslie, Matt."

Leslie waved at me, a little too cutesy for my taste. I waved back, proving I could be cutesy with the best of them.

"Not to worry, Leslie. Matt's sense of humor takes some getting used to, it's an acquired taste like gefilte fish and anchovies. In his secret heart, though, he's one of us, and he has a huge heart."

Recalling the sage advice I'd gotten earlier that evening *sobriety won't be a plus where we're going,* I had some more wine.

"Leslie's looking for a lawyer, but Matt, if you need to leave..." Our hostess looked at the spot on her wrist where a watch would be.

"It's so early," Leslie said. "I don't know who you've met so far, but this group is... Well, we certainly think highly of ourselves...and of Freya."

"I see that."

"Matt represented Johnny Walker, got a fabulous result in record time."

Our hostess tilted her head to the other side of the room, where Walker—wearing evening clothes with a red bowtie, cummerbund and turban—was involved in animated conversation with a gaggle of tall bejeweled women and their shorter, dumpier male counterparts. Except for Walker, they all were in noticeable states of intoxication. He stood straight, exuding a prim, condescending arrogance. A pretty young man—Hakan, I assumed, although I wouldn't have expected Walker to appear in public with him— hovered close by, as if he were part butterfly and Walker were coated with nectar.

"Really?" Leslie said, with excessive enthusiasm.

My gut told me to leave—there had to be a Faustian price to pay for all these offers of new business—but my feet failed to follow my brain's instructions as if they'd been set in a tub of concrete, a prelude to my being dumped in New York Harbor.

After holding up a finger to indicate to Leslie that I would be coming back in one minute, I, having recovered the power of locomotion, guided Non-Madelyn to a place beyond the range of Leslie's hearing.

"When I'm ready to leave, you'll have a car take me home?" I asked her.

"Just let me know when," she said. "You have any more questions, or can I go back to making sure that the rest of my guests are enjoying themselves and drumming up yet more legal business for you?"

"Just one: what the fuck?"

"Through my *excessive efforts to be mysterious,* I've gathered together some of the city's, actually the world's, most interesting and influential people. If we decide to invite you back—and it is a big if—it would be the best thing that ever happened to your practice and your intellectual life since you dumped The Lyin' King."

"You didn't answer my question about why you made such an effort to bring me here. I'm far from being one of the country's most influential people."

"You'd definitely be punching above your weight," she said. "Stay or go. Your choice."

Rays from her gray, gold-flecked eyes lasered into me, and I began to understand what inspired people to refer to her by the names of mythical goddesses of death and vengeance. No use agonizing over whether to stay or go; she'd already spun the thread of my fate and would determine when and how it would be cut.

"So by what ridiculous, pretentious mythical name should I address you?"

"Kate will do. That's what my parents chose for me." She blew me a kiss that caused the hair on the back of my neck to stand. "Go talk to Leslie."

I did.

"Sorry about that," I said. "She and I just needed to straighten something out."

"No problem." Leslie had a sweet smile, although a little

64

crooked, perhaps from too much expensive spirits. "I gather you're new to the group. The initiation is a bit weird but… Well, she keeps it interesting."

"Kate said you had a legal problem."

"Kate?" She raised her meticulously trimmed eyebrows.

I tilted my head toward our hostess, who was being picked up and swung around by a distinguished-looking new arrival obviously delighted to see her.

"Until last week my husband was the head of M & A for a major investment bank. Then just before the close of their fiscal year, they canned him, claimed it was a *restructuring*, which was crap. I'd introduce you, but he couldn't be here tonight because… he refused to come."

"I'd be happy to see if I can help. Have him call me." I handed her my card. "Why did he refuse? A glittering gathering like this would seem to be hard to pass up."

She stuck my card in a little black bag.

A waiter refilled her wine glass, 2012 Jadot Louis Le Montrachet Grand Cru, according to the label.

"I'm good," I said, and he departed.

"I'm curious about our hostess," I said once it became clear that she wasn't going to answer my question. "It appears you two are quite close."

"It *appears* she and many people are quite close."

"I get the feeling she has plans for me, like I'm a turkey," I said. "It's October and all seems fine, but Thanksgiving's coming and there's an ominous chill in the air."

"She has plans for everyone. I used to think that the whiff of danger was just part of her shtick, her endless effort to be interesting, but…"

"But?"

A cloud seemed to pass in front of her face, then she looked over my shoulder, smiled and waved.

"Excuse me, someone I need to talk to." She took a quick step away. "I'll have Ellis, that's my husband, call you."

She exchanged greetings with the woman she'd waved to. The woman's slightly stunned look, as if she'd just taken off her glasses, made me think that she didn't know Leslie and had no idea why she'd come up to her. They separated after two strokes of conversation.

I washed down the remains of my food with the remains of my wine and graciously consented to a waiter's request that he refill my glass.

Johnathan Walker detached himself from a couple he'd been talking to and staggered in my direction. He looked thoroughly soused. Maybe he hadn't been as sober as he'd appeared just a few minutes earlier. The young man I'd pegged for Hakan hovered behind, steadying him when he seemed to be about to topple over.

Perhaps embarrassed by his condition, he avoided making eye contact with me.

I said, "Jonathan, are you okay?"

Still ignoring me, he brushed past, bumping into my left shoulder and grabbing onto my jacket for support.

"Jonathan," I repeated.

He seemed oblivious to the chair he tripped over, sending him sprawling into a matronly woman's lap. Hakan mumbled an apology, then helped him to his feet.

Walker turned toward me, eyes pleading for help.

I was about to go over to him, when Hakan got him seated in a chair, and a pair of waiters came over to tend to him.

In any event, the pastry table beckoned.

I came abreast of a scrum of people who had the look of malefactors of great wealth with a heavy foreign presence.

A bejeweled Asian woman said, "You're Matt Bloom?" Her tone would've been appropriate for addressing Queen Elizabeth, if she'd unexpectedly appeared at a community bake sale.

"That's what my mother told me, and she stuck to that story till her dying day." At least when she didn't mistakenly call me by her brother's name.

Several seconds passed, then one of the men smiled, and smiles spread through the group like the metachronal rhythm of a wave at a football game. After an exchange of looks among the group, the crowd parted. A cannibalistic attention focused on me.

"We've been told that you represented Mr. Trump," said a South Asian woman. She wore a *haute couture* version of a sari and a gold necklace featuring a large sapphire. "What is your impression of him?"

"That was over a decade ago."

I stepped toward the dessert table.

"Please." A man who, from his skin-tone and heavy accent, I pegged as hailing from the Middle East put a hand on my shoulder and nudged me back toward the group. The sleeve of his elegant jacket slid up exposing a Patek Philippe Sky Moon Tourbillon, which carried a seven-figure price tag.

"No legitimate bank will lend to him. We pulled the plug on him years ago," said a black woman with a Parisian French accent. If not a banker herself, she'd gone to great lengths to look like one. "If it wasn't for the Russian kleptocracy, he'd go under. I can't imagine any sensible businessman letting himself get involved with that crew. He must've been desperate."

The attention of the group again focused on me. I felt flattered and fought the urge to comment.

"I'm sorry, but I'm not at liberty to discuss anything I learned in the course of my representation of him."

"Everyone I know who has done business with him refuses to have anything further to do with him," said a light-skinned black man with an Oxbridge accent, a perfectly fitting tux and a stunning dark-skinned companion wearing a clingy low-cut sequined dress.

"I know nothing about his banking relationships," I said.

The man with the multi-million-dollar watch cast an irritated look toward Kate who'd been observing us from a comfortable distance. She caught my eye and by an economical motion of her upraised palms, directed me to be more forthcoming. At least I now knew, or thought I knew, the reason I'd been forcibly invited to this event. But couldn't Kate have found a more expert authority on Trump's inner workings? Certainly she could have kidnapped someone less constrained in his ability to offer an opinion. I pivoted away from the group and responded to her gesture with a one-fingered one.

"Certainly we're not looking for you to breach any confidences," said the South Asian woman, "but you must have some impressions and insight into what he thinks. We would be most grateful if you would share them."

"I don't know what he really thinks," I said, "and, based only on what I read in the press, neither does most anyone else, including he himself. Although he freely blurts out his passing thoughts, he's a hard guy to get to know."

"He must have been a terrific litigation client. I gather that virtually everything he does results in a lawsuit," said a tall, thin, pale blonde man, in the accent of a movie Nazi commandant. He resembled Andy Warhol, yet was even more effete. He had his arm around the Parisian-accented banker's waist either out of affection or the need for support, in the event a strong breeze were to sweep though the room.

"Did he pay you?" asked a man who looked familiar. Perhaps a Hong Kong real estate magnate whose photograph I'd seen in *The Financial Times* or *The Economist*.

"We parted on good terms," I said, the line that my non-disclosure agreement required me to say.

"I do not desire to be impolite or to intrude on confidences, but we have been told that it would be acceptable for us to inquire about your impression of working for him." He punctuated his statement with a slight bow, which I returned.

Everyone in the group leaned forward like a team of synchronized swimmers. I reminded myself that each person there was a potential client who could have substantial business in New York but might not have a lawyer in the Big Apple. Would it hurt for me to capitalize on the buildup that Kate had apparently given me? My observations would be no less reliable than those of the so-called experts who mouthed off on TV every night.

"In his tweets, just in the past couple weeks, he exhibited gluttony, lust, greed, pride, wrath, envy and sloth—all of the seven deadly sins," I said.

That drew encouraging smiles. These wealthy, influential people leaned yet further forward, hanging on my every word. I was under no obligation to refrain from commenting on what I'd gleaned from public sources after the termination of my relationship with him. While I wasn't thoroughly comfortable bad-mouthing a candidate for my country's highest office, I was far more uncomfortable with Trump being such a candidate

"Based only on what I've read or seen on television after he and I parted company, it appears that he has no close friends, no hobbies, no interest in art or literature and doesn't read anything other than articles about himself. I think he cares for his children, but as an archetypical narcissist, he might see them merely as an extension of himself, but as I said, I don't know." I cast an angry glance at my wine glass, as if my loquaciousness had been its fault. "Maybe there's a good side, or *human* side to him, that I never got to see. After all almost no one is all bad or all good—even Hitler loved his dog, Blondi, and purported to like children."

"Does he have a pet?" asked a blonde woman of indeterminate age and aristocratic bearing.

"Not that I know of."

"So in comparison to the previous worst person in history, he comes up short?" a hitherto silent woman asked.

I pretended that I thought her question had been rhetorical.

"I can't tell if he loves or hates the media," another woman, said, rescuing me from the hyperbolic hole I'd dug for myself. An elaborate silk confection covered her hair, and she wore pants and a jacket and long gloves, so the only skin that showed was her face and upper neck. The height of Islamic fashion, I assumed.

"Both," I said. "Although he claims to hate the media, he yearns for their love."

"Sounds like he is easy to motivate by flattery," said the man I thought to be a Hong Kong real estate tycoon.

"So Mr. Putin has realized," the pale blonde man said.

A short, stocky man with coppery skin, and straight slicked back black hair made fleeting eye contact with the tall, strikingly beautiful, raven-haired woman next to him. She shuddered. I had the feeling that any glance that lasted longer than a few hundred milliseconds from those dark dead eyes could be fatal. If he wasn't a Mexican drug lord, Hollywood was missing out on a golden opportunity to cast him as one.

Apparently, his glance had been a cue, as the woman said, "The wall, his tax plan, his supposed ability to bring back manufacturing jobs lost to automation…why would anyone in his right mind believe any of that?"

Before I had a chance to respond, the blonde man, who I realized was actually an albino, said, "Our people have concluded that he is exactly what he appears to be."

I seemed to be the only one who didn't know who *our people* were, but whoever they were, it seemed that their opinion counted.

The drug lord doppelganger glanced again at his companion.

"Have you spoken to…?" She tilted her head toward Lev Georgorovich Zhukov.

The albino responded with a dismissive wave.

"There's nothing to his honey trap pee story," he said, and I was grateful that the conversation had passed me by. "It's a cover for something far worse. The FSB is all in for Trump, and it would be a mistake to underestimate their influence."

"So that is your opinion or that of Goldman?" asked a hitherto silent Asian woman on the fatal side of fifty, her tone out-condescending his.

Goldman Saks. So the man was worse than the Nazi manqué I'd at first imagined him to be.

"Naturally I don't speak for the firm." He seemed to shrink by several inches.

"They're among Hillary's biggest contributors." She stepped toward him, closing in for the kill.

"Wouldn't be the first time they played both sides," the Asian woman said.

Several people looked at me, awaiting my sage pundit-speak.

"It's clear that Putin would prefer the Republican," I said.

"Which most American voters would count as a strike against the candidate?"

"One would think so."

"Putin sees Trump as a useful idiot," the man from Goldman said.

"I enjoyed talking to you," I said. "But it's almost time for me to leave, and I haven't yet gorged on the pastries."

"Thank you for your time," the Asian man said.

Others nodded.

I took several steps toward my just desserts. The man whom I'd mistaken for a drug lord and now believed to be a sophisticated Latin American businessman, broke from his group and caught up to me. I chided myself for my initial impression of him, but told myself it hadn't been fueled by racism but rather resentment that such a ravishing woman was stuck with this unattractive, squat man. Usually I was less given to snap judgments and more accurate on the occasions when I made them. I told myself that Kate had caused me to lose my bearings.

"I was very much taken by your insights."

In spite of my susceptibility to flattery and my high self-regard, I didn't recall having imparted any *insights.*

"Thank you."

"Your opinions are far more level-headed than those of our hostess," he said.

"Oh, really, what does she say?"

He looked at the back of his hand as if he'd written crib notes on it. His manner would have made me more suspicious of Kate and her motives, if my capacity for suspicion hadn't already been stretched to the limit.

"I would like to be able to follow up with you regarding mutually profitable business," he said.

He handed me a calling card that read *Enrique de Caldas*, no address, telephone or email.

"I would like that," I said, believing that he wouldn't follow up and that this would be just as well.

On my way to the desserts, I noticed that the flap on my left jacket pocket had become tucked in.

In untucking it, I found a cocktail napkin on which was scrawled *Flynn Turkish $$$, Kislyak. I was played. Hakan Russian agent. Big trouble. Need to talk to you 646 678 0320 ASAP JW.*

I recalled Walker brushing into me as he staggered past and his grabbing onto my jacket.

Kate appeared beside me. I shoved the note back into my pocket.

"You were just speaking to the collective net worth of over fifty billion dollars," she said.

Still slumped in the chair, Walker was being attended to by the waiters and Hakan.

"They seemed to take me more seriously than I deserved."

"I gave you a big build-up, not that I expect anything back from you in the way of thanks."

"Thanks," I said in my most insincere voice, "but I wonder why."

"The election is having a depressing effect on interesting conversation," she said. "Hardly anyone here realizes that Creep Throat's going to win. It'll be quite a shock when he does."

"You sound pretty sure—"

"You too, based on your investment pattern."

I shot her my most hostile look.

"It's one thing for you to hack into everything I do, quite another for you to tell me about it."

71

"Matt, I'm trying to be up front with you."

"Far better would be for you to leave me the fuck alone."

"You're not enjoying—"

"The food and drink is first-rate. It seems that this group of yours has great business-development potential. Still, I can't shake the feeling that something's not right here. Among other things, it doesn't make sense that you've fixated on me." I maintained my hostile stare. "Your continued failure to give me a straight answer as to that, among other things, has pushed my concern well beyond the level I can tolerate."

She took both my hands in hers.

"Matt, we're going to need each other."

I yanked them away.

"God, I hope not."

Again, she brought her lips close to my ear. "Hair Hitler must be destroyed," she whispered.

If Cato had spoken with such vehemence when he'd regularly declared on the floor of the Roman Senate *Carthago delenda est,* Carthage would have fallen without Scipio Africanus ever having to sail to North Africa. Plenty of people were profoundly offended by the Republican candidate, but Kate's vehemence was beyond the pale. Too intense to be believed, I told myself.

"That's your agenda?" I asked.

"My agenda? Heavens, no." Her bewitching stare made the hair on my arms stand up and my fingers feel prickly. "It'll be yours. Some have greatness thrust upon them."

"No. And don't even say anything in my presence that even hints at violence toward the candidate or anyone else."

"Understood," she said in a high-pitched comic voice that communicated the opposite.

"Walker doesn't look so good," I said.

"You don't want to be involved in his latest *mishigas.*"

"If his problems are in Yiddish, they must really be serious."

"Delusions of persecution," she whispered. "We're trying to get him help."

"First priority would seem to be to make sure he gets home alright."

"Yes. Please be sure to do that."

"I'd be happy to. I'm ready to leave. Is there a car available?"

"Waiting downstairs. You'll be blindfolded again. Once you're in Manhattan, you can take it off and they'll return your phone, but are you sure you want to leave? The real fun's just about to start."

"There's only so much fun I can handle. I'm sure Lauren's already worried, and Walker looks like he could use my help." I looked back toward the chair he'd been sitting in. "Where is he?"

"If I can do anything to help with Lauren or anything else—"

"Yeah, that'd be great. Here's what I need." I motioned for her to come closer, and when she did, I whispered in her ear, "Leave me and my family the fuck alone."

"Eau de sweet sickly smell of death," she said, apparently having noticed my nostrils flare from the odor wafting off her. "Some here find it overpoweringly erotic. For others, it fuels their fantasies of my otherworldliness."

"Count me in the third category."

Her tongue made a slow transit across her lips and bared teeth, an exaggerated comic gesture perhaps, but I felt it in my groin.

"You really are going to have to trust me here, Matt."

"That wouldn't happen, even if you were to start being truthful with me."

She squinched up her face in a pantomime of hard thought.

"It will, when you realize it's your best option."

Deciding that further conversation would be pointless, I asked, "Where's Walker?"

She scanned the room. "Wait here."

She disappeared behind a scrum of revelers and didn't emerge on the other side.

"Seems he left," she said on her return. "I guess he got tired of waiting for you."

"Waiting for me?"

"I'd told him you'd be leaving soon and suggested he share a car with you."

"When? You only just suggested it to me a few minutes ago?"

"I'm entitled to anticipate more than a few minutes forward."

"I guess if he took one of your cars and drivers, he'll be okay," I said. "His problem seemed to come on suddenly. A little while earlier he appeared to be sober as a—"

"As a judge?" She tilted her head toward one end of the room, where I noticed a judge I'd appeared before wearing a plate as a party hat and laughing hysterically while his companions looked on, aghast. Kate dropped her voice to a whisper. "I don't trust that weaselly little rent boy Hakan. He's too pretty to be honest. I'm told he's older than he looks and has been involved in some dirty doings."

I made a mental note to call Walker when I got home.

"Well, I'll be on my way then."

I had another long look into her gold-flecked gray eyes and wished I hadn't.

VII
Don't Hi, Honey Me

I think that [Hillary Clinton's] bodyguards should drop all weapons. They should disarm right? I think they should disarm immediately. Take their guns away. Donald J. Trump, September 16, 2016

Lauren was waiting up for me, a bad sign. CNN was on in the background, the channel that Trump had dubbed the *Clinton News Network*. Never mind that it and other media outlets had already given him two billion dollars in free publicity, which substantially helped his successful efforts to secure the nomination.

"Hi, Honey!" I said.

"Don't hi, Honey me. Where the hell have you been?"

While I told her, her cheeks reddened and her eyes narrowed. If she'd been a cartoon character, steam would have come out of her ears. Then she'd have hit me so hard with a rolling pin that tweeting birds would've flown in circles around my head.

When I finished, she said in the quiet voice she used when too angry to yell, "A little hard to believe."

"If I were making it up, I'd have come up with something more credible."

She sighed.

"After all these years of courting danger, you've finally landed her."

"I was kidnapped at gunpoint."

"You stayed an extra hour."

"And I seem to have gotten significant business."

"Maybe they'll call, maybe not, but if they do... You said yourself that this *Kate* isn't what she seems."

"That's good because she seems to be part harpy, part gorgon."

"Spare me the classical allusions."

I hung my head like a penitent.

"If she's trouble, you think clients you get from her won't be?" Lauren said.

"If they call, I'll be cautious, but most of the people at the party seemed legit."

"You're not going to attend any more of these *soirées* or have anything more to do with her?"

I placed my hand on my heart but pulled it away when I remembered that Kate had done the same.

On the theory that Lauren was already as angry as she could be, I confessed to what I'd done on the investment front.

She stared at me, apparently searching my face for a hint that I was joking. Under the force of her gaze, my cheeks felt warm. I broke eye contact.

"YOU WHAT?"

"I—"

"AND YOU DIDN'T THINK TO CONSULT ME?"

"I did."

"You didn't!"

"Yes, I thought to. In fact, I *mean*t to."

Her look communicated so much anger that words were unnecessary.

"If Hillary loses, I'll make a bundle, which would soften the blow of having to live through four years of a megalomaniacal, ethically amnesiac president. If she wins we'll probably be okay. We don't spend all that much."

"Seventy-five thou a year in college tuition."

"Only another two-and-a-half years."

"And graduate school?"

"He hasn't decided—"

"And what about your extravagant charitable contributions."

"I'll cut back."

She sighed, as if her anger had exhausted her. More likely she was fed up with me. I understood; I was fed up with me as well.

She tilted her head, perhaps she thought viewing me from a different angle would change what she saw.

"Do you know anyone who actually thinks Trump will win?"

"No. That's what concerns me."

It seemed unwise to mention Kate.

"Please, be serious." Her furious quiet voice. "You've

committed a hell of a lot of money to this… gamble."

"When I was in law school, everyone I knew favored McGovern. I thought Nixon would lose in a landslide."

She shook her head as if trying to dislodge what I'd said. Her hair flinging out like in a shampoo ad, she looked quite attractive.

"You're almost seventy. Not a good time to take financial risks."

"Sixty-eight."

"How many productive years do you think you have ahead of you?"

"Not all that many." Maybe one, but I had to allow for the possibility of things being better than they seemed. So it could have been as much as two.

"You actually like being under financial pressure." She paused, allowing her epiphany time to sink in as deeply as my consciousness would permit. "You can't stand prosperity."

"Maybe. I don't know. There's lot I don't know these days."

"Your self-destructiveness is getting worse." She sounded concerned. I'd have preferred it if she was still angry.

"I'm not self-destructive."

"What then?"

"I have a pathological antipathy to boredom."

She buried her head in her hands.

Just when I thought things couldn't get any worse, Kellyanne Conway's face appeared on the TV screen. I could tell she was lying because her lips were moving. No amount of money could compensate for having to listen to her for four years.

"Perhaps you can come up with some more productive outlet for your boredom?"

"Working on it."

"In the meantime sell those stocks, please."

"But they're all down."

"Of course they're down; the market anticipates a Hillary win."

"I suppose I could sell calls against them to cover my loss."

"Just take the loss and consider it a lesson learned."

"Good advice," I said, seeing no reason to remind her that I only took good advice after I'd exhausted all other options. Of course, my not having taken her advice would only make her reaction more extreme when the stocks got hammered.

"How much would we lose if you sold at today's closing price?"

"I haven't calculated—"

"Ballpark?" she said. Annoyingly she'd long before learned to see through my bullshit.

"Two hundred K." I wiggled my hand.

Her jaw hung open in amazement.

"You invested...."

"All my available cash, supplemented by a margin loan or two." I sounded sheepish, but not nearly as much as I should have.

A small bet wouldn't have alleviated my boredom. I wouldn't have had to make the big bet if I'd known that I'd be facing a huge, unquantifiable future risk from someone who might or might not have been named Kate.

"I... I don't know what to say."

Bad sign that I'd rendered her speechless. Quick to criticize me for any little offense, but in the face of serious crises, Lauren cleaved to my side and was hardly ever at a loss for verbal support. Her speechlessness seemed to mark her transition from one mode to the other. Perhaps I really did fuck up.

An uncomfortable silence descended.

I changed the channel to Bloomberg. When Lauren didn't object, I turned up the sound, hoping that the blathering of talking heads would provide a benign distraction.

A respected market guru said, "One thing we can absolutely count on is that Hillary will tighten regulations on banks. Even if she doesn't fully believe that to be necessary, the Bernie-Sanders-Elizabeth-Warren wing of her party will not tolerate her not doing so. The banking stocks are down but the market hasn't fully priced in the cost of such regulation."

"What effect would that have on stocks such as JP Morgan and Goldman?" the host asked.

"At the least, the very least, twenty percent down from here."

"So big shot," Lauren said, "what would a twenty percent drop do to your investments, or rather, gambles?"

"Margin calls would take ten percent off the top. With regard to the rest, if I can afford to wait it out..."

"Meaning?"

"I'd have to work until I'm a hundred and five."

"Matt, I've had enough for the evening."

"Oh, in the interest of full disclosure, one more thing," I said.

Her look didn't bode well for my disclosure.

I reached into my pocket for the note from Walker. It wasn't there.

I shouldn't have been surprised. Kate had already shown herself to be a skilled pickpocket. No real problem, though, as I remembered his phone number.

"Nothing, random thought."

She switched the channel to *Law & Order* reruns which she'd listen to, with eyes closed, when trying to get to sleep.

I went out to the living room and called the number in Walker's note. No surprise given his intoxicated condition, my call went into voicemail. I left a message asking him to call in the morning. Then I started reading a novel about a Russian aristocrat condemned to spend the decades following the Russian Revolution in a Moscow hotel. Although, unlike the main character, I wasn't a gentleman, I related to him as a man out of step with his times.

I fell asleep on the couch.

The front door swung open with an ominous creak.

I sprang to my feet.

Our once-a week housekeeper, who'd been with us since Jason was a month old, had unlocked it.

It was 8:30, the latest I'd slept in months.

"Good morning, Esperanza," I said in as cheery a tone as I could manage.

Lauren, rushed out to meet her. They talked in hushed tones as if they were discussing me. Perhaps, though, people spent a good deal less time talking about me than I thought. Nah, unlikely.

When I arrived at the office, I called Walker again, and again reached voicemail.

When I got home, I started to tell Lauren about my day, but transfixed by the TV news, she flicked her hand: not now.

"It's normal for the polls to tighten as we approach Election Day," a TV pundit said, with the confidence of someone who actually knew what she was talking about.

"To win, Trump would have to run the table," another expert on the panel said. "It would be a virtual statistical impossibility for him to climb Hillary's blue wall."

"Absolutely," a third panelist said. "The bottom line is that Hillary's *ground game* and organization outshines Trump's to the nth degree."

"What about the emails?" the host asked.

"Already baked-in," the fourth panelist said, punctuating her statement with a dismissive wave of her hand.

Lauren asked, "Did you sell your stocks today?"

"They were down big. Rather than sell on a downtick, I hoped to catch them on an uptick."

"I hope you enjoy a diet of peanut butter and jelly with the occasional treat of black beans."

Several weeks after the soirée, Leslie's husband, Ellis McKuen called, and we set up a meeting for three days hence.

McKuen showed up in my office precisely on time. Although unshaven and wearing a black watch plaid shirt, jeans and running shoes, he carried himself with the arrogance of the prosperous investment banker he'd been until a few days earlier. I led him into the conference room and offered him water, tea or coffee, which he declined, with an impatient wave of his arm.

"You represented Johnny Walker?" he asked, portentous tone, as if his question, pregnant with deeper meaning, demanded an in-depth response.

"That's right."

Staring, he appeared to be studying my face for clues to I knew not what.

I stared back. His lips were clamped together so tightly that they made a faint bloodless line. Was there something he was afraid to say to me? Hard to imagine what that might have been.

After an awkward silence, he said, "He recommended you highly, before…"

He shifted his weight from one foot to the other back and back again. He looked down at his shoes, then gave me another searching look.

I responded with a quizzical one, trying to encourage him to finish his sentence.

He made a windshield-wiper movement with his left arm, broke eye contact, then took a seat at the middle of the table. I sat across from him.

"Walker's recommendation is enough for me," he said. "So spare me the canned speech you use to sell yourself," he said.

Canned speech? Well, his loss.

He handed me a file folder, containing emails and other documents relevant to the termination of his employment, with selected portions highlighted.

"Read, this, then we'll talk."

While he drummed his fingers, I skimmed his papers enough to get a general overview, then put the file back on the conference room table. I wasn't about to devote the time and attention necessary to read with care with him sitting there.

Before I had a chance to speak, McKuen said, "I know I'm an employee-at-will and the payment of a bonus is discretionary, but to be fired two days before the end of the fiscal year, when my entitlement to a bonus would have vested, reeks of bad faith."

"How much bonus would you have been entitled to?"

After a hand-to-forehead gesture that communicated impatience and frustration—hadn't I just read the file?—he showed me a spreadsheet entitled *Approximate Bonus Calculation*. The figure $6.5MM appeared on the bottom right hand side with a double underlining. I was in the wrong business, but then again so was almost everyone else.

"What reason did they give you for—"

He brought his finger hard on the lower part of another page, where he'd highlighted the word *restructuring*.

"Look, Ellis, I understand that when you were an investment banker you felt a professional obligation to be an arrogant asshole, but now that you're unemployed... Either dial the attitude way the fuck back or find a lawyer with greater tolerance for condescending bullshit."

I matched his wide-eyed look of shock with one of my own.

Finally, he laughed.

"Actually, I could use a glass of water, with ice if you have it," he said.

When I returned with his tap water and a coaster, he asked, "Is it true that you represented Donald Trump?"

"Until he became so insufferable that I had to fire him," I said, a minor breach of the mutual non-disparagement clause in my agreement with Trump that I immediately regretted.

McKuen shot me an annoyed look.

Time to turn the conversation back to business.

"So they didn't give you a reason beyond *restructuring*?" Once it had become clear that he wasn't about to respond, I said, "They just called you into HR, gave you the bad news, then had security goons escort you back to your office, so you could pack up, your phone and computer having been already disabled?"

He nodded.

"You must have some understanding why they fired you, beyond a desire to save the bonus money."

"They canned two managing directors the same day. The three of us were white male Trump supporters." He held up his hand. "And please spare me the liberal political bullshit about him being the second coming of Hitler. I get enough of it at home from my wife."

"No, I was just surprised. I thought the other night's *soirée* and its promoter were heavily skewed toward Hillary, with a strong anti-Trump agenda."

"Don't get me started on that," he said. "The firm contributed a pant-load of money to Hillary. So perhaps I was unwise to express my opinions, but this is America, and at least as of now, I'm still endowed with unalienable First Amendment rights."

"Which protect you against the government, not private individuals or companies," I said. "Did any clients complain about your political opinions?"

His wince told me that my question had hit home.

"The client on a mega-deal I was working on requested that I leave the team."

"Just out of the blue?"

"Not entirely." He broke eye contact. "A few days earlier, the client's CEO asked what I thought about the election, and I'd told him that Hillary should be locked up."

Fighting my desire to respond, I clenched my teeth.

"You don't think I have a case?" he asked.

"From the little I've heard so far, you probably don't under the law, but under the lore, you have a claim worth pursuing," I said, then lapsed into auto-pilot. "Typically when terminating senior executives, big companies give a low-ball offer, holding something back in case the employee hires a lawyer, and if the lawyer seems to know what he's doing they offer yet more."

"They gave me a no-ball offer."

"Might be the opening shot in a negotiation, like your candidate's plan to deport eleven million immigrants, or it might be their bottom line, like your candidate's plan to deport eleven million immigrants."

His lips, pressed together, turned thin and white—it being his turn now to fight a desire to respond.

Finally, he said, "Okay, let's give it a shot."

"Enough about you. Let's talk about me. I'll need a five-thousand-dollar retainer, against which I'll charge for my time at my usual seven-hundred-fifty-dollars per hour."

"I want the same deal Walker had. Straight contingency."

"But given the numbers involved, if I get you anything, you'll do far better on an hourly—"

"Having been stiffed on my bonus, I'm strapped for cash and...." Sheepish grin. "If up to me, I'd go with the hourly. But Leslie...someone told her that that's the way to go, and she was quite adamant. As you may know, in marriage, one has to decide what's important enough to argue about, and your fees didn't qualify."

"Okay," I said, even though I wanted to ask who this *someone*—Kate, I assumed—was, what she'd told Leslie, why Leslie was so adamant and why this sophisticated banker felt compelled to follow her instructions, even though he knew they were not in his financial interest. "If you have a few minutes, I'll have my assistant prepare a retainer agreement."

"Sure," he said.

After telling my assistant what I wanted, I turned back to McKuen.

"While we wait, may I ask you a question?" I asked, drawing a *noblesse oblige* nod. "What do you know about these *soirées* and the woman who throws them?"

"You mean the fraudster sometimes known as *Freya*?"

"I think that's your wife's pet name for her, but—"

"Total scam, even worse than The Clinton Foundation," he said. "Some of the attendees pay up to thirty grand for an annual membership, which entitles them to the bargain basement price of five grand per head for each event. They're happy to pay, thinking that doing so marks them as the *crème de la crème,* as opposed to members of the schlemiel of the month club and that it entitles them to hobnob with real movers and shakers, all of whom have far better things to do than attend one of her events."

"Leslie seems to have her head screwed on straight, and she's an enthusiastic proponent."

"She's a high-end real estate broker. She's sold half a dozen nine- and ten-figure condos to Chinese, Middle Easterners or Russians, with more money than sense, whom she's met there. For her it's been a good investment, even if it means buying into some of the nutsy rants and flattering her with that ludicrous nickname."

"The food and drink is first-rate."

He had yet to take a sip of his water.

"The supposed Wagyu Kobe Strip steak is normal U.S. grade A. In beef Wellington it's hard to tell the difference, particularly when combined with the power of suggestion. The *Iberico ham* is serrano sprinkled with a smidgen of acorn essence. The wine is decent mid-price stuff with counterfeit labels. The secret meeting places are abandoned South Bronx warehouses. The blind waiters have 20/20 eyesight and are armed with cameras and recording devices."

"How did you learn all this?"

"Her files on the attendees make J. Edgar Hoover's look benign. If any attendees were to speak to law enforcement, the exposed files would destroy them."

"You've seen them?"

He shook his head.

"But I know from—"

His lips came together with an audible plop.

"What were you about to say?" I asked, still hoping to determine whether what he was telling me was based on hard knowledge or rumor and speculation.

He again shook his head.

I leaned forward, eyes wide and encouraging.

Finally, he said, "She's covered her tracks so it's hard to pin anything on her, particularly with this latest but…"

He placed his hand in front of his mouth, an unconscious gesture, I assumed.

"This latest?"

His brow creased with concern, and a cloud passed across his face.

"Best that we leave it that she's a fraudster."

"So the soirées are kind of a Trump University for the *nouveau riche* and those who prey on them?"

His eyes narrowed. By giving too free a rein to my curiosity, I'd yet again run afoul of my rule not to anger prospective clients before they signed retainer letters.

"Sorry, my sense of humor is an acquired taste," I said, an apology I seemed to be having to make more and more frequently. "I had the feeling that she had an agenda, with strong political overtones."

"Her agenda is to accumulate a maximum amount of assets, probably in untraceable offshore accounts, while avoiding commitment to an institution for the criminally insane." He enunciated each word as if he'd chosen it with great care.

"You needn't hold back on my account," I said, punctuating my statement with a smile.

He responded with a crooked smile that could've meant anything from enlightenment to indigestion.

"On the other side of the ledger, she's as charming and entertaining as anyone I've ever met." His tone, just short of sing-song, reminded me of mine when I'd parrot what my non-disparagement agreement with Trump permitted me to say. "According to Leslie, she's a genius, with skills that border on the supernatural."

"I gather you're concerned about her influence on your wife?"

After a long pause, he said, "Wouldn't you be?"

I nodded.

While Kate was the best source of business I'd had in some time, I'd have been foolhardy to ignore the warning signs. I wanted to know if McKuen had first-hand knowledge to support his statement. If I pushed him too hard, though, I might scare him into silence or worse cause him to walk out without retaining me.

"Leslie sees the money pouring in via foreign condo buyers and thinks she's being clever stroking the woman's ego, by calling her that farcical nickname and sucking up to her," he said before I had the chance to change the subject. "All the while, I fear, Leslie is the one being played. That the con-artist-currently-known-as Freya is reeling her further and further in, and one day Leslie will find herself flopping on a deck, gasping for air." He held his palms out at his sides. "She assures me she can take care of herself, and one of the keys to a successful marriage—like knowing what fights not to pick—is knowing when to keep your mouth shut." He grimaced. "I guess that rule applies to jobs as well."

"I understand what you're saying about these *soirées* being scams, but do you really think Leslie is in some sort of danger?" I asked, hoping that he would answer in the negative, allowing me to put a lid on my curiosity.

"You ever look into the woman's eyes?"

"Makes the hair on the back of my neck stand up and causes a pricking in my thumbs, but I thought that was just me."

"Leslie thinks having a witch on her side is a good thing. She doesn't realize the woman is only on her own side."

"When you said *witch*, you were speaking metaphorically?"

My assistant put the retainer letter on the table and left. I looked it over, then slid it across the table to McKuen.

He screwed up his face, and I readied myself for a tirade. Most clients signed my retainer letters without reading them. Investment bankers, though, tended to view everything as a negotiation in a zero-sum game where one was either a winner or a loser.

Rather than pick up the retainer letter, he whispered, as if afraid he'd be overheard, "The woman's psychotic, perhaps an unusually well-organized schizophrenic. Her brilliance allows her to function successfully, but there's a tension there, and the stasis won't last."

"Other than your psychological diagnosis of her, is what you've told me fact or opinion?"

He stroked a non-existent goatee, then grimaced.

"Can I count on you to keep this confidential?"

"Of course."

"Her former partner was a frat brother of mine," he whispered. "That's how Leslie and I came into her orbit."

"He's the source of what you told me about the phony beef Wellington, etc.?"

After another long pause, he whispered, "He was until he disappeared."

"Disappeared à la Jimmy Hoffa?"

He squinched up his face, an expression of discomfort and

something else that I couldn't discern.

"I shouldn't have said anything," he said, his fear now easy to discern, but what was he afraid of? "I don't think she capped him or ordered a hit, if that's your question."

"Then what do you think happened to him?"

"Please, no more about this. I probably know more about her than is healthy for me." He picked up the retainer letter, then set it down again. "I wouldn't have mentioned it but, with…"

"With?" I unfurled my arm.

He shook his head.

"So in the least, you'd advise me to stay as far as possible from *Freya* and her soirées?" I asked.

"I'm sure they'll be a good source of business, but it doesn't matter what I tell you. When she sets her mind on something, or someone, she gets it…or him. Resisting her is like fighting quicksand. Just be *very* careful not to be sucked in deeper than you want to go."

Accepting referrals from her but having no additional involvement seemed the appropriate resolution of my issues with her, his warning—and Lauren's *diktats*—notwithstanding.

"I wonder why she invited, or rather dragooned, me to attend. I'm hardly a mover and shaker."

"She needs a constant flow of new blood to make her gettogethers seem vital and growing. She probably told others that, as a former Trump lawyer, you had unique insight. People will need to cover their asses if he wins, and no one seems to know quite how to do that. That, though, I'm sure is only part of the story."

"And the rest?"

"Unknowable, her mind doesn't work like a normal person's."

He signed the retainer letter without reading it.

As I walked him out to the elevator, I reflected on his curious undertone at the beginning of our conversation and his evident discomfort mentioning Walker.

"Have you spoken to Jonathan Walker recently?" I asked.

His face went white.

"I didn't know if you'd heard and didn't want to say anything if you hadn't," he said after a several second hesitation. "Actually, it's not what I wanted. Leslie told me, in no uncertain terms, to steer clear of the subject, presumably repeating a direct order from commandant Freya."

"Is Walker okay?" I asked, concerned.

McKuen studied the wood grain on the table top.

"He and that weird Turkish rent boy he used to skulk around with…" He bit his lip. "On the way back from the soirée, their car jumped a divider and ran head-on into a beer truck. They were both killed instantly. Truck driver died on the way to the hospital."

"My God!" My throat became so constricted that I felt like I was speaking through a straw. "My impression was that our hostess had arranged for a ride home for them."

Between the note Walker slipped me, Kate's pickpocketing it, her agreeing that I should see him home and then him disappearing; could I close my mind to the possibility that she might have had a hand in their demise? But why would she have? Walker literally worshiped her; he thought she was a demigod. Perhaps it was dangerous even to accept referrals from her, but there seemed to be nothing untoward about McKuen or his case.

"From what I understand, Walker never touched liquor." Although he was standing next to me, McKuen's voice sounded like it was coming from far away. "Leslie spoke to him briefly at the soirée, and according to her, he seemed to be his usual arrogant, prim self. A little while later, she saw him staggering around, as if he'd been slipped a mickey." He shook his head. "Ignore that. Leslie's read too much Raymond Chandler and Dashiell Hammett."

I decided not to tell him about the note, as he'd tell Leslie, who'd tell Kate. I'd make up my mind later whether to talk to law enforcement. I had no evidence that Kate had caused Walker's and Hakan's deaths and was certain, though, that if she had, she'd covered her tracks.

We stood by the elevators each of us waiting for the other to say something; neither of us knowing what to say.

The elevator doors opened, but he didn't get in.

"Had you and your wife socialized with him?" I finally asked.

"We'd been to a dinner party at Walker's *pied-à-terre*, which he'd set up to introduce us to a couple of Russians and a Turk with gobs of hot money. No, now that I recall, *Freya* had set it up. One of the Turks ended up buying an eight-figure condo, through Leslie. Hakan was there. The nature of their relationship was unclear, but Walker's wife wasn't present."

"He didn't drink then?"

"Perrier and lime. Hakan teased that that was too strong and he should dilute it with water."

"Did the police investigate the accident? Did Leslie speak to them, tell them that from what she'd seen at the soirée Walker hadn't been drinking?"

He shrugged.

"She told them what she'd seen and tried to get details from them, but all they told her was that Hakan was driving and he tested clean for drugs and alcohol was well within the limit." He grimaced. "Turns out he wasn't here legally, had way overstayed his green card and didn't have a license—maybe he barely knew how to drive."

"So because he was drunk, Walker had someone, who didn't know how to drive, sitting behind the wheel, following his directions?" I said.

"Doesn't make much sense, does it?"

"Kate had cars and drivers available. One dropped me off at my front door."

"Apparently he was in one of those cars but rather than use a driver..." He shook his head. "I only know what Leslie told me, and none of it holds together. *Freya* claimed the cars were new prototype self-driving vehicles and only needed someone at the wheel as a precaution. She claimed the drivers were blind, but even Leslie didn't believe that. So..."

While I waited for him to continue, it occurred to me that self-driving cars could be hacked and made to crash. Could have been that Walker and Hakan were murdered, but that Kate had nothing to do with it. Russian spies? My inner Lauren told me that what happened to them wasn't my business and I should stay as far away from any investigation—and from Kate—as I could, further even. If I were to buy into McKuen's theory on the keys to a good marriage, I'd have followed those directions.

"If you hear anything more, please let me know," I said, once it became clear that he wasn't going to complete the sentence he'd barely started.

"Please don't repeat anything I said to you about our mutual acquaintance."

"Would it be okay if I call Leslie to get the name of the detectives she spoke to?" I asked. Even though I knew Lauren wouldn't like my inquiry, I felt I had to do something.

"Oh, God." He buried his head in his hand. "She instructed me not to tell you about Walker and was quite adamant."

"From what you said, she'd told you not to mention it if I didn't know. What if you tell her I knew?"

He sighed.

"I suppose that's okay. Give me a chance to talk to her first."

A few hours later, I called Leslie and asked for the name of the detective in charge of the investigation of the Walker traffic *accident.*

"*Investigation* is an exaggeration," she said but gave me the name and phone number.

"Ellis told me that Walker doesn't drink and that you'd said he looked like he'd been slipped—"

"Christ, that was a joke. Very bad taste but…"

"Walker did seem to be—"

"I thought he was ill, a bad stomach bug or something of the sort. Hakan seemed to be caring for him."

She paused. I waited.

"Matt, let's not get carried away. Hakan was certainly creepy, but, if he wanted of kill his benefactor, he could have come up with some way that wouldn't involve his own death as well."

"But if someone wanted to do in both Hakan and Walker?" I asked.

She sighed.

"It's a tragedy but let's not read more into it than is there."

"It sounds suspicious."

"That's partially because you heard it from Ellis. He thinks Freya's a bad influence on me. Her opinion of Trump drives him up a wall. Even Freya told me to have him put a lid on it." She spoke quickly, like she wanted to end the conversation before she said something she'd regret.

"He told me a frat brother—"

"Oh, God! He didn't? Please, Matt, forget that. We don't know what happened to him. Could be entirely innocent."

"Ellis sounded frightened when I spoke to him, and now you do," I said, trying for a calm, conversational tone. "If I'd thought I might have offended a goddess of revenge, I'd be scared, too."

I steeled myself for her hostile response.

"After we heard about the accident and spoke to the cops," she said, mournful, not angry, "I spent the night with Freya. She was besides herself, overwhelmed with grief. She needed someone by her side. I think Ellis was jealous. Among his other weird fantasies, he suspects Freya of being a predatory lesbian."

"How did you hear about what happened?"

"I…I'm not sure. One of Freya's drivers, I think. She doesn't carry a phone and… I don't really know."

I called the detective and told him about the note Walker had slipped to me. I explained who Flynn and Kislyak were, told him about Hakan's and Walker's relationship and expounded on my realization that self-driving cars could be hacked. From the background noises it sounded like he was playing a videogame while I spoke.

He told me that Hakan had been the driver "not some damn robot," thanked me for my public-spiritedness in coming forward and said he'd get back to me if he needed additional information.

I wasn't holding my breath.

Pushing from my mind all thoughts of Kate and the ramifications of Walker's suspicious demise, I drafted a demand letter and emailed it to McKuen for comments.

VIII
The Best *and* The Worst are Full of Passionate Intensity

It was almost raining...the rain should have scared them away, but God looked down and he said, we're not going to let it rain on your speech. Donald J. Trump speaking to the CIA staff, January 21, 2017

"I got a new client today," I told Lauren on my return home.

"That one from that *soirée*?" It was amazing how much negative connotation she could give to an innocent word like soirée.

"An investment banker who was fired because his political rants antagonized a big client."

"Didn't they have a right to fire him if he pissed off clients?"

"Well, technically."

"Meaning, yes, they acted within their rights?"

"Yes."

"Hope you got a huge retainer."

"He thought he was being clever by making me agree to take it on a contingency."

"Sounds clever to me."

"Look on the bright side. If I'd gotten a retainer, I'd probably have sunk it into my Trump-stocks." Before she could react, I said, "He gave me his take on Kate and her soirées."

"I don't care what he told you. You promised me you'd have no more contact with her."

I told her what McKuen had said, and she had the good manners not to say, "I told you so."

I was mulling over whether to tell her about Walker. On one hand, there was no reason to scare her unnecessarily, and I wanted to believe that the cops—the professionals who'd examined the evidence—had rightfully concluded that there hadn't been any foul play. On the other, I knew she'd want to know.

Deciding to do the manly thing—avoid the discussion—I hit the power button on the remote, then punched in the code for CNN.

It showed a video of Trump in a van having a discussion with the nephew of the 41st president. I watched and listened in disbelief.

"Well, that's a new low, even for a campaign steeped in new lows," I said. "Did you ever think you'd see the candidate from a major party bragging on TV about grabbing pussy?"

Not that I should've been surprised, he'd said cruder things to me about women, and I wasn't as encouraging as Billy Bush had been. Nor was talking to me as flattering to his huge but fragile ego as speaking to an actual Bush.

"Well, at least now he's done for," Lauren said. "No woman in the country will vote for him."

"I hope you're right."

"Of course I'm right. While he was out there trying to seduce married women"—another admission on that tape—"his wife was pregnant with their son."

Lauren changed channels from CNN to MSNBC, so she could see it again. The story seemed destined to dominate the airwaves for days, or at least until the candidate distracted the media with his next outrageous tweet. Perfect for each other, Trump and the media each had a five-year-old's attention span. I hoped the electorate's was longer.

"There must be other, similar tapes and incidents of women he harassed," I said. "His treatment of women was one of his few consistencies."

"They'll all come forward now."

Lauren went to the bathroom, and as luck would have it, Emily took that moment to call.

"It's Emily," I said. "Should I let it go to voicemail."

"No. Please tell her I'll call back in the morning. This latest Trump thing…I can do without dealing with her now."

"Double for me."

"Come on, Matt."

I picked up the phone, "Lauren's residence."

"Hi, Matt—"

"She told me to tell you she'll call in the morning."

"Actually, it's you I wanted to speak to."

"I have nothing relevant to say about the Billy Bush tape."

In fact, I'd advised Trump not to appear on *Access Hollywood*, but he said something along the lines of, "The show's number one in its timeslot. I've got an amazing new line of steaks coming out. Vodka, going to be tremendous. A mortgage company. A university." Impressed, I'd replied, "You're starting a university, like John Harvard, Cornelius Vanderbilt or Leland Stanford?" In spite of his immense inherited wealth, the man had given almost nothing to charity, but maybe he'd been saving up for one big plunge. Then he told me he planned to "charge like fifteen-hundred for a three-day lecture given by some unemployed loser, who I'll pay on commission, based on the bigger losers he signs up." Fine with me that both my non-disclosure agreement and attorney/client privilege prohibited me from sharing any of that with Emily.

"You owe me for sending me on that wild goose chase," she said. "Trump had no such assistant."

"I told you names aren't my strong point."

"Yeah, right," she said. "Unless…Could he have been paying her off the books?"

"No idea. I had the feeling that, like a lot of young attractive people in the city, she was an aspiring actor and probably didn't intend her work for Trump to be a long-term career. She sometimes disguised her voice on the phone, pretending to be various fictional officers of his company, so it would appear that Trump had more employees, and more women in senior positions, than he actually did."

"That's all you have?"

"It's all I remember." Assuming Kate was listening in, I decided to send her a message that I wasn't going to continue to play the role of the passive dupe—a role I might or might not might not have been playing. "I might have sort of a scoop for you."

"I'm waiting."

"I'm sorry, it's a little vague."

"Why aren't I surprised?"

"Four weeks ago, A former client of mine, Jonathan Walker, died the in a head-on crash on the Bruckner Expressway."

"Oh, that's some scoop, current too."

"He was coming back from a party, and the hostess provided rides home. I heard the car was a porotype Google self-driving vehicle—shouldn't have been on the road."

"Your source?"

"Rumor, third hand, but I spoke to a Detective Morris at the 43rd Precinct. He seemed strangely disinterested."

"So you want me to check out this moldy, unverified, unsubstantiated rumor?"

"I don't want you to do anything, but it seemed suspicious to me."

"Because the detective on the case was disinterested?"

I hesitated, but then said, "No, because Walker had slipped me a note, 'Flynn Turkish money, Kislyak. I was played. Hakan Russian agent.' Hakan Yaldiz was his several-decade-younger male lover, an unlicensed driver who was at the wheel, also died in the crash."

"You have the note?"

"No."

"Where exactly was this party?"

"Not sure. I was driven there, didn't pay attention."

"Who threw it?"

"I think her name was Kate."

"Right, you're pathologically bad at names."

I couldn't come up with a credible explanation. Certainly the truth didn't qualify.

"Jonathan Walker and Hakan Yaldiz are dead, and there could be a claim against Google. Self-driving cars are a controversial issue. Google is always newsworthy."

"Maybe I'll look into it. You've been a big help, as usual."

"You called me. I could only give you what I had," which, I realized, was practically nothing.

Having not heard back from McKuen for two days, I emailed him: *Do you have any comments on the draft demand letter?*

He responded: *All sorts of issues here. Nothing to do with my termination. I'll be back to you when I can. Ignore everything I told you about that woman and her soirées. As you already know, I have a problem with being too forthcoming with my opinions and prejudices some of which, like most of what I said to you, don't have any real basis.*

I told myself not to wonder about the cause of McKuen's *volte face.*

Emily called later that day.

"Thank you for the tip," she said. "I shouldn't have been quite so dismissive."

"Are you going to run a story?"

"Detective Morris was suspiciously closed-mouth, claimed not to know the location of the party Walker was coming from. According to him the wreckage has already been sent to the crusher, so there's no way to tell if it was equipped with self-driving apparatus."

"Sounds strange that a car involved in a fatal collision would've already been destroyed."

"Sure does," she said. "The editor nixed the story, told me it was too speculative and not sufficiently supported, but...I don't know. I had the feeling he was being disingenuous. Something's not right here."

Quite the understatement.

"I'll let you know if I hear anything more on my end," I said. "Please do the same."

James Comey announced that the FBI was reopening its investigation into Hilary's emails. The email *scandal* dominated the TV news even though nothing had changed since June when the FBI found that Hillary had not committed any crime. Like her primary opponent, I became *sick and tired of hearing about [her] damn emails*. Her poll numbers began to fall.

"What makes it a s*candal*?" Lauren asked. "Comey admitted— as has everyone else who's looked at the issue—that there's nothing there. The FBI could have examined Weiner's emails without making an announcement until they saw what was in them."

A news report that Russian hackers had been the source of the release of emails stolen from the Democratic National Committee got Lauren's attention, particularly as Trump had, in a Florida campaign appearance, encouraged Russia to hack her emails—*I will tell you this, Russia: If you're listening, I hope you're able to find the 30,000 emails that are missing*. Those facts, however, got buried in a blizzard of reports about the content of the DNC emails, even though they were totally inconsequential.

Trump said the hackers might not have been Russians and that the wrongdoer could have been "somebody sitting on their bed that weighs 400 pounds" or "some guy in New Jersey."

"I doubt Chris Christie did it," I said to Lauren.

"Why is no one outraged that the Russians are trying to influence our election?" she asked.

"Not no one. *You're* outraged," I said, drawing a look of disdain. Being married to me was no picnic, although it might have been a day at the beach—complete with metaphoric sunburn and sand abrading intimate places. "If she wins their interference won't matter. If he does then he'll suppress all evidence and fire or demote anyone supporting the story, so it also won't matter."

"I still think she'll win."

"When I ran into her on the subway, over a year ago, Kate claimed that Russian hackers were reading everything she sent or received."

"Even paranoids can be right," she said. "I can't wait for this damn election to be over and for things to return to normal."

She swept both palms over her face and into her hairline as if emerging from the ocean.

"Of all the possibilities, a return to normal seems the least likely. Or, rather, dysfunctionality is now normal...until something worse takes its place."

"What could be—"

"The five horsemen of the apocalypse: Conquest, War, Famine, Death and Trump."

"You're impossible," she said but smiled and gave my hand an affectionate squeeze

"Just unlikely."

We watched the final episode in the fourth season of *House of Cards*. Last line: Frank Underwood looks into the camera and says, "We don't submit to terror. We make the terror."

Lauren looked into my eyes. "Hillary will win, of course."

I looked away.

Finally, I heard from McKuen about the draft letter: *Good job I couldn't have done better myself. Send it ASAP.*

Of course he couldn't have done better himself. That was why he retained an experienced professional.

Three days later I got a call from the general counsel of McKuen's former employer.

"Once I get around to it, I'll respond to your letter," she said, "but dealing with more of McKuen's chauvinistic bullshit not being high on my to do list, that might not be for a few weeks. So, I wanted to call to give you a heads-up."

"Okay, shoot."

"No way, José. It was him or lose a mega-merger on which we stood to earn a high eight-figure fee."

"A small price to pay for supporting free speech."

"Did he treat you to any of his Crooked Hillary rants?"

"We didn't delve into the details."

"They start with her killing Vincent Foster, then move onto her enabling Bill's *multiple rapes.*"

Maybe his comments about Kate were no more reliable than his anti-Hillary bullshit.

"Hyperbole is the mother's milk of political satire."

"Not when directed at someone who's made seven-figure contributions to Democratic candidates. Then it's just stupid."

"Still, a public lawsuit would be ugly and bring to light—"

"We'd welcome it. Your case would be dismissed in a heartbeat, we'd hit you with a claim for substantial sanctions for bringing a frivolous suit."

"Wouldn't everyone's best interests be served by a nuisance settlement, a couple hundred K? A fraction of the six mil bonus he was entitled to."

"Bonuses are discretionary," she said. "And the answer to your question is 'No'."

She slammed the phone down so hard it caused ringing in my ear.

On Election Day, I manned a lawyers' hotline at the Hillary campaign's downtown Brooklyn headquarters. The level of organization and dedication of the many volunteers impressed me as did the sheer size of the place. I didn't expect to have a positive impact, but if the American people were to elect a con-man with an antagonistic relationship with the truth, I didn't want to feel guilty about not having done my share to oppose him.

The majority of the callers inquired about the location of their polling places or whether it was too late for them to register to vote. Using materials the campaign had given me, I had no difficulty answering those questions. The calls regarding problems my minimal training hadn't covered I referred to a higher level. Those included about a dozen calls from residents of the Midwest, whose accents marked them as African-American or Latino and who had received emails inviting them to vote online. Others working with me had received similar calls. There must have been many people who'd received such emails, thought they'd voted and had no reason to call the hotline to confirm the propriety of that process. *Russian spearfishing*? I wondered, but I never heard any more about that scheme.

Lauren and I watched the election returns, hoping that they would mark the end of the long national nightmare.

The early results from Florida were disappointing, but CNN— the self-described *most trusted name in news*—assured us that its predictions were on track, Hillary's blue wall continued to be unassailable and Trump's ability to "run the table" was still a statistical impossibility.

Hillary was getting *schlonged* in Ohio, but neither CNN nor the other networks, wavered in their predictions. Apparently the Buckeye State was no longer the pivotal battleground state it had been in prior national elections.

"This doesn't look good," I said.

Lauren pretended she hadn't heard me.

Based largely on early returns from Philadelphia and Pittsburg, Hillary led in Pennsylvania, but the big city returns lagged behind predictions.

Changing channels had no effect on the results that were coming in.

"Matt, stop squirming. You're getting me worried."

Michigan, what the fuck?

In search of distraction, I poured myself three fingers of Irish whiskey. Although aware that I rarely drank at home and never shy about criticizing my alcohol consumption, modest though it was, Lauren didn't comment. Another bad sign. At this point, a Roman seer would've cut open a sacrificial animal and seen that it had no entrails.

The impossible began to look possible.

"It's inconceivable," Lauren said. "The man's a clown. On average, he lied every minute of the debates, both primary and general election."

The S&P started falling. A double impossibility: Trump would win and the predictions of financial gurus that his victory would cause a massive drop in the stock market would turn out to be correct. When the fuck did the stock market begin to act rationally?

Florida wavered. Wisconsin—the keystone in the unassailable blue wall—began to crumble. The world was fucked.

The Peso collapsed against the dollar. Financial markets kept tanking, my stocks leading the retreat. Panic scattered through me like rats behind a baseboard.

"How could she possibly lose Pennsylvania?" Lauren asked, her voice seemingly coming from a long way off. "What about the minority vote in Philadelphia? What about the women?"

"Same way she could lose Michigan and Wisconsin."

"That won't happen," she said, with the vehemence of the uncertain. "It's… How can we elect a vulgar con-man with no experience who is incapable of focusing on anything but himself?"

"Hillary's not an appealing candidate," I said.

She looked like she was about to slug me. This impending catastrophe had to be my fault. I was about to remind her that I'd contributed the maximum amount to Hillary's campaign and worked a hotline, but I realized that none of that mattered. Nothing mattered anymore.

"I'm going to be *very* upset if he wins," she warned.

"You'll have plenty of company."

CNN called Florida *and* North Carolina for Trump.

Retreat turned to rout, as the bottom began to fall out of the stock market. The bank stocks I'd counted on to rally on a Trump victory continued to lead the market down, even the pharmaceuticals, which would benefit from the immediate repeal of ObamaCare, faltered. Of course, the market hates uncertainty and Trump was uncertainty in spades. Why hadn't I realized that before? What had I done? I couldn't look at Lauren. This actually was my fault.

"I'm going to try to go to sleep and hope that when I wake up sanity will have been restored," Lauren said after a long ominous silence.

"Good night," I lied.

S&P futures began to turn, then started to move violently up. Goldman and J.P. Morgan led the charge, followed by the pharmaceuticals.

Oh my God! This might not be a total disaster.

The upward move continued. The country was going to hell, but I was going to get rich. I felt like Cassandra. Well not exactly like her. She became Agamemnon's property and was later murdered by Clytemnestra. I intended a more felicitous fate for myself.

And speaking of the she-devil, I received a text from an unknown number, *We were right, now you'll REALLY need to be more paranoid and a lot more careful.*

As soon as I read it, it disappeared. I suspected that if I called the number I'd reach a recording that said it had been disconnected. I was smart enough not to try.

Like I had in the wake of 9/11, I woke each morning, hoping the election had been a bad dream. Most of those who voted for Trump would end up being worse off, not only unemployed but also deprived of their health care and other governmental benefits and protections. Ironic though it was, I'd do fine as long as my beach house weren't wiped out as a consequence of global warming and my family and I weren't burned to a cinder in a nuclear conflagration. My Goldman and J.P. Morgan stocks were up thirty percent from where I had bought them, the pharmaceuticals up twenty. If the prices held through the New Year, as I was pretty sure they would, I'd sell, so my profits would be taxed at 2017 reduced-to-benefit-the-rich rates. Trump's damping down of free trade, irresponsible tweets, and soaring deficits would eventually lead to a recession. Then I'd jump back into the market, buy at substantial discount and sell on the eve of the next election. Unhappy about the situation though I was, I had to admit that there were worse things than white privilege, as long as one was white and privileged. So I decided to leave agonizing about politics to others.

Having not received the promised written response to my demand letter, I called the general counsel of McKuen's employer.

"Just checking in to see if senior management wants to be known as a company that fired someone for supporting Trump."

"We terminated Mr. McKuen's employment because he put one of our biggest deals in jeopardy by antagonizing—"

"Surely the President-Elect will understand that subtle distinction."

"Not sure we care what he understands."

"There's talk about several senior people at the bank vying for cabinet posts and influence, but not to worry, Mr. Trump's probably not the sort of guy who holds grudges."

"Still angling for that nuisance settlement? Too bad we don't give points for persistence."

"I'm not angling. I'm demanding McKuen's full six-point-five-million-dollar bonus."

"Well, first of all, many factors go into bonus calculation. The process isn't nearly as straightforward as your client led you to believe."

I admired her ability to squeeze so much condescension into two short declarative sentences, but rather than compliment her, I said, "Fair point. Make it an even seven mil. You have until noon tomorrow."

"That's when you plan to file your baseless lawsuit?" She punctuated her statement with a condescending snicker.

"No, that's when I have a telephone conference scheduled with the bank's former employee Steve Bannon. My call with Sean Hannity starts a half hour later."

For veracity, I'd entered both calls on my calendar even though it was doubtful that either man would take my call, if I were to make it.

"You're blowing smoke," she said, although her voice lacked all conviction.

"Where there's smoke, there's fired. I'd hate to see you being the one who gets burnt."

"Big on threats, aren't you?" she said, voice shaking with anger.

"Adjusting to the times," I said. "Talk to senior management and get back to me. I bet they're adjusting, too. 'You better start swimmin' / Or you'll sink like a stone / For the times they are a-changin'.'"

"I suppose I have a duty to report on our conversation." She sighed, deep and unpersuasive. "If there's any change in our position, I'll get back to you."

"Before noon or the settlement price goes into eight figures."

"You're insufferable."

"I used to represent Mr. Trump. He insisted on insufferability," I said. "You might want to look up my record. You'll see that over a decade ago, I won a series of cases for Mr. Trump. After that, there are no reported decisions in cases where I represented him. Everyone on the other side learned their lesson and cases were settled confidentially and favorably."

My assistant came through on the intercom. "I'm sorry to interrupt, Matt, but I have Mr. Priebus on the line for you."

"Got to go," I said to the general counsel, then hung up.

There being no call from Mr. Priebus, I went back to my important newspaper reading but was interrupted by an email advising me that a Columbia Law School classmate and friend, Peter Lawson, had died—massive myocardial infarction upon the announcement of the results in Pennsylvania, I later learned—and advising me of the time and place of his funeral.

Several hours later, while composing a eulogy, I received a call from another law school friend, James Kaplan.

"Hi, James, I gather you heard about Peter," I said.

"My God, terrible. I didn't know him nearly as well as you did. Too much the knee-jerk, phony radical for me, but... Well, we've reached that age where there are more funerals than weddings, brisses and bar mitzvahs put together."

"You can say that again, but please don't."

"Actually, I'm calling about something else."

"A new favor, no doubt."

The man already owed me big time. On the strength of a large real estate developer I'd referred to him, he'd made partner at a major law firm. I'd represented him in a lawsuit, in which he was in danger of losing his license to practice, even though he *probably* hadn't actually done anything wrong. Although I had grave doubts about it at the time and later regretted what I'd done, I'd covered for him when he cheated on his wife. One day I'd collect. Well, maybe in another life.

"Depends how you look at it," he said, meaning yes. "Can I count on you to buy a table for the AIPAC dinner? Jared Kushner is speaking."

"Sorry. I'm a big supporter of Israel but I don't much like the Netanyahu government. I don't see that they have an endgame. Putting aside the various moral issues, without a two-state solution, Jews will be a minority and Israel won't be a Jewish state. Having two classes of citizens is morally and practically unacceptable. And

I can't totally put aside the moral—"

"Yeah, yeah, bullshit, bullshit, bullshit. I forgot about that bleeding heart of yours. Okay, we disagree, but you really don't want to pass up the opportunity to hobnob with Jared. He's going to be a real power in the new administration. You've noticed that Trump's craziest tweets come during Shabbat, when Jared's not available to hold him in check?"

"His weekday tweets don't seem to me to be of a much higher caliber."

"Jared is—"

"I know. I had lunch with him a couple times, back when I represented Trump. But my hobnobbing days are over, as are my sucking-up-to-evil days"

"He and I have become quite close. I've been doing quite a bit of real estate work for him and his company. In fact, he's become my largest client."

"Good for you," I said.

To my relief the receptionist buzzed in with a call from the bank's lawyer.

"Sorry, James I need to get off, for an important call. Talk later?"

We settled on five million with a confidentiality agreement, non-disparagement clause and an exchange of releases.

My ten percent contingency worked out to a hundred grand per hour of my time.

A week later, I received an email from Jerome Curtis, the guy who'd given me the plate-and-glass-clip at the soirée, asking to set up a meeting later in the week.

Trump was going to make me a rich man. He and Kate.

Maybe she wasn't complicit in Walker's and Hakan's murders; maybe they weren't even murdered but died in a traffic accident. I wanted to hear her side of the story before I judged.

I led Curtis into our conference room.

"May I get you something to drink, coffee, tea, water?" I asked when he took his seat across the table from me.

"You have any organic, fair-trade, pesticide-free, herbal tea?"

My laugh died in my throat when I realized he hadn't been joking.

In the kitchen, I found an old mint teabag that had been left there by a temporary secretary with aspirations to be a professional bodybuilder, who'd drunk the stuff to wash down her protein supplements and testosterone pills. I returned with a steaming mug of green stuff that smelled like masticated chewing gum.

"I enjoyed meeting you at the soirée," he said, after thanking me for the beverage.

That had only been four weeks ago? Time seemed to have divided into pre-election and post-election, with everything pre-election having receded into the distant past.

"I enjoyed meeting with you as well."

"That was your first time at one of her events, yes?" he said. "What was your impression?"

"I had some interesting conversations and no complaints about the food and drink," I said.

"How did you come to be invited? Had you met Erinye before?"

"Only once, when she picked my pocket."

He laughed, apparently on the misapprehension that I had been joking.

"She's a remarkable woman."

"Yes, the last time I had the occasion to remark on her someone told me the Wagyu Kobe Strip Steak is really normal U.S. grade A and the wine mid-price stuff with counterfeit labels."

While I usually tried not to be off-putting until the retainer check cleared, my curiosity about Kate overwhelmed the usual. Anyway, with Trump as president, there was no longer such a thing as normally.

"Probably there never was a genius or visionary whom someone didn't call a fraud. Freud, Newton, Edison. Hell, they crucified Jesus."

"Which is she, genius, visionary, or the Princess of Peace?"

"I don't know anyone who ever left one of her soirées disappointed."

Unable to help myself, I said, "So you didn't know Jonathan Walker?"

He sipped his tea but finding it too hot—or perhaps not sufficiently organic, free-tradey or pesticide-free—put the mug down so quickly that some plopped out, and a small puddle formed several inches beyond the coaster. Rather than wipe it up myself, I stared at it until he utilized his napkin. Then I again directed my gaze at him, willing him to answer my question about Walker.

Finally, he said, "Erinye's been cleared of all wrongdoing."

"I have an uneasy feeling around her, like she's playing me and has some hidden agenda," I said, seeing no reason to ask the basis for that claim as it clearly had come from her and was of dubious believability. "The strange circumstances surrounding their deaths add to that concern."

"Certainly unfortunate, but hardly *strange*. Impatient to get home, a little sloshed and finding the car unlocked, they took a car—"

"An unlicensed driver and a sick or drunk man?"

"I don't know exactly what happened, but Walker had a reputation for being unstable and a secret drinker, and Hakan... Well, everyone knew he was trouble from the get-go." He spoke quickly, like someone unsure of the truth of what he was saying who wanted to speed through it in order to get it behind him. The *reputation* he'd referred to was likely as secret as Walker's supposed drinking. "As to your first point, she *plays* everyone, always for their benefit, not her own," he said, his cadence now back to a more normal speed. "I gather I'm not the only client you've gotten through her, and you only attended one of her events."

"That's her entire agenda, to help people? I'm surprised you didn't compare her to Mother Theresa."

True believers and their hagiography always rubbed me the wrong way, but I admonished myself to cut out the sarcasm. Notwithstanding the Kate connection, Curtis could turn out to be a good client.

"Of course, she makes money out of her soirées, but there's nothing wrong with that." He pointed at me. "I presume your services don't come free of charge."

"Fair point," I said. "So what can I do for you?"

He smiled, perhaps for no other reason than to show off his blinding white teeth, highlighted by the contrast with his tawny skin and black moustache.

"You think my pet name for her is a bit much?"

"As deities of vengeance, the Erinyes weren't exactly promoting the public welfare. But what led you to come up with that nickname, or was it her suggestion?"

"Suffice it to say that when someone made the mistake of

offending her, he paid the price many times over."

"Vengefulness sounds incompatible with the a self-sacrificing demigoddess you described."

"Even God was vengeful, dealing with the iniquity of the fathers by punishing the children to the third and the fourth generation."

An electric current shot though my nervous system ending with a now-too-familiar painful pricking of both my thumbs.

His eyes narrowed and lips compressed.

"A large part of my conversations with Erinye is just flirtatious play, not to be taken seriously," he said, seemingly attempting a lighthearted tone and failing. "She has a pet nickname for me as well."

"Which is?" I asked.

His face reddened.

"She sometimes calls me by the name of a University of Michigan basketball player with a killer foul shot."

I unfurled my hands, indicating he should tell me the name, but his face just became more flushed.

"Do you know how I fit into her schemes?" I asked, not wanting to subject him to further embarrassment.

His face squinched up, as if thinking was an unpleasant experience.

"She's violently opposed to Trump, but beyond that...."

He picked up a paperclip from the table and straightened it.

"How *violently?*"

He focused his attention on the paperclip, apparently concerned that, in spite of his efforts, the implement still wasn't sufficiently straight.

I was about to repeat my question when he said, "Her mind works in strange and wondrous ways."

Give me a fucking break.

If I wanted to keep open the possibility of landing him as a client, I needed to get off this subject and get on to discussing the concerns that brought him to my office.

"I apologize for the digression," I said. "I want to discuss your legal matters straight away. But, as I said, she makes me uncomfortable. I don't like playing games when I don't know the rules."

He stroked his moustache.

"She won't force you to do anything you don't want to do."

"She already had me kidnapped at gunpoint."

"Likely wasn't a real gun."

"That's a comfort."

After a lengthy silence, which probably had lasted no more than a minute in real time, he extracted a laptop from his briefcase, set it on the conference room table and powered it up.

"At her party you gave me the bare bones of your idea," I said. "Something about providing low-cost drugs, particularly in the South and Rust-Belt Midwest, circumventing regulations, big pharma and insurance companies."

He wiggled his hands, communicating that I had it pretty much right.

"I gather Trump's victory and the likely repeal of ObamaCare will be good for you, even if terrible for most everyone else," I said.

"Looks that way."

"How can I help?"

"We're constrained from beginning the big rollout until we see what, if anything, they replace the Affordable Care Act with. In the meantime, I've been working through my business plan, doing test marketing and consulting with FDA counsel in Washington, generally getting all our ducks in a row."

"You'd said something about needing a *consigliere*?"

"Someone familiar with my business, whom I can trust."

"What can I tell you about myself?"

"Erinye's told me all I need to know. I have tremendous respect for her judgment. She's the most intuitive person I know."

"I barely know her, so I'm not sure that her recommendation—"

"She knows you."

No reason to argue against myself.

"Do you have any written materials concerning your company? The most current draft of your business plan would probably be a good place for me to start."

"I'd like to formally retain you. Erinye suggested a twenty-five thou evergreen retainer."

"I'm not yet comfortable—"

"You can bill me for your time as we go along. A thou an hour?"

"My rate is seven-fifty."

Fee discussions often involved negotiations, sometimes

unpleasant ones. Rarely, had I felt obliged to negotiate a client down.

Mindful of Upton Sinclair's dictum, *It is difficult to get a man to understand something, when his salary depends on his not understanding it,* I wondered if my desire not to believe the worst about Kate had been influenced by the business she sent me. Had it been part of an effort to suck me into her *coalition*? Didn't seem that I was worth the effort. What the hell was she up to?

"Erinye suggested that a bonus would motivate you, push me to the head of the line."

"I'm already motivated, and all my clients are at the head of the line."

He slid a $25,000 check across the table. I left it there.

"Are you doing any business now?" I asked.

"We've got a test website which is generating some sales and helping us get the bugs out of our system. We've still got a long way to go, but it's a start." He turned his laptop toward me.

I didn't like what I saw.

"This looks like one of those sites that sell prescription drugs online, from Canada, India, or elsewhere, without legitimate prescriptions," I said.

"Yes, there are a heck of a lot of disreputable—"

"You're selling quite a variety of pills," I said, "at least some of which appear to require a prescription?"

"We have doctors on staff."

"Do they actually see the patients?"

"Via skype."

"Sounds dodgy."

"There's a real need—"

"I admit this is way out of my area of expertise, but I do know that selling controlled substances online without a valid prescription is a felony. As is importing drugs into the United States and shipping them to a non-DEA registrant."

"You do understand that drugs in this country are vastly overpriced due to collusion between the government and the drug companies? Same pill in Canada can be a tenth the cost here, often less."

His self-assured smile seemed intended to communicate that sophisticated men of the world like us should ignore all those ill-advised governmental regulations that serve no purpose beyond oppressing the poor and maintaining the monopoly power of the rich. Perhaps, though, his smile was just a smile.

"But that doesn't make what you're doing legal."

"Many people, particularly poor and unemployed middle-class whites in the Rust Belt, don't have the luxury of paying through the nose, just to enrich the drug companies." He pointed a finger at me, displaying the perfection of his manicure. "The drugs we sell are identical to those sold at the jacked-up monopoly prices imposed by the government-drug-company cabal."

"Why just white people and why just the Rust Belt? Aren't all poor in the same leaky boat?"

My comment drew a nasty scowl.

"Yes, of course, all poor people, but the current crisis happens to most affect unemployed white males in particular states." He spoke quickly while staring at his tea cup.

"I'm not questioning the righteousness of your goal," I said, but his self-righteousness was starting to grate.

"So I gather you understand why I need to be extra-careful and squeaky clean."

"Selling illegally imported controlled substances online without valid prescriptions might be so squeaky as to get the attention of the both FBI and the FDA."

"You're saying I should take down the website?"

"Based on what I've heard so far, it sounds dodgy to me, but I'm not the right guy—"

"Spoken like a true lawyer, unwilling to commit to anything." He chuckled. "You've given me a lot to think about, and I assume I've done the same for you."

"Your goal is laudable, but you have to carry it out legally, if that's even possible."

"That's why I'm here."

He pointed to the check. I left it where it was.

"Just thinking out loud here." He held his hands out to the side, a studied casualness. "What if we were to set up an off-shore company, say in the Caymans or somewhere, create a labyrinth of subsidiary and parent companies—all on the up-and-up of course—that eventually would lead to a phony passport for someone who doesn't exist?"

"Labyrinths of off-shore companies run by non-existent people to do something illegal are by definition on the down-and-down."

He smiled. Each time he did so it was slicker than the last.

"Lawyers do that kind of thing all the time."

He began to bend the paperclip back and forth. I stifled a desire to take it from him.

"I don't." I stopped myself from adding *that's why I'm not rich but sleep well at night,* as I realized I was getting rich and wasn't sleeping all that well. "I wish you the best of success, but I'm not the right lawyer for you."

I slid the check back toward him.

His brows drew together, his lips stretched horizontally, and his eyes opened wide—a look of sheer terror. I'd seen a variety of reactions from potential clients when I'd declined to represent them but never that one—though I did recall that I'd seen a similar look when I told Zhukov that I was unwilling to hold his phone for safekeeping.

"May I at least pay you for your time today and call on you for advice from time to time?" He bent the paperclip back and forth until it broke.

"I won't be able to give you worthwhile advice without thorough research into areas of the law in which I have no expertise or experience, and as I said ''

"But you'll meet with me and advise me from time to time?"

He reached across the table.

I drew back.

"Maybe, on the understanding that, without my having put in the required time and effort, my advice won't be worth much, other than, I suppose, acting as a sounding board for you."

He looked at his watch, then began to write a new check.

"By the time we're done it'll be well over an hour," he said. "So, I'll make it an even grand."

"Half the time we spent chatting about *Erinye.*"

"All you have to sell is your time, and if I chose to take up your time with a conversation that helped us to get to know each other… Well, that's part of the process, right?"

He completed the new check, slid it across the table. I hesitated, then took it. After all, I did put in the time.

He wiped his brow with his hand, which I first took to be a

sarcastic gesture but then realized otherwise.

"Why is it so important to you that I represent you?"

"People are dying because they can't afford the drugs they need. This is a serious problem that's about to become a national tragedy."

"You didn't answer my question."

"Did you see that mega-bitch Kellyanne on CNN last night? Incredible, the gall of that woman."

"You still haven't—"

"She's almost worse than Trump. At least he has the excuse that he's insane."

"Did *Erinye*, insist that you retain me?"

His head kicked back as if I'd taken a swing at him. What was I to make of these extreme reactions?

"I trust her judgment." A forced smile appeared on his face, then disappeared as if it had been chased away. "You should, too."

"That almost sounded like a threat," I said, punctuating my statement with an insincere smile: there had been no *almost* about it.

"Oh, come on." He matched my smile with an even more disingenuous one. "I didn't mean...."

"I know what you meant," I said my pleasant tone adding ambiguity to my statement. "By the way, do you have a mailing address, email, phone number for...*Erinye*"—I couldn't make myself say that name without an ironic tone—"I'd like to thank her for the referral."

The fearful look returning, he shook his head.

"She doesn't communicate by those means."

"That doesn't make you suspicious?"

"No." He sounded startled that I'd even ask such a question. "Why would it?"

Not coming up with a polite way to ask whether he was being disingenuous or merely naïve, I stood.

When he continued sitting, I said, "I guess we're done."

"I'll follow your advice and take down the website and consider a different structure."

"I didn't give you advice because I don't know enough to advise you."

"There are numerous websites like ours. My guess is that the FDA had made a decision not to prosecute."

"I don't know what the FDA is and isn't prosecuting, but I sense that what you're doing is illegal and will end badly for you," I said. "Maybe a lawyer with the appropriate expertise will tell you something different."

"The Trump Administration is going to cancel many regulations and not bother to enforce the rest," he said. "It's going to be the Wild West. I'm getting in on the ground floor. I intend to hit the ground running."

"I don't know," I said, forcing myself not to comment on the clichés and mixed metaphor.

I didn't know why Kate had put us together, but I did know that infernal goddesses don't bestow benefits on people. I didn't accept what Curtis told me at face value—I never accepted what any client told me at face value—but I had no doubt that the fear I saw on his face had been real. I wondered what he was afraid of.

IX
Too Weak to Knock on Death's Door

Watched protests yesterday but was under the impression that we just had an election! Why didn't these people vote? Celebs hurt cause badly. Donald J. Trump, January 22, 2017

According to the news, the leading candidates for secretary of state were Rudolph Giuliani, the man who'd made his fortune by figuring out how to monetize the 9/11 terrorist attacks, and Mitt Romney, the man who'd called Trump a fraud and a phony. I rooted for Romney but drew comfort from the fact that Rex Tilleson's name was nowhere on the list, putting the lie to that video Zhukov had played for me at the soirée. I hadn't given his story much credence at the time, but it was comforting to have my initial view confirmed.

On an unseasonably warm January day, I wanted a break from the office but couldn't bear another lunch where the only item on the conversational menu was Trump, so I went out to buy a sandwich to eat at my desk.

"Come with me," said an all-too-familiar woman's voice behind me.

"No, thank you."

"He's dying, he's asked for you. Sloan Kettering. It's a few blocks from here. A pleasant walk. On the way I'll fill you in on what's going on."

She held a large bouquet of exotic flowers. Her platinum blond hair shimmered under a sunbeam that appeared to be aimed directly at it, the way movie stars in the thirties and forties were lit more brightly than the supporting actors. While not a classic beauty...I shut down that line of thought.

"Kate, leave me alone." I purposely didn't ask who was dying.

"Ever hear of *bikur holim,* the Jewish commandment to visit and aid the sick? It's a prime aspect of *gemilut chasadim,* benevolence, selflessness and loving kindness," she said. "Jerome is one of your biggest fans, and that's *really* saying something. He greatly appreciated your advice."

Curtis was ill? He'd seemed fine a few weeks ago.

"I didn't give him any."

"Oh, of course, I get it. Attorney/client privilege and all." Bringing her hand to her lips and twisting, she made the irritating key in lock gesture. "Far be it for me to tell you how to run your business, but you should've taken the retainer check. I fear you deeply offended him. You accepted Trump's money but not his. You have any idea how small that made him feel?"

"I'm sure he'll recover even without my visit."

"Try to rise above that cold-heartedness. It's unattractive."

"Can't. According to my wife, I'm on the spectrum."

"Come on, we both know that your put-on cynical detachment is a defense measure you employ because of your extreme emotional sensitivity." A size extra-large thug appeared on my left, another came up from behind; neither Kate's tone nor her stride changed. "Matt, I'm only asking for an hour of your time, max, and it would mean so much to him."

"Dismiss the goons," I said, realizing that there was something I wanted to ask her.

She flicked a hand, and they departed.

"Goons?" she asked.

"In a way I'm glad you showed up," I said. "I've wanted to ask you about Walker. He slipped a note into my pocket. Shortly after he did that, an experienced pickpocket was talking to me. When I got home the note wasn't there. Walker and Hakan ended up dead."

"That's awful," she said. "The Russians seem to have their hands in everything these days."

"Except that of the two people who had their hands in my pocket, one is dead and the other I'm walking with."

"You can't be accusing me." She pointed to herself. "If the Russians would be in league with anyone it'd be Boss Tweet."

"I'm trying to think that through."

"Don't try too hard. At your age any strain can be detrimental to your health."

"True. It's probably not in either of our interests that we spend any more time together."

I turned to go.

She pulled on my sleeve.

"Matt, I'm sorry. This is hard for me. I don't know whom to trust." Her sincere tone, so different from her usual flippant one, almost had me wanting to believe her. "You have to know I'm broken up about Johnny Walker. He was an early member of our group and a loyal friend."

I turned to face her. She tried to hold my hand. I pulled it away.

"I want you involved in the group I'm putting together. Not just the soirée, also the coalition. That's why I took the note from you. I knew he was in trouble, and I didn't want to expose you to any danger." There was a hitch in her voice and her upper lip trembled. "I had no idea they'd get to him so quickly."

"They?"

"Oh, come on, Matt. You have to know that Trump's deathly afraid of what Flynn knows, and if Hakan was involved with him and there was a danger Walker would go public—"

I recalled that Walker's employer's lawyer had mentioned a meeting between Walker, an intimate of Erdogan and a Director of the United States Defense Intelligence Agency, Flynn's former title. Surely, some people around Trump wouldn't want that to get out.

"So, you're sure it wasn't an accident?"

"I'm not sure of anything. You've accused me of being paranoid. Paranoia is a useful adaptation to the world I find myself in." Her lips quivered in a way that, with a normal person, would indicate she was working through whether or not to say something. Then she continued in a whisper, "I fear we have a mole."

She'd actually sounded afraid.

I didn't respond, and she started walking again. I matched step with her, planning to part company once I heard everything she was prepared to tell me about Walker's and Hakan's deaths. Figuring that if I appeared too curious, she'd shut down or dissimulate even more than she ordinarily would, I waited for her to speak, even if that meant listening to her rant more about this supposed mole. Probably I'd be better off not knowing as there wasn't much I could do about it, but I felt an obligation to find out.

We walked half a block in silence, with Kate perusing each of our fellow pedestrians while maintaining a casual air. She abruptly turned uptown and, with me tagging behind, she double-timed it across 42nd Street, just as the light changed, drawing honks from cab drivers.

"Is this part of a plan to get me killed?" I asked, not bothering to disguise my annoyance.

"When you represented Walker, had you learned about his exploiting his—or rather Hakan's—Russian and Turkish connections to bring deals into the firm?"

"I'm not allowed to discuss privileged information," I said, although what the company's lawyer had told me wasn't privileged.

"At the soirée, Walker told me that he had explosive information on Flynn and the Russians coordinating their efforts to defeat Hillary and that Hakan was instrumental in facilitating their backchannelling," she whispered. "That was one of the reasons I decided it wouldn't be a great idea for you to help him get home. Rather, I sent one of my most experienced and trusted drivers."

"I'd heard that Hakan was behind the wheel and he and Walker were the only occupants of the car."

"My driver has disappeared." She exhaled and looked at her shoes. "I told the police everything, and they directed me not to talk to anyone about it. So please, keep that between us."

"No way I'd be involved with anything that smacks of murder and espionage."

"Me neither," she said.

"Okay, then. This is where I leave you. Goodbye and good luck."

"Please, Matt, come with me. There's something you have to see and a question I need to ask you after you've seen it."

I continued to match step with her, not because her cryptic statement had aroused my curiosity but because I still had questions I wanted her to answer.

"Curtis seemed terrified when I turned down his extravagant retainer—not disappointed or hurt but terrified."

"I congratulate you on so quickly having gone from being on the Asperger's spectrum to becoming an expert on reading the facial expressions of people you hardly know."

"His fear was clear enough for a blind man to see."

"He had plenty of reason to be afraid," she said, again scanning the street. "If he pulls off this business idea, he'll run afoul of rich and powerful interests. Perhaps I over-sold you as someone who'd help, and when you turned him down, he feared you might be in league with them."

"His fear expressed itself when I turned down his retainer. I had the feeling he was scared of *you*, not *them*. Same feeling I had when I saw Zhukov's expression when—"

"Paranoia is like cholesterol. There's a healthy and an unhealthy kind." She again made eye contact, and I felt drawn to her, even as my thumbs prickled. "Matt, I've been only good to you. Okay, the kidnapping pissed you off. Apparently, your sense of humor isn't all that well-developed, when it comes to other people's frolics. You have to admit, though, that you enjoyed the evening and it worked out quite well for you."

"Less well for Walker and Hakan."

"You can't really still be suggesting..." Her face turned red with outrage. "How can you lay that tragedy at my feet?"

I thought her reaction overdone, but I had no evidence to contradict her, beyond her pickpocketing Walker's note, and she'd sort of explained that.

"You happy with the Russian election tampering?" she asked.

"Such an abrupt change of subject, I'm surprised I didn't get whiplash."

"If I could tell you all I know and explain what I'm planning to do about it, you'd be an enthusiastic participant."

"Since you can't, I'll be on my way."

"Please, Matt, just come with me. It will, in the least, help you in your Diogenes-like search for the truth."

"I'm not quite the philosopher you think I am."

Her smile could have charmed the most fervent cynic.

"Don't I have the right to respond to your accusation that I played a role in the death of one of my oldest and closest friends?"

"I'm listening."

"Come with me."

Her gray gold-flecked eyes locked onto mine. The next thing I knew I was accompanying her as we walked toward Memorial Sloan Kettering.

I thought it possible that accompanying her to the hospital would clarify what happened to Walker and might ease the suffering of a sick man. Also, the allegations of Russian hacking did concern me. I didn't have the slightest inclination to join Kate's supposed coalition, but I was curious about what she had in mind. Knowing that Lauren would have said that I accompanied Kate because I preferred danger to boredom, I resolved not to allow myself to get sucked into anything dangerous or borderline illegal. Lauren's analyses, however, generally proved more reliable than my resolutions.

As it turned out, Curtis wasn't in the hospital. Kate had someone else for me to see. I didn't know why she'd misled me; perhaps, like the parable of the scorpion and the frog, it was just her nature.

Zhukov looked tiny in his hospital bed. Red-eyed, clumps of hair missing, skin deathly gray, he didn't appear to have the energy to knock on death's door. Not that he'd need to—it seemed about to swing open to admit him. His appearance was so shocking that any question I had about why Kate had led me to believe that Curtis was the one who was sick seemed superfluous.

"Thank you for coming, Matt," he said, voice a strained whisper.

"If it eases your suffering in any way, I'm glad I have, but I have no idea why you wanted me here."

"When I showed you that tape at the soirée..." A coughing fit cut off the remainder of his sentence, and when it subsided, he appeared not to have the energy to finish it.

"I wondered why you showed it to me," I said.

"He received a lethal dose of polonium-210," Kate said.

"Oh, my God. I'm so sorry," I said.

"It's just like former FSB and KGB officer, Alexander Valterovich Litvinenko, who'd fled from Russia and received asylum in England, where he suddenly fell ill and died three weeks later, becoming the first confirmed victim of polonium-210-induced acute radiation syndrome," Kate said, appropriating my pedant role.

"Unlike him, my death will go unnoticed," Zhukov whispered. "Everything on tape true.... But one thing no one will see...." Too weak to cough, he semi-coughed. "I had only copy." Another aborted cough. "You I have to ask..."

He extended a trembling hand toward a nearby table.

I half-filled a paper cup with water from a shiny insulated metal pitcher and handed it to him. His hand shook so much that I had to hold the cup to his lips. He took several sips. Then his hand dropped away from the cup and his eyes closed.

"You had only one copy of the tape showing prostitutes Trump paid to pee on him?" I asked.

Zhukov's eyelids fluttered.

"No, the short-fingered vulgarian never pays anyone. The FSB paid them," Kate said. "The whores were graduates of Sparrow School, the FSB unit that trains women in the art of honey trapping. That's—"

"I've read enough thrillers to be familiar with the lingo," I said.

"Lev's poisoning is part of a pattern," Kate said. "He joins Oleg Erovinkin, the former KGB chief who helped MI6 agent Christopher Steele draft the dossier on The Apricot Hellbeast and was recently found dead in the back of his car in Moscow."

"Two isn't a pattern," I said, becoming irritated by her ever-more-absurd nicknames for the President. Although I was impressed by her ability to remember which ones she'd used and to not use the same one twice, at least not so far.

"Also, Russia's permanent ambassador to the UN, Vitaly Churkin, recently died mysteriously," Kate said. "As did Russian diplomat Sergei Krivov, having suffered severe head injuries at the Russian consulate in New York on Election Day. Both died from Trump-connectionitis."

"Lev, you wanted to ask me something?"

His lips moved but no discernable words emerged.

"Kate, why am I here?" I asked.

"The Mango Mussolini won by less than one percent in three states," she said. "The Russian hacking, false news and manipulation made the difference."

"I hope there's an investigation that uncovers the truth," I said. "But I asked why—"

Zhukov whispered, "I fear it'll all be swept under rug, along with murders of Oleg and me."

"It's awful what you're going through. I wish there was something I could say or do to make you feel better, but I'm not the one to publicize your situation," I said, then directed my attention to Kate. "I have no media connections beyond my home delivery subscription to *The Times,* and my knowledge of social media is on a par with Trump's familiarity with *Spinoza's Ethics.*"

Zhukov started shivering.

I didn't want to get into a discussion that would upset him and certainly didn't want to commit to whatever crazy scheme Kate had in mind. Indeed, I no longer cared why she'd brought me there.

"The Commander in Grief used to say that Julian Assange is a Russian stooge who deserves the death penalty," Kate said. "Now he calls Assange a hero. There are only three possible explanations." She held up one finger. "Putin owns him because of the sex tape, his debts to FSB-controlled Russian banks and his involvement in money laundering." Second finger. "He and Putin have a business deal regarding Eastern Europe, the Caucasus and Russian oil." Third finger. "Or he truly believes Putin has our best interests in mind, is an exemplary leader and is a model for this country. If either of the first two are correct, he should be impeached and tried for treason. If the third is correct, he should be allowed to resign to spend less time with his family."

"Somewhat simplistic" I said.

"The Sociopathic Seventy-Year-Old Toddler says he's so smart, he doesn't need intelligence briefings," Kate said. "That's because he gets all the information he wants directly from the FSB."

"Such overstatements don't add to your credibility," I said.

Kate shrugged.

"It was very nice of you to come," she said. "Lev wanted very badly to see you."

"I can't imagine why, but in any case, Lev, I should leave, let you rest. If there's anything I can do to ease your suffering…"

"Beyond help I am, but thank you for coming," he whispered. "I need to know if…" His lips trembled, then his eyes closed.

"Matt, do you know what happened to Lev's phone?" Kate said. "His phone, and with it the only copy of the pee tape, disappeared at the soirée. Last time he's sure he had it was when he showed it to you."

The question was too ridiculous for me to respond to.

"According to the doctors, he was poisoned at the soirée," she said in the tone of a police detective interrogating a suspect who'd been caught wearing a suicide vest and holding a subway map with Times Square circled. "You were also the only one he'd eaten with."

"I've been very careful otherwise," he whispered with what sounded like one of his last bursts of energy.

"You've *got* to be joking, Kate," I said, losing my patience. "As

121

you well know, I refused to take the phone, and my access to polonium-210 is quite limited."

"We're still investigating," she said.

"Well, don't stop on my account," I said. "And don't feel compelled to share your conclusions with me."

"Relax, Matt. I assured Lev that you hated The Tiny-Handed Tyrant, but obviously, we had to ask."

"Actually, you didn't. Also enough with the Trump nicknames; you're giving me a headache," I said. Then I turned from her to address the dying man. "I don't understand any of this, but, Lev, I'm terribly sorry about what happened to you."

He responded with a weak nod.

"She said you'll help."

"*Ceterum autem censeo Trumpinem esse delendam*," Kate said, presumably on the not unrealistic belief that one of the roads to my heart was paved with classical references.

"You might not want to express that opinion within the hearing of a Secret Service agent," I said.

"I don't want The Tangerine Nutsack to die a martyr's death." Her eyes glowed with a zealot's passion. "We need a deep recession, or some other event that would lead to a sweeping mid-term victory for the Democrats, followed by a swift impeachment."

"That might be beyond even your ability to achieve," I said, hoping to end the conversation.

"The Red Staters must be made to squeal like the pigs they are." She flicked her tongue. "Worse than they got from William Tecumseh Sherman's March to the Sea."

"As you must know, there's no way I'd condone that," I said.

"Don't even start with the shit about innocent people suffering!" Kate shouted. "Under *The Cheeto Benito's* presidency, everyone will suffer."

Clearly she'd emphasized the nickname to further irritate me, but why would she want to alienate me? Hadn't she asked me here to recruit me? Seemed she wanted to keep me guessing. The solution: stop guessing, stop caring.

"The question is whether civilization will come through it intact," she said. "We haven't faced a challenge like this since the Battle of Britain."

"Well, with you on the side of civilization, I'm sure we'll all be just fine," I turned toward the sick man. "Lev, I wish you the best."

I stepped toward the door.

"We need your help," he whispered after me.

"Are you willing to let Lev die in vain?" Kate asked.

I continued walking.

"You never thanked me for all the business I sent you and will send you in the future," she said to my back.

"Thanks."

"'Someday, and that day may never come, I will call upon you to do a service for me'," she said in a gravelly voice.

Her words cut through me like a salted rusty grapefruit knife and filled me with at least as much dread as they'd filled the mortician, Amerigo Bonasera, in *The Godfather*, but I continued waking.

She cut ahead of me and looked me in the eye.

"You do know you're in grave danger."

"Is that a threat?"

"The Dangerously Deranged One has an elephantine memory for slights and an unquenchable thirst for revenge. You fired him. You don't think he'll forget do you? And now that he has real power... One of the reasons I'm recruiting you is you have a compelling reason to be afraid."

"We parted amicably."

"You think he sees it that way?"

I was certain he didn't. Just the same, I walked away as fast as my arthritic knees would permit.

I had a bigger problem to deal with than the threat to civilization. How was I going to explain to Lauren why I'd let Kate persuade me to accompany her on another bizarre venture, albeit a harmless one? I planned to tell her that I now knew Kate's agenda and was fully on board with not having anything further to do with her. Or, as I'd say it to Lauren, *even more* fully on board.

X
Torture Works

Frederick Douglass is an example of somebody who's done an amazing job and is being recognized more and more. Donald J. Trump February 2, 2017

Trump gave a horrifying inauguration speech, the essence of which was that patriotism and loyalty to him trumped— *Trumped?*—the Constitution and the rule of law. He spent the next week claiming the press lied by printing photographs showing how sparsely attended the event was and decrying *fake news* that consisted of quoting what he actually said.

The next day, Lauren and I and over 3.5 million others attended women's marches that were being held around the world.

During the campaign Trump had claimed that torture works, and he might have been right. After weeks of listening to him, Kellyanne and Spicer, I was willing to do or say almost anything to make it stop—anything, that is, short of aligning myself with Kate.

The Republican Congress rubber-stamped most of Trump's cabinet picks, which included: a surgeon, who'd announced that he knew nothing about public housing, to head HUD; a creationist, who opposed public schools and believed keeping guns in school was necessary to protect the children from a grizzly bear attack, for Education Secretary; a fake news disseminator, who was on the FSB and Turkish government payrolls, for National Security Advisor; a congressman, who'd traded pharmaceutical stocks based on his knowledge of pending legislation, for head of the Human Health and Services Department; and a climate change denier and shill for the energy industry as EPA chief. Trump campaigned as the candidate of change, and, in that regard, he seemed to have been truthful. Anyone who'd believed that would be a change for the better would get what they deserved, but what about the rest of us, a clear majority? JFK was onto something when he said, "Life is unfair."

Based on a False Story

I sold my stocks at an ample profit and changed channels whenever Trump, Kellyanne or Spicer came on the TV news. The rest of the news, however, was no cheerier. One example out of many: middle-aged white men were dying at unprecedented rates, due primarily to alcohol and opioid abuse. The uptick in their rates of death was so substantial that the life expectancies of Americans as whole had taken a substantial hit. That, to some extent, explained the anger of uneducated white men. Perhaps they were too zonked-out to understand that their preferred candidate was a con-man who hated *losers* like them.

A brief, paid-for obituary notice in *The Times* announced Zhukov's demise.

After having been caught lying to Congress about his meetings with the Russian ambassador, i.e. spymaster—meetings that Zhukov had mentioned—Attorney General Jeff Sessions recused himself from any investigation of the Trump/Russia connection. News of the deaths of Oleg Erovinkin, Vitaly Churkin and Sergei Krivov, which Kate had mentioned, received passing comment by the news media, then sank like a cement encased corpse.

In the weeks following my hospital visit, I heard nothing from Kate, Curtis or anyone connected to them. Kate had been the best source of legal business I'd had in years, certainly the most lucrative in terms of dollars per hour. While I didn't want to kill the goose that laid the golden egg, I didn't want the goose to kill me; and the vehemence of her anti-Trump rants scared me even more in retrospect. Surely she didn't expect her diatribes to result in my joining up with her, but what *did* she expect?

A month went by without any calls about new cases. Then, Enrique de Caldas, the man at the soirée whom I'd embarrassingly pegged as a Mexican drug lord, contacted me via an assistant. She and I set up a meeting with de Caldas for the following day. In response to my question, she said she didn't know what her boss had in mind, besides that he wanted *to discuss legal matters*. My quip that I wasn't going to discuss illegal matters landed flat.

As soon as I hung up, the phone rang again. De Caldas' assistant calling back to cancel or Kate calling to take credit?

Neither.

"Hi, Mr. Bloom, this is Susan Cohen. Peter Lawson"—my law

school classmate and friend whose heart had given out on the night of the election—"represented me for many years."

"I still haven't gotten over his...."

"You gave a beautiful eulogy at the funeral."

"Thank you."

"We don't have any current legal problems, but we seem to become involved in litigation from time to time, so I'd like to be ready in case a new one develops," she said. "May I take you to lunch sometime next week? Wednesday maybe?"

"Let me check." I called up my electric calendar, which was as blank as it had been minutes earlier when I'd entered my meeting with de Caldas. "That works."

"Great. I'll have Alexa send you an evite."

A few minutes later, I received an invitation to lunch at Agern, an exorbitantly expensive Scandinavian restaurant in Grand Central Station. Perhaps, never having eaten a meal or paid for it with its—her?—own money, the Amazon virtual assistant hadn't learned to be price sensitive or that beef heart with salt and ash-baked beet root weren't everyone's idea of a treat.

After an initial exchange of pleasantries, I asked de Caldas how he'd gotten involved with Kate and her soirées. At first, my mention of her appeared to confuse him but then he realized from context to whom I'd referred.

"I think it is best for both of us that we do not have such discussions," he said. "Suffice it to say that I know you and she have worked together on many projects with excellent results, as have she and I, and I am grateful to her for the introduction." Many projects? Perhaps she built up her having referred Walker and McKuen. Still... "She shared none of the particulars, and I'm sure she's shared none of our particulars with you."

My concern-o-meter flashed red, but I interpreted that to mean I should be cautious, not that I should refuse to represent him regardless of what he wanted me to do for him. I practically heard Lauren demanding that I take the later course, but I could take care of myself.

"She and I have parted company," I said.

"All the better."

His smile, brilliant due to his dark skin and black moustache, didn't spread to the dark eyes that I'd found so scary at the soirée.

"I've concluded that Mexicans should stop worrying about Trump's wall and just get over it," he said, a clear effort to change the subject.

It took me several seconds to realize that that had been a joke. I smiled.

"So what brings you here today?" I asked.

He spoke non-stop for several minutes, ignoring my attempts to inject questions. In essence, he told me he wanted to set up a business in New York, via a corporation or LLC that I would help him to form. He also wanted me to look over an office lease that, being almost half an inch thick, made a loud plop when he dropped it on the conference room table. He intended to use the corporation/LLC as a vehicle through which to do a series of acquisitions of U.S. businesses and asked about Foreign Investment Adviser exemptions from the Investment Advisers Act and inquired about whether I thought Trump would change the way large investments from abroad were taxed.

"None of that is within my areas of expertise," I said, when he finally paused long enough for me to do so. "I'm a business litigator with some recent experience negotiating packages for high-level executives whose employment has been terminated."

"Concepción told me you have partners with the expertise I require."

I was disappointed that he didn't know Kate by the name of a bloodthirsty Aztec goddess.

"Shall I see if my corporate and real estate partners are available now?"

"Please."

They were, and when they arrived, I left the conference room, hoping to obtain more clarity when I debriefed my partners.

My corporate partner reported back that he'd have expected a sophisticated Mexican businessman like de Caldas to have gone to a large international law firm with offices in Mexico City, of which there were at least a dozen in New York, and certainly to have contacted a lawyer with the requisite expertise, rather than a small-firm litigator.

"I suspected that de Caldas is looking to set up a company behind the backs of his partners, shareholders or government, and that he came to us because we didn't have ties to other entities with which he did business," my partner said.

"Are you okay with that?" I asked.

"I emphasized that we would not be involved in anything the least bit shady, and he responded that if he detected even a hint that I'd cut corners, he'd have gotten up from the table."

"If anything you learn raises even the slightest ethical or moral concern, please let me know," I said.

"He told me that his desire to have a U.S. presence grows out of concern about Trump's immigrant ban and trade policies and that he intended to make several substantial acquisitions in the near future. Maybe Trump will be good for our business," he said. "Like how the booming demand for Zyklon-B helped IG Farben's bottom line during WWII."

Tired of the Trump/Nazi comparisons, I didn't acknowledge his historical reference. Maybe, though, I was just irritated that I hadn't come up with it myself.

"Having been involved in large, international deals, he's accustomed to paying substantial legal fees," he said.

"Makes me wonder why he came to us and not one of those firms. If he'd wanted to avoid large firms, there are plenty of boutique firms that do the types of deals he's talking about."

"He said he'd met you at a party and had been impressed by your perceptive take on world and national affairs." He smiled. "I restrained myself from saying that he must have you confused with someone else."

"I didn't say anything that even I thought was perceptive."

"You've become quite the rainmaker lately."

"I sold my soul to the devil."

I came to work two days later and the receptionist, clearly shaken, showed me *The New York Post*, a Murdock-controlled tabloid I rarely looked at and never read.

At first I thought she was calling my attention to yet another story about the plague of deaths from opioid overdoses among middle-aged white males in the Rust Belt. Then I looked down the page. *Murder of Trump Supporter*.

Oh my god! The picture showed a very dead McKuen with posters scattered around the body: one featured Trump's photo inside a circle with a line through it and had the caption *Bad Hombre*, another showed Trump, in front of Putin, bending forward pants around his ankles with the caption *Nyet My President*.

I went into my office and closed the door.

After composing myself, I called McKuen's wife, Leslie, to give my condolences even though I'd only met the woman once. I reached a recording: "Thank you for your call, but we are not taking or returning calls." Then a hang-up, no beep to leave a message. I felt an urge to contact Kate, but luckily I had no way of doing so.

I remembered McKuen's fear when he told me about his frat brother and Leslie's shock when she learned he'd told me.

When I got home, Lauren had CNN on. Her addiction to Trump-related news was starting to concern me. I understood, however, that she was unable to look away from a train wreck, particularly as a seemingly endless line of railcars were continuously piling into each other, jackknifing and bursting into flames.

On the tube—or rather the flat-screen; it hadn't been a tube for over a decade— Kellyanne said, "This cold-blooded murder is the inevitable result of the irresponsible liberal media's concerted campaign to undermine and slander the President of the United States."

Having developed a visceral hatred for the woman, I changed the channel only to see the Reichsminister of Public Enlightenment and Propaganda, Sean Spicer, blaming McKuen's murder on "paid agitators." In spite of my dislike of Nazi analogies, sometimes I couldn't help myself.

"Wasn't that your client?" Lauren asked.

I nodded.

"You never before had a client murdered. Now you've had two."

"We don't know that Walker was murdered and certainly have no reason to believe that Kate had a hand in—"

"Oh, sorry. One murdered and one who died under suspicious circumstances. Half the clients she sent you died shortly afterwards. Being a client Kate refers compares unfavorably to having an aggressive brain tumor."

"I can't explain—"

"Was it Curtis who told you that when someone made the

Robert N. Chan

mistake of offending *Erinye*, he paid the price many times over?"

I nodded.

"And McKuen said she'd made his frat brother *disappear*?" she asked.

I nodded again. One of Lauren's few flaws was her near perfect memory for everything I told her. That might come in handy if I begin to slip into dementia.

"Then there's her Russian pal who died of radiation poisoning, not exactly an everyday occurrence."

"Yes, it does seem suspicious. Maybe I should cozy up to her and surreptitiously search for evidence. Be like that mystery writer played by Angela Lansbury, who lives in a small town with a murder rate many times that of Chicago's."

"Or maybe you should be solicitous of your wife who doesn't want to be a widow at least until you load up on life insurance."

Not the right time to remind her that I didn't like life insurance because it seemed like betting against myself.

On TV, Attorney General Jefferson Beauregard Sessions, III called for more funds, "to combat political hate crimes, such as this one."

I picked up the remote and gave Lauren a questioning look to which she responded with a nod. Having gained her permission, I shut off the television. Now, all I had to do was persuade her to keep it off until after the 2020 election.

We went out for a lovely dinner at Red Farm, an upscale and up-priced Chinese restaurant in the neighborhood. We didn't even turn the news on when we returned home.

A few minutes after we stepped through the door, though, a reporter for FoxNews called, asking, "Is it true McKuen was fired because he was a Trump supporter?"

"No comment," I said, then hung up.

As I hadn't filed any papers in court, there was no legitimate way the reporter could have known of my representation of McKuen. If the reporter had called his former employer, they'd have responded with a no comment and certainly wouldn't have told them about me, giving me a a platform to bad-mouth the company.

"Who was that, Honey?" Lauren asked.

"A solicitation."

Then Emily called.

130

"I don't know anything about what happened to McKuen other than what I read in *The Post*," I said in lieu of hello.

"If you learn anything?"

"How did you know I represented him?"

"You don't expect me to reveal my sources, do you?"

"Actually, I'd thought you just made the stuff up." I said. "You hear anything more about the Walker slash Yaldiz accident?"

"No. Have you?"

"That McKuen was killed by anti-Trumpsters who left posters lying about like calling cards seems preposterous. Certainly sufficient to merit an investigation."

"May I quote you for a story about lawyers whose clients die suspiciously?"

"I assume you'd meant that as an attempt at humor. What gave it away was that it wasn't funny," I said. "You might want to follow up with your secret source about Walker."

"Why is there some connection between the three deaths other than you?"

"If there was, it would make a good story." I heard a click. "Emily, you still there?"

A new message appeared to come from an unfamiliar source: "Matt, be smart, promote yourself, this is a chance to be on national TV. Say you're shaken by his death but understand the fury of the loyal Americans whose values Benedict Donald is betraying on a daily basis."

Before I had the chance to delete it, Kate's message disappeared.

I left my office bound for lunch with Susan Cohen. The half inch of snow on the sidewalk and a squall reduced visibility to a few feet. I'd neglected to wear a coat because, once I crossed the street, all I had to do was walk through Grand Central.

Windblown snow and sleet made the wait for the light to change seem endless.

A tall, attractive black woman appeared in front of me, materializing out of nowhere, a reprise of one of Kate's better tricks.

"We decided to hold our lunch at a more secure location." She tilted her head toward a black SUV parked at the crosswalk. It had tinted windows and an Uber decal on the windshield. "Funny, you don't look like a Susan Cohen," I said assuming that it was who'd contacted me to have lunch.

"I'm not."

She flashed what appeared to be an FBI badge, identifying her as Azealia Grae.

I leaned forward. The photo on the badge looked like the woman in front of me. The badge said *Federal Bureau of Investigation* on the top and *Department of Justice* on the bottom. I'd read that fake badges often used the abbreviation *FBI*.

"I would've thought a real FBI agent would come by my office."

"If your office wasn't bugged, we would've."

I asked for her agent number. It matched the number on the photo ID.

"Give me a minute," I said.

"The longer we're exposed, the greater the danger."

I suspected she wasn't referring to the risk of freezing to death, but that one felt real enough. I'd begun to shiver, and the SUV looked warm and comfy. I cast a covetous glance at the agent's black Canada Goose parka—pricey for an FBI agent—and a pink wool cap and matching scarf that looked like her mother might have knitted them for her.

"We still have a few minutes until our Agern reservation," I said. "If that was a ruse and it worked, whoever you're afraid of will be there."

"You're the one who should be afraid."

I took out my phone.

She snatched it from me.

"No!"

"It's 'yes,' if you want me to get into that car."

"You better not be alerting—"

"I'm not."

"Your calls aren't secure."

"We'll have to risk that."

She handed me back my phone, as if it—and I—were coated in dogshit.

With the assistance of Siri, I called the local FBI field office and gave the person I spoke to the agent's number. She confirmed the agent was Azealia Grae.

"Now turn off your phone," Grae said.

Not waiting for me to comply, she took it from me and turned it off. I wondered if she had the right to do that.

"I'll return it when we're done."

My instinct was to tell her that we were already done. "What's this about?"

"Why don't you tell me?"

"Because I'm not clairvoyant." My teeth started to chatter, not only because of the cold. "Am I a target?"

"You think you should be?"

"I should have counsel present."

The wind picked up, and icy snow scoured my face. My inquisitor looked supremely comfortable.

"You're not under arrest."

"Then I'll be on my way."

I stepped back toward my office.

She grabbed my sleeve.

"You are a target, just not the FBI's target, at least not yet," she said. "Mr. Bloom, you have to know you're involved with some very dangerous characters, who are doing very bad things."

"No one has asked me to do anything illegal or to assist them to do anything illegal," I said. "If anyone were to, I'd decline, and that includes such a request from the FBI."

Her eyes narrowed to crinkling slits, a sign of distrust or a reaction to the blowing snow?

"You heard what happened to Ellis McKuen?"

I nodded. The image of McKuen dead on the sidewalk flashed in my head.

"I'm losing patience, get in the fucking car," she said. "If we wanted to harm you, we could do it right here."

I hesitated.

"This isn't the way the FBI makes contact with potential witnesses—or whatever I'm supposed to be—in books and movies," I said. "Given the constant interaction between life and art, I'm sure that, even if the fiction had started out incorrect, real-life agents have modeled themselves on it and vice versa."

"Books and movies." She rolled her eyes.

"I understand why NYPD would be investigating McKuen's death, but the FBI?"

"Fine, freeze your skinny ass off. Just tell me one thing, then you're on your own and may God have mercy on your soul," she said, barely audible, over the howling wind. Her last phrase didn't sound nearly as hokey as I'd have imagined it would. "Where's Jerome Curtis?"

"No idea. I haven't seen or spoken to him since—"

"Since he told you he'd embarked on a criminal scheme to make opioids available on a massive scale to white men in the Rust Belt states where Trump had razor-thin margins of victory?"

"I'm not going to disclose attorney/client communications, but I assure you he never said anything like that to me." I hoped I didn't sound as shaken as I felt. "If he had, I would've reported it."

"You did know about his intent to shift the demographic balance in the Democrats' favor?"

Jesus, was that actually Curtis' intent?

"Absolutely not."

"We have evidence otherwise."

"I'd be curious to see that," I said, my voice pitched an octave higher than usual.

"Your failure to disclose that ongoing criminal scheme has led to over a hundred deaths, and those resulted from his brief rollout of the test website he showed you."

"I told you…" No reason to repeat myself. It would just make me sound more defensive. Over a hundred deaths?

"You want to see evidence?" She unfurled her arm toward the car.

My having been lured out on false pretenses and then accosted on the street had set alarm bells ringing, and in spite of confirmation from the FBI that Grae was who she said she was, I had my doubts. It was about time, though, that I told law enforcement about Walker, McKuen and Zhukov and their connection to Kate, even though I didn't have evidence of wrongdoing on Kate's part. And—why should paranoia be limited to the paranoid?—if Grae was aligned with Kate? Well, I wouldn't be telling them anything Kate didn't already know.

I got in and was surrounded by warmth. The driver didn't acknowledge me, but a man in the back seat—cheap dark suit, white shirt, stained rep tie, sports watch with fraying band—flashed his badge.

"Good afternoon, Mr. Bloom. I'm Agent Anderson," he said in a formal tone. He didn't extend his hand.

"Hello." I didn't say *Nice to meet you,* because it was a felony to lie to a government agent.

Agent Grae got in, and the car pulled away from the curb. Between the tinted windows and the blowing snow outside, I couldn't see a damn thing. At least no blindfold needed this time around.

"Where are we going?"

"Just driving around," Anderson said.

"It's a sorry state of affairs if the FBI is so terrified of being eavesdropped on that they have to conduct business by Uber," I said, "or has the new administration rented out your offices so more money can go to tax relief for the super-wealthy?"

"You only now noticed the sorry state of affairs?" Anderson said.

"No, Director Comey opened my eyes to it in his late October speech."

"Asshole," the driver said, a comment that I realized had been directed at me.

He showed me his badge, then removed the Uber logo, which hadn't actually been a decal but something more temporary.

Grae turned on her tablet and started to play a video of Curtis showing me the test website from which he intended to sell Canadian drugs at cut-rate prices.

As I recalled our conversation, Curtis had told me that Kate was *violently opposed to Trump* and I'd told him that she'd had me kidnapped at gunpoint. In this version, though, the audio had been edited. It contained no reference to Kate. Instead, Curtis said that *he* was violently opposed to Trump and I replied that I was, too, and offered to be his *consigliere*—a word that now carried its full *Godfather* connotation. The $25,000 check he'd slid toward me was plainly in evidence, as was the list of drugs on his website—all opioids and other controlled substances, according to Grae. After Curtis, on the tape, explained his plan to market controlled substances to white males in red states, I said, "Your goal is laudable" and suggested setting up an off-shore company, in the Caymans or somewhere, to create a labyrinth of subsidiary and parent companies that eventually would lead to a phony passport for someone who doesn't exist.

I began shivering again, and this time it had nothing to do with the temperature.

"I assume that, with your sophisticated forensics, you know that tape has been extensively edited," I said.

"You'd be best advised to keep you assumptions to the absolute minimum," Anderson said, hostile as Sean Spicer caught in a lie. There was something to the old Head & Shoulders advertising tag line, *You never get a second chance to make a first impression.* "You're in way over your head."

"When you have that tape unscrambled—unless, of course, you're the scramblers—you'll see I told Curtis that I wouldn't be involved in anything illegal and I expressly disapproved of setting up an off-shore company." Although I had no idea whether unscrambling an edited video was easier than unscrambling eggs, I believed a close examination would reveal that the lip movements didn't square up with the words. "I don't know if he actually set up an off-shore company, but I assure you I didn't assist with that. Indeed, I don't know how one would go about doing that."

"Playing stupid is just plain stupid." Anderson's eyes bored into me. "What did you think his twenty-five-grand check was for? Seems a pretty steep price for a short meeting where you told him you wouldn't help and counseled him against violating the law."

"That's why I didn't take it," I said, now sweating as well as shivering. "I told him I don't have expertise in FDA regulations or other relevant legal areas and that his entire scheme, which he presented as a charitable endeavor to help those who couldn't afford needed medication, sounded dodgy to me."

"You're getting stupider and stupider right before my eyes. It's like watching a time-lapse video of an insect going through metamorphosis," Anderson said, sounding unexpectedly erudite.

He handed me a print-out of a statement from my money market account, with the $25,000 deposit highlighted in fuchsia.

My stomach shrank to the size of a cherry pit.

"I... I, um, haven't received this statement." I pointed to the date, indicating that it was due to be mailed that day, or rather I tried to. My finger shook too much for me to point with any degree of accuracy. I folded my hand into a fist.

"Ah, the now ubiquitous fake news defense," Anderson said, drawing a chuckle from the driver. "Us humble civil servants aren't as stupid as you seem to think we are. Neither are prosecutors, judges or juries."

"How the fuck did you get that without a court order?" I asked hoping they didn't have a court order, because to get one they'd have to have presented evidence to the court and I'd have to be a serious target.

"A concerned friend of yours sent it," Anderson said.

My stomach blew up to the size of a watermelon and then shrank to the size of fish egg.

"We compared what Curtis and McKuen paid you with the time you put in. Either you're the most expensive lawyer in the Western world or you were paid for something else."

Fuck! Of course it was too good to be true.

"Enough bullshit!" I slammed my fist into my lap. Ouch. "Where did you get this tape?"

I didn't expect an answer, but a former client had taught me that sometimes one had to counterpunch; when attacked take the offensive.

"The late Ellis McKuen," Grae said. The corners of her mouth turned up. Apparently, her enjoyment of this encounter had become too great to hide. "Appears he bugged the room when you left the conference room to get him water. We're guessing he did so at the direction of his wife."

"For you to know that, you'd have to have already bugged my office," I said, fuming.

Unless this same *concerned friend* told them.

"Your office has more bugs than a week-old corpse," Anderson said. "And not just those planted by McKuen."

"None by us," Grae said.

"What do you want from me?" I asked, making an effort to make my tone convey impatience and annoyance, rather than fear and more fear.

"Cooperation," Grae said. "We're not inclined to charge you, *for now*, but that decision totters on a knife-edge."

"If we decide to take the other route, the charge will be conspiracy to murder with terrorism enhancement. That's a capital crime." Anderson smiled, presumably enjoying the image of a fatal cocktail being injected into my veins—after sterilizing the needle to avoid infection.

Dizzy and nauseated, I asked Anderson to roll down the window. After a cruel snicker, he complied.

We passed the Bowling Green subway station, where protestors were holding signs purporting to commemorate the Bowling Green Massacre—an event conjured up out of thin air by Kellyanne Conway to justify Trump's Muslim ban.

"Fucking assholes," the driver said, then pushed a button causing the window to roll up.

"I didn't do anything wrong, and I'm fully confident that I could never be convicted on the basis of this trumped-up evidence," I said, although the tremolo in my voice conveyed my lack of confidence.

In the face of alternative facts, *1984* had become a bestseller, but when it came to dystopian fiction, I related more to K in *The Trial*. Once one became ensnared in the criminal justice system, the outcome was unpredictable. Almost a hundred deaths attributable to my supposed silence, Christ. They'd probably try me in the red state where most of the deaths occurred. Half the jurors would already believe that, as a Jewish New Yorker, who'd supported Hillary, I deserved to die as a matter of principle.

Did Curtis really want to kill middle-aged white men because they had a disproportionate likelihood to vote for Trump? How did things get this bad?

"Start by telling us about how Curtis came to you," Grae said.

"In minute detail," her partner added.

As I spoke, my words scrolled out on the screen of Grae's laptop. She highlighted certain phrases in yellow, but from my angle I couldn't see which ones.

My throat became dry, and scratchy and my voice turned harsh.

She handed me a bottle of Islandic Glacial water. I might be facing the needle, but at least my inquisitors had a sense of humor.

Finally, the car skidded to a stop in front of my office building. Grae returned my phone.

"You're free to go."

"For now," Anderson said. "And don't go far. We'll be watching."

"For your sake, I hope this *Kate* actually exists," Grae said. "Before we part company, is there anything else you'd like to tell us."

"No, nothing that I'd like to, but I guess there's one thing I *should* mention."

I told her about Walker and Hakan, including Walker, a non-drinker, suddenly becoming drunk or sick, his note, Kate's pickpocketing of it and her version of what had happened.

"Sounds like being your client is more unlucky than walking under a ladder, while a black cat crosses your path, on Friday the Thirteenth," Anderson said. "You should give out rabbits' feet, like pediatricians hand out lollipops."

"They don't do that anymore, bad for the teeth."

My knees and back were so stiff, Grae had to help me out of the car.

The snow had stopped, and the setting sun cast an eerie magenta glow on the miraculously still-white streets. In New York newly fallen snow turns gray and slushy in a manner of minutes, except in the parks and now apparently on 42nd Street—a metaphor for my situation that I was too thick to interpret.

XI
Cool as a Cryogenic Cucumber

The opinion of this so-called judge, which essentially takes law-enforcement away from our country, is ridiculous and will be overturned! Donald J. Trump, February 4, 2017

"You *are* going to fully cooperate?" Lauren said, a rhetorical question.

"I can't violate attorney/client privilege, of course, but otherwise—"

"ATTORNEY/CLIENT PRIVILEGE?"

I jerked back as if she'd slapped me. I suspected that if I looked in a mirror I'd have seen a hand-shaped red mark, complete with ring indent, on my cheek

"Yeah, probably doesn't apply. After all I never represented Kate. McKuen is dead, and the privilege died with him, I think."

"You will, because I say you will."

I saluted.

"I have no idea where Curtis is or what he's up to. In any event, they have a tape of my meeting with him, saying what they want it to say. So they don't need me for what's on it, and apparently they've decided that it's not enough to merit charging me with a crime. Just the same, I'd like to know who altered it to make me look guilty."

"Altered or not, you're cooperating fully."

"Yes, but—"

"Did you tell them about the Mexican guy?"

"They didn't ask, and I don't know of any laws he's violated."

She buried her head in her hands, then looked up again.

"Tell them anyway."

I nodded.

"I wish I knew what Kate's anti-Trump endgame is and what part she plans for me to play."

"You're better off not knowing. Just tell them everything, answer their questions fully, then answer those questions they don't ask," she said. "Also, hire a lawyer. Actually, hire a lawyer first."

"I probably should but…"

"But what?" Her stare bore into me. "You're afraid they may interpret it as a sign of guilt, like every other dumb-shit who blows his right to counsel?"

"I haven't even been Mirandized."

"If you were representing a client under these circumstances, you'd tell him not to hire counsel?"

"Well, no, but—"

"What's that expression, a lawyer who represents himself is a total asshole?" she asked, rhetorically, I assumed. "And you think you needn't worry about psychopathic Kate because you have your consummate charm to protect you."

"Okay, sure, I have an inordinate faith in my ability to work my way out of whatever jams I get myself into, but even if that faith is misplaced, I'm not sure what a lawyer would do for me at this point."

While I didn't fully understand why I was being so obstinate, I did know that the reason I gave her was only a small part of it. I needed to fully understand my motivation, because I suspected Kate already had that figured out and would use it to my detriment. Clearly, she had something in mind for me, given all the energy she'd devoted to manipulating me.

"For one thing, a lawyer would insist that law enforcement not talk to you except in his or her presence, insist that he or she speak for you and insist that you have no further conversations with Kate or anyone associated with her."

"If I become a target, I'll—"

"Once you talk yourself into trouble, it'll be hard for a lawyer to talk your way out of it."

I took a deep breath, then let it out slowly.

Lauren shot me a questioning look.

"Give me a minute," I said. "I'm trying to cage my thoughts."

I decided not to add *that are flitting about my head like hummingbirds on amphetamines.*

I splashed cold water on my face, which accomplished nothing.

I returned from the bathroom.

"I figured out why I'm not hiring a lawyer."

"We already resolved that one: it's your overweening faith in your own cleverness."

"It's more that Kate is far cleverer than the FBI, and I'm pretty sure that she's a greater threat than the Feds. First, I need to get a better handle on what's going on, something a criminal lawyer won't be able to do."

"You're kidding?" she shouted, then dropped her voice as if afraid that someone was listening in, and as far as I knew, they might have been. "You have to know that that makes no sense at all."

"Hard to explain."

"I'm sure of that." Lauren didn't do snide all that often, but when she did, she did it well. "They're threatening you with conspiracy to commit mass murder with a terrorism enhancement."

"But they haven't done it. They say they want my cooperation, and I'll give them that."

"Did it occur to you that they're building a case against you?"

"Sure, I know how these things work. I've watched almost as much *Law & Order* as you have." If I could mimic the look Lauren gave me, I could intimidate anyone who came after me. "I don't think a lawyer would be of help in dealing with Kate."

"Dealing with Kate is easy, just don't do it."

"I'm certainly not going to reach out to her, but back to the Feds. I'm hopeful that if it comes down to it, I can get immunity as a material witness."

"Witness to what?" She pointed a manicured finger. "Curtis' website which you didn't report to anyone; Zhukov's radiation poisoning, which you didn't report to anyone; conversations you'd had with McKuen, which you didn't report to anyone? Or the guy you'd pegged as a drug lord, who seems to be here buying businesses so he can launder money through them?"

Shit, that hadn't occurred to me. I'd been so appalled by my having stereotyped him that I'd shut down that thought.

"Yeah, okay, I don't know what the Feds could use me to testify about, but neither are they from what I can tell. As long as all they're doing is threatening, I'm okay. As soon as it appears that I'm actually a target, I'll stop talking to them and retain counsel."

She rolled her eyes.

"Jesus, Matt. When Trump was running, I couldn't shut you up about the value of experience and why a politician experienced in the ways of Washington would be a far superior choice for president than a businessman without such expertise," she said. "Don't you get it? The right lawyer, maybe a former U.S. Attorney, would know how the FBI and prosecutors think, be able to speak off-the-record to people in the U.S. Attorney's office with whom he or she has a relationship and—"

"Only if I had something to offer, which I don't *yet*," I said, all too aware that that undercut my hope of being a material witness.

"So you're planning to go undercover and crack the case wide open?"

"I'm not *planning* anything, but both the FBI and Kate seem to think I'm important, and I intend to figure out why. Once I do, I'll come up with the next step."

"Your faith in the power of pure intellect is misplaced."

"But it's all I have. *Cogito ergo sum*."

"Play your cards right, and you might be the most thoughtful guy in the entire Federal Prison System."

Leaks from inside the White House described an almost empty West Wing, where aides, unable to find the light switches, held meetings in the dark and stumbled around trying doorknobs in search of exits. Lacking sufficient focus to read, Trump was signing whatever executive orders Steve Bannon—a self-described Leninist and Alt-Right extremist, contradiction in terms though they might be—placed in front of him. The President spent much of his day watching FoxNews and spent his lonely nights, abandoned by his wife and ten-year-old son, wandering around in his bathrobe, watching more FoxNews and sending out deranged tweets based on what he'd just seen on TV. Spicer and Kellyanne pushed back against those reports, claiming that Trump didn't own a bathrobe, but the mental picture of him wandering around naked was too terrible to bear.

Trump claimed that the media was covering up terrorist attacks in order to undercut his Muslim ban—which Spicer said shouldn't have been called a Muslim ban, except that that was what Trump called it. In fact, the media had covered most terrorist attacks *ad nauseam*; the Orlando and Paris attacks, for example, had dominated the news for days. Certain terrorist attacks I thought I knew about, however, such as the polonium-210 radiation poisoning of Zhukov and Curtis' alleged poisoning of red state middle-aged white men, appeared to have been covered up.

Weeks went by without further communication from Kate, the FBI or anyone else connected to them. I searched for news of the Curtis mass murders and found none. I did see, however, yet another piece about a further spike in opioid-connected deaths, particularly in certain red states. Maybe the Feds had clamped down on news about their investigation.

Having slept all the way to sunrise one fine February morning, I woke in an unusually good mood and told Lauren that I thought the storm had passed me by.

"Don't jinx it," she said.

Grae and Anderson were waiting for me when I entered my office reception area.

She paced like a caged predator. When he saw me, Anderson's right hand went to the gun in his shoulder holster, a reflex action that had nothing to do with me—I hoped.

"Why the fuck didn't you tell me you'd represented this Kate?" Grae said, face so close to mine that, even if I'd been deaf, I could have made out her words by the impression they made on my cheek.

"Because I didn't represent her."

I led them into the kitchen and turned the water on high.

"I'm in no mood for amateur tradecraft," Anderson said, shutting it off with a violent twist.

"Fine," I said, trying to play the unaccustomed role of the only adult in the room.

I led them into my office and sat behind my large teak desk, leaving them to the two ancient client chairs, with a fine view of framed finger-paintings that Jason had done in preschool—now badly faded, but I couldn't part with them. The morning sun back-lit me and made them squint. I'd designed my office to lord my majestic power over my visitors, something I'd learned from…a former client.

"I'd love to help," I said, "but I think we've reached the point where I need to have counsel present."

"Think again. We're this far from charging you with a capital crime." Grae held her thumb and forefinger a few millimeters apart.

"If you force us to go that route, you can have an entire quarrel of fucking lawyers for all we care."

Quarrel, the term I'd made up for a group of lawyers at the soirée. I realized that I'd better be careful about what I said; they had extensive recordings.

I told myself she was bluffing, that the charges would never stick, but myself already knew that listening to me was ill-advised. Being less than an inch away from an indictment for a capital crime merited criminal counsel, but in spite of Lauren's deafening screaming in my mind's ears, I decided to wait until the meeting was over. I hoped that I'd then have a better idea of what they were up to.

"I thought you didn't want to talk here because my office was bugged," I said.

"We've passed the point where we give a shit," Grae said.

"You implied that I'd represented Kate. I didn't."

The agents exchanged pissed-off eye rolls. A vein in Anderson's temple began to twitch—hard thing to fake.

"18 U.S. Code Section 1001 makes lying to a federal officer a felony," Grae said.

"I make it a point not to lie to anyone, makes it easier not to have to remember what I say to whom."

She opened her laptop and began to play a tape.

"Mr. Bloom, my name is Hilaria Bormann," said a well disguised but now sickeningly familiar voice. "I've come here from the twenty-fifth millennium to kill the Short-Fingered Vulgarian. *"

"Time travel is beyond my area of expertise," I said on the tape.

"Don't be so modest. I've chosen you because, in my time, you're one of the Twelve Revered Martyrs."

I buried my head in my hands. Why the fuck hadn't I put this together long ago? I had many conversations in the course of a typical week, many crazy, but not that crazy. In fairness the recorded voice did sound different from her actual voice.

Perhaps when Kate asked me about whether I'd had any fun cases recently, she was testing to see if I was stupid enough for her to manipulate. I passed with flying colors.

This conversation took place long before I met her. The FBI wouldn't have been taping my phone. Seems they'd been on to Kate for quite a while—unless a *concerned friend* had passed them the tape.

"I'm flattered but I'm busy working on twenty-first century matters," I said on the recording.

"I need your help, I'm illegally confined in the Manhattan Psychiatric Center."

"If you send me the commitment papers I'll take a look, and if I agree your confinement was illegal, maybe I'll make a call, but..."

I must've been bored out of my mind at the time to entertain her call.

"You already have them. I sent them telepathically."

"I prefer email."

"You needn't worry about money. I'll pay you in Federation Bitcoins, once I receive my fee for the successful completion of my mission."

"I assume Hilaria Bormann isn't her real name?" I said to the agents, the most coherent thought I was capable of expressing.

"The guy's brilliant," Anderson said to Grae. "A regular Sherlock Fucking Holmes."

"I got her released due to a defect in the medical certification that had led to her confinement. It took me a couple phone calls," I said. "Quite obviously, I had no idea that Hilaria Bormann and Kate were the same person. You've heard how different her voice sounded in that call from how it sounded in the call I'd thought I'd made to Madelyn. You do have that recording?"

"You were the sixth lawyer she'd called," Anderson said. "The others were smart enough to decline to have anything to do with her."

"She got me on a slow day. Lucky for her, as it appears she was down to her last half dozen revered martyrs."

"Judges trying terrorism cases are notoriously challenged in the sense of humor department." Grae fixed me with an unblinking stare. "Wising off like that might get you the needle."

I stared back, willing myself to stay calm, or rather to become calm.

"What do you want from me?" I asked.

"To start, we're curious about why you neglected to tell us about Enrique de Caldas," Anderson said, voice wet with menace.

"I... I didn't know you were interested in him. As far as I knew, and still know, he's a businessman seeking to establish a U.S. presence to do legitimate transactions."

"You met him at *Kate's* so-called *soirée*?" Anderson said.

"I did."

Grae continued her unblinking stare. I recalled that snakes don't blink because they lack eyelids.

"Didn't it occur to you that it was strange that someone as well-connected as he claimed to be would call an obscure litigator from a small firm to do sophisticated corporate work and would do so after only a brief meeting at a party?"

"It didn't even occur to me that I was *obscure*, but to answer your question, there's a huge gulf between strange and illegal."

"But why you?" In spite of the malice that infused Anderson's tone, I wondered why a sense of calm came over me. Sure, I thrived on conflict and at least I wasn't bored…but still. "As opposed to a lawyer with expertise in setting up businesses for foreigners, perhaps one with offices in Mexico City."

"He said I impressed him at the soirée." I shrugged and held my hands out to my side. "Also, he told me that Kate gave me an enthusiastic recommendation. She's a skilled promoter, although I still have no idea why she chose me to promote."

"So you just took it on faith that she'd acted out of the goodness of her heart, not expecting anything in return?" Anderson asked

"No. It seemed that the primary purpose of her soirées was to provide a platform for the attendees to make mutually beneficial introductions, and she charges handsomely for that service."

"Really?" Grae said. "How much did you pay to attend?"

"Nothing. I was kidnapped at gunpoint."

"That happen to you often?"

"She'd portrayed it as a hazing ritual. In any event, I decided not to have anything further to do with her, and I haven't," I said. Then, remembering, I added, "Except that she recently dragooned me into visiting Lev Zhukov in the hospital. He's—"

"We know who he is, or rather *was,*" Anderson said.

"Your hostility is unnecessary. I'm happy to help. Understand, however, I'm this far"—I held thumb and forefinger a few millimeters apart—"from shutting up and retaining counsel."

"That wouldn't be in your interest," Grae said.

"That's for me to decide," I said. "While I work that through, here's something I don't get—since you know so much, what do you need me for?"

147

"Representing four clients she sent you doesn't sound like having nothing to do with her," Grae said, using the tone of a prosecutor springing a trap on cross-examination, "two of whom were murdered under *very* suspect circumstances, another is a terrorist responsible for several hundred deaths and the fourth—"

"Several hundred?"

"The number keeps climbing as we investigate," Grae said. "As I started to say, the fourth client she referred to you is in league with him. We picked up, at the Mexican border, five million tabs of extra-strong, tainted and mislabeled OxyContin, in a container bound for one of de Caldas' U.S. companies. That's more than enough to actually change the demographics in the three states which Trump won by less than one percent and which your clients focused on."

"Oh my god! I had no indication that he had any agenda beyond making money." I paused to catch my breath. My heart was beating so fast I felt it in my eardrums. "I met with him only once, then referred him to my partner. He said he had big plans for investing in the U.S. but neither my partner nor I have heard from him since."

"Probably because he's in detention." Anderson smirked.

Perhaps one day I'd learn to follow Lauren's advice.

"As you undoubtedly know, he didn't call me to represent him in connection with that."

"He probably didn't think it wise to have a co-conspirator representing him." Anderson gave his shoulder holster an affectionate pat.

"More likely he wanted someone experienced in criminal law," I said. "You didn't answer my question. What do you need me for?"

"At this so-called soirée," Grae said, "did you say to de Caldas, when talking about the President, 'According to the news reports, augmented by his tweets, in the past couple weeks he's exhibited gluttony, lust, greed, pride, wrath, envy and sloth—all of the seven deadly sins'?"

Sure, I probably should've retained counsel long ago, but it was useful to know about these recordings. I wondered what their purpose was in telling me. Clearly, they wanted to intimidate me, but to what end?

"I probably said something pretty close to that." I tented my fingers, trying to determine why my heart rate had returned to normal and why, in spite of the overwhelming evidence to the contrary, I felt as if I had some degree of control. "If those were my exact words, I commend you on your surveillance techniques and your verbatim recall, but such comments are protected by the First Amendment."

"And did Kate say to you, 'Trump must be destroyed'?" she asked.

"If I recall right, she used one of her many nicknames for him, but it was clear from context."

"What did you think when you heard that?"

"That it was a play on the way Cato would end all his speeches to the Roman Senate, and that she was playing on my fondness for the ancient Greeks and Romans."

"And partially as a result of Cato's speeches, Carthage, a city of approximately seven hundred thousand souls, was destroyed, her inhabitants killed or sold into slavery and her fields sown with salt?" Grae said.

"The salt part might have been a later excrescence added to intimidate Rome's enemies. By the time of St. Augustine, it was again a thriving metropolis."

"At least you'll be able to put your death sentence in its proper historical context," she said.

"I thought Kate had intended her comment to be understood as hyperbole, but as I told you, I vowed not to have anything to do with her anyway. It had also occurred to me that her vehemence was too intense to be real…unless, of course, she was deranged."

"I assume you immediately informed the Secret Service?" she said, to my growing irritation. I interrogated people for a living and took offense when it was done badly.

"If I called them every time I heard someone speak ill of Trump—"

"You hear a lot of people saying he should be murdered or enslaved?"

"No, and I've never heard anyone threaten to plow salt in his hair, either." I stood. "We're done here. I've got work to do. I'll have my attorney call you. All further communications will go through her."

"Sit!" Anderson commanded, in a tone that sounded as if, if I disobeyed, he'd hit me on the nose with a rolled-up newspaper.

I sat, but to maintain a *soupçon* of dignity, I scowled at him.

"So after making this supposed vow, you represented Curtis and de Caldas, each of whom you'd met at the soirée and each of whom expressed a violent anti-Trump bias?"

"Note for the record, I asked for an attorney."

"So noted," Anderson said, his tone indicating that he believed the phrase to be a synonym for *go fuck yourself.*

"Neither said anything that implied violent action. The great majority of the people I talk to during the course of my day are opposed to him. Several weeks ago, over three million women marched—"

"When this *Kate* said, 'Trump must be destroyed,' was her tone serious or jocular?"

"Serious as a stiletto," I said, assuming they had a recording.

"You remember from law school that any act in furtherance of a criminal conspiracy makes the actor responsible for the entire consequences of the conspiracy?"

"Vaguely."

"Here we have several hundred deaths," Anderson said, voice an angry whisper. "That's over several hundred counts of conspiracy to commit murder. We continue to dig. I suspect we'll find evidence tying you into Curtis' schemes."

"Suspect to your heart's content, but the fact is I did nothing in furtherance of any criminal conspiracy." Unless falsified evidence proves otherwise.

"Bullshit!" Anderson said, a few decibels short of a shout.

"Well, seems you've got plenty to do," I said, calm and quiet. "Don't let me waste even another minute of your valuable time."

Standing again, I leaned forward, hands on my desktop and shot him my most hostile look. One thing my notorious former client liked about me was that I didn't back down and met hostility with greater hostility. Of course, none of my litigation adversaries had the power to arrest me for a capital crime. But if that was the way this was going to go, might as well get on with it. The key to any negotiation is to always be willing to walk away from table. My former client had taught me that, even though he was a mediocre negotiator. On reflection, I learned quite a bit from him. That he learned nothing from me, or anyone else, might yet turn out to be his downfall.

"You better not be terminating this interview." Anderson

pointed at me. His finger shook with anger.

"Oh, but I am. I know you're serious people who don't make idle threats that you're not prepared to carry out, because that would make you appear weak and pathetic." I held out both my hands to make cuffing me easier. Getting no reaction, I said, "Would you prefer that I turn around, so you can cuff me with my hands behind my back and frog-march me out of the office in full view of my partners and employees?"

"We're continuing to investigate," Grae said.

I sat. Having made my point, it wouldn't do for me to gloat.

"You seem to have done a remarkably thorough job of investigating me and haven't come up with diddly squat, and you know it," I said, now cool and calm as a cryogenic cucumber and perhaps stupidly, disinclined to retain counsel, at least as yet. "So please get out of my office. It's time for my morning nap."

"You made a huge multiple of your hourly rate off her referrals," Anderson said.

"No crime there. They were contingency fees. If I recovered nothing for my clients, they'd have owed me nothing."

"How often in the past had you done so well on contingencies?"

"Never," I said, no longer calm.

"And you expect us to believe she asked nothing in return?" Anderson raised his bushy eyebrows in case I'd missed his sarcastic tone, or more likely become inured to it. I refrained from suggesting that he have them trimmed. "And that she helped you out of the goodness of her heart?"

"I suspect there's very little goodness there and am pretty sure she was using me, but I never figured out to what end. She says she wants to destroy Trump and seems to make good money from her soirées, but I haven't a clue how referring clients to me helped with either purpose." Actually, I had several clues, but I'd been unable to put them together in a way that made sense, at least not yet. The only way I could come through this alive and not incarcerated would be to figure out what Kate was up to. No lawyer would be able to do that at least not in time to help me. "So if there's nothing else, I hope the balance of your day is as pleasant and productive as your morning has been."

We exchanged hostile stares for what felt like several minutes but was probably considerably less.

"Okay, then," Grae said.

They both stood.

I did the same.

"One more question," she said. "Why do you think Kate is so interested in you?"

"I've asked myself the same thing. I asked her, too. She told me that it was because Trump had me in his sights as I'd fired him as a client and that she thought I hated him, but neither reason rang true."

"It would be in your interest to figure that out sooner rather than later," Anderson said.

Sure would.

"I'll walk you out," I said.

"No need," Grae said.

When they left my line of sight, I collapsed into my chair.

XII
The Truth Isn't What It Used to Be

Nobody knew that health care could be so complicated.
Donald J. Trump February 27, 2017

Over dinner I told Lauren a sanitized version of my encounter with the two agents. She responded with such fury that I wondered why I'd bothered to sanitize it.

"If they'd wanted to arrest me, they'd have done so. My gut told me to call their bluff."

"This the same gut that told you to stay at the soirée, then to represent the criminals and terrorists a psychopath referred to you, and then to refrain from hiring a lawyer until it's too late?"

"No, the one that made us a pant-load of money on the Trump trade and helped me over all these years not to break any laws or to do anything ethically questionable."

She rolled her eyes.

"Lauren, I told you—"

"Oh, right, you need to first figure out what Kate is up to, and you are the only one who can do that. It's like how Trump knows more about ISIS than the generals."

"There's something obvious I'm missing. I've set my mind to work on the problem. It's like how, when I see someone whose name I can't remember, my mind goes to work on it and sometime later the name pops into my head. Of course, by then it's too late but…"

"Sounds more like the initial stage of dementia than genius."

"Maybe by the time they get around to arresting me, I'll be so far gone, I'll be unable to tell if I'm in jail or a luxury bordello."

"You're not the least bit funny."

"That's 'the most unkindest cut of all,'" I said, using a tone of high dudgeon. Perhaps I'd organize a Shakespeare troupe in prison.

Robert N. Chan

She buried her head in her hands.

"Let's watch TV," I said. "How 'bout that new show you mentioned, *This is Us,* or...?"

She shook her head.

"It's *Two of Us.*"

"Oh right, you said it was too feminine for me."

"No, I said it has emotions, so you wouldn't understand it."

"Right." I understood my emotions at that moment and that it wouldn't be wise to express them. "Let's watch *Game of Thrones.* I'll probably not be able to get HBO in prison."

"Or in the mortuary."

A boring few weeks followed. No contact from Kate or anyone referred by her. Nothing from the Feds. I should've been thankful, but I knew it wasn't over, even as I didn't know what *it* was. Questions about Kate, her real agenda and what she had planned gnawed at me, an itch I couldn't reach to scratch.

Trump didn't let up, and I was starting to take it personally. He referred to the media as *the enemy of the American people.* The next day, based on a debunked FoxNews story, he decried "what happened last night in Sweden." Strange that the President of the United States was relying on *the enemy of the people* for information, rather than his own State Department and security advisors. Surely just a coincidence that Stalin and Mao had used the phrase *enemy of the people* as a death warrant.

I had a nightmare that Trump punched me in the nose and an even worse one that we were friends. Never before had a president had the temerity to invade my dreams, and I had no doubt that he was doing it on purpose.

At least there were only 201 weeks left in his term.

Posts from *Breitbart* and *InfoWars* mysteriously appeared on my Facebook newsfeed. Each claimed that, with the intention of swinging future elections to the Democrats, a terrorist had been targeting middle-aged, white male, high school dropouts in states that had gone to Trump by slim margins. While that sounded disturbingly like the plot Grae and Anderson had attributed to Curtis, I dismissed anything appearing on those sites as fake news. So I unfollowed them and thought about it no further, or at least tried to.

154

The next day a new post appeared, this one identifying the supposed terrorist—Muhammad-Ali Abdur-Rahkman, a U.S. citizen whose parents had immigrated from Egypt before he was born. By coincidence, that was also the name of a University of Michigan basketball player with no connection to terrorism, except that his foul-shooting percentage bordered on the terrifying. According to the right-wing propagandists, the non-Wolverine Muhammad-Ali Abdur-Rahkman had been found dead of an opioid overdose in Milwaukee and the police had ruled it a suicide. At least they weren't blaming Curtis.

Annoyed to be on the receiving end of right wing disinformation, I was about to again unfollow them and complain that my earlier request hadn't been honored. But then I saw the photo of the dead terrorist.

Oh shit! I remembered Curtis telling me that Kate had a *pet nickname* for him—that of a University of Michigan basketball player with a killer foul shot.

When I first met him, I'd thought he could have been Jewish, Indian, Turkish or Arabic, and as we were in New York, I assumed he was Jewish. In the photo, he looked like the archetypical Islamic terrorist.

I searched on Google for corroboration. All I found was an small article in the *Milwaukee Journal Sentinel*, containing the same photograph of Curtis and reporting that he'd been found dead in the Milwaukee Riverfront Holiday Inn.

It was hard to believe that the guy was a terrorist responsible for hundreds of deaths. I doubted that Muhammad-Ali Abdur-Rahkman was Curtis' real name and suspected that the infernal goddess of vengeance wannabe had played puppet-master to his puppet.

Knowing I was making a mistake, I called Grae.

I told her what I'd seen on the websites and asked if the reports were true.

"I'd never have pegged you as a follower of those websites."

"I'm not."

"Mr. Bloom, you know I can't comment on an ongoing investigation."

"You'd already told me you linked hundreds of deaths to opioids sold by Curtis. He told me that Muhammad-Ali Abdur-Rahkman was a pet name Kate had for him."

"Well, now he's dead—having been tipped off that we were coming to arrest him," she said in a most disturbing, accusatory tone.

"I'm sure you've been monitoring my communications and know that I've had no communication—"

"There's a full court press to identify his confederates," she said. "So it's interesting that one of the prime suspects has just now called. Should I attribute it to a guilty conscience or fear that the noose is tightening on your skinny neck?"

I actually did feel such a tightness but forced myself to focus on another part of her statement. My neck was trim, not skinny.

"I found it perplexing that I couldn't find anything about these attacks in the legitimate media," I said.

If tipped off, why he didn't run? More likely, someone killed him to shut him up.

"My job description doesn't include being a guide for the perplexed."

"It's comforting that Federal agents are steeped in semantics and capable of making allusions to the great work of Maimonides," I said.

She sighed: dealing with clueless, intellectually arrogant suspects is so tiring.

"We've been instructed to keep all mention of opioid terrorism out of the news until our investigation is complete and Abdur-Rahkman's associates have been rounded up. Some of the media have been more cooperative than others."

"I assume these *associates* include Kate?"

"You're free to make all the assumptions you'd like."

Yeah, it's a free country—at least for now.

"Having recorded my conversation with Kate from the mental hospital, you must have her records, fingerprints, etc. right?" Grae didn't respond. "With all your resources, facial recognition software etc. why don't you arrest her?" I hoped she'd say that they had her under arrest, but I suspected that Kate was endowed with superpowers that protected her from such travails. "In any event, as you have recordings of all the conversations she and I have had, I'm irrelevant."

More silence.

"Agent Grae, I really do want to help. I apologize if I conveyed the opposite impression."

"The documents regarding her involuntary commitment that she'd emailed to you were falsified," she said, voice barely above a whisper. "She might not even have been committed. Could've been a ruse. She's created a labyrinth of ruses and blind alleys."

"So when she claimed to have been involuntarily committed, she'd already planned to suck me into…whatever?"

"Since she's never used the same alias twice, it's hard to know. She might have been trolling for suckers and then targeted you due to your animus towards Trump. I gather your prior representation of him didn't go well."

Grae's forthrightness—if that was what it really was, as opposed to a scheme to manipulate—unnerved me. She must've been desperate if she had to fall back on honesty.

"When I thought I'd dialed the wrong number, could she have already had me in her sights and rerouted the call?"

"Possibly. She, or those connected to her, have cyberwar-level computer skills."

"I don't understand what role she expected me to play in her scheme, or indeed what that scheme might be."

"Did you consider that you're just a pawn in a larger game?"

"Yes, but that line of thought pretty much dead-ended."

"I'm sure it did." Her tone was as enigmatic as her statement. "Rest assured, we'll give all the weight they deserve to your efforts to direct our attention away from yourself and onto the elusive, possibly non-existent, Kate."

"I assure you she exists."

"Well, that's an enormous help," she said, voice dripping with sarcasm. "Now, if you can only send me a birth certificate, photograph or other document in a government file."

That damn prickly-thumbs feeling returned.

"You're kidding. You're the fucking FBI, aren't you?"

No response.

"Could she or someone associated with her have scrubbed the government databases?" I asked.

I took her silence for an affirmative answer. If it was true, the scrubber would have to have been either someone with the highest possible clearance or an extremely accomplished hacker.

"Hundreds of people attended her soirées or worked there."

"Those we've located won't talk or have contradictory things to say. People paid her in cash and have reason to be silent. McKuen told me that she maintained a database with damning evidence on all of them, so it's unlikely that any would come forward."

"Leslie McKuen and she were pretty tight."

"For one thing, she goes by Tomkins, her maiden name, for another…"

"Yes?" No response. "Well, if I can be of help, please—"

"We haven't forgotten you."

Her threatening tone had no effect on me. I was already as frightened as I could be.

While Kate's plans remained a mystery to me, I now had some insight into how the FBI intended to use me: they suspected Kate would contact me and that would lead them to Kate. Maybe they'd thought the same about Curtis before he checked in at the Milwaukee Riverfront Holiday Inn and didn't check out or rather checked himself out.

XIII
A Dark and Stormy Night

How low has President Obama gone to tapp [sic] my phones during the very sacred election process. This is Nixon/Watergate. Bad (or sick) guy! Donald J. Trump, March 4, 2017

It was a dark and stormy night, my arthritic hip throbbed, and I couldn't bear the thought of taking the subway. Due to the bad weather and the rush hour traffic, flagging down a cab on the street would've been impossible. Uncharacteristically indifferent to surge-pricing, I contacted Uber and watched the car approach on my phone.

A black Toyota Land Cruiser pulled up to the curb. I walked up to it. The driver unrolled his window. "Matthew?"

"Yes."

I got in. By the time I'd wrestled the seatbelt locking tongue into the proper receptacle, we were already snaking through traffic.

The car stopped at the light. The door on the far side opened, and in hopped…

"Oh, shit!"

The locks on the doors clicked shut. I pried at the handle but they were apparently child-proofed, or rather old-man-proofed.

The driver hit the gas as the light turned green, and the car fishtailed through the busy intersection.

"Hey, what a nice surprise!" Kate said.

With her butterscotch blond hair in a French twist and oversized glasses hiding her crow's feet and making her eyes look huge, Kate appeared younger, prettier and less harried than she had at the hospital. Her appearance enhanced the usual sensation I'd had that I knew her from a former life.

"Please let me out of the car. I don't want to have anything to do with you."

"Didn't you notice that the license plate is different from the one Uber sent?" She extended her index finger in a manner reminiscent of the gesture on the Sistine Chapel ceiling with which the Prime Mover transmitted the spark of life. "Not to worry. I'll cover the cancellation fee. It's just that…Matt, when are you going to learn to be more careful? There's a limit to the amount of time and energy I can devote to protecting you from yourself." Her cadence accelerated like when a poor liar is uncomfortable with dissimulating. Kate, though, was an expert liar. So what was that about? "Curtis, or rather Muhammad-Ali Abdur-Rahkman, turning out to be a mass murderer. Amazing, right? You think you know someone and then… But I guess you suspected all along? That's why you turned down his retainer, right? CYA could be your initials."

When she paused for a breath, I said, "I didn't suspect, but your involvement seemed clear."

"Mine?" She pointed at her chest, more cleavage showing than appropriate given the weather and circumstances. "I'm not nearly that smart. That's why I brought you into our large functional family to help suss those things out before they spin out of control. I'd have appreciated a heads-up but… Anyone ever tell you that you're not much of a team player? Guess that's why at your age you're still playing singles tennis. God forbid you lose a point because your partner flubs an overhead, or you let him or her down by failing to cover the alley."

"You don't *have* me to suss things out, or for any other purpose," I said, struggling to keep control of my anger.

"Oh, Matt, Matt, Matt. The man doth protest too much, methinks. I get that you're trying to position yourself for maximum deniability, but you must know that that compromises your effectiveness."

Again, I struggled with the door handle.

"Let me the fuck out of here!"

"Please don't yell. It's been a hard day, and I already have a headache brewing. Anyway, it's pointless, the driver is stone deaf."

Like the waiters were stone blind? I took out my phone.

"It won't work in here." Sure enough, it showed a blank screen. I pushed and prodded, but my phone remained unresponsive. "Anyway, it'd be a bad move to call the Secret Service. I'm basically a ghost. No one can find me. No two people even know me by the same name. You, though... Both Lauren and I told you to be more careful, but did you listen?" She tsked. "Typical male."

"I've been wondering, where did we first meet?" I hoped to extract a kernel of information that might provide the key to unlock the mystery that was Kate and lead me to evidence I could take to the FBI. A longshot, particularly as I had no reason to expect the truth, but hope springs eternal among the desperate.

"On the subway, of course, when I performed a magic trick for your amusement. Remember how delighted you were to find your wallet, phone and keys all wrapped up in a nice little package. You don't remember?" She tilted her head and furrowed her brow. "Matt, you're not losing it, are you? Not now, when I need you more than ever. The Orange Terror Clown's done. All he needs is one yuuuge bigly shove and he'll fall over, *believe me.*" Her smile seeming to take up her entire face, she put her hands on my shoulders and shook me. "Don't you get it? We're almost there."

"You're right, I'm losing it. I'm no good to you anymore, if indeed I ever was."

"You're such a kidder." Gleeful smile. "Given what's happened to Curtis—I can't bring myself to think of him as Muhammad-Ali Abdul-something-or-other—Walker, and McKuen, some might say you're a regular Jonah. To lose one client may be regarded as a misfortune; to lose two looks like carelessness, but three—"

"The FBI told me that de Caldas is under arrest for drug trafficking, in league with Curtis. When interrogated, de Caldas may tell the agents about your soirées and your connection to him, Curtis, Walker and McKuen."

"My connection?" Her head kicked back in astonishment. "Don't be silly. I barely knew them, You, though.... Not to worry, de Caldas won't roll over on you, unless given a big juicy inducement, and I'm quite sure Walker, Abdur-Rahkman and McKuen won't talk."

"The FBI has tapes of conversations at the soirée."

"Only yours. I've warned you time and again to be more careful, but no, you knew better." She rested a hand on my thigh. I shoved it away. "You have an amazing talent. Although you've been unfailingly nasty to me, somehow I still find myself drawn to you."

"Yeah, right, I'm one of the *Twelve Revered Martyrs.*"

"Ah, you remember that!" An irritating brilliant smile, with an infuriating false undertone, like those I saw on centerfolds in my adolescence. "I knew your mind wasn't going. By the way I really was committed to an institution for—utterly incongruous though it may be—the criminally insane. It's a funny story, when he have more time and can kick back over some fine wine and a thick steak."

I was pretty sure she was just trying to piss me off. Probably so I wouldn't focus on where she was taking me and what was really going on. Whatever the hell that was.

"Enough, Kate. Let me out of here."

We reached the far east end of 42nd Street, and it appeared that we were about to get on the FDR, although in the fog it was hard to know for sure. Then the driver swung the wheel.

Tires screeching, we went into an abrupt U-turn, cutting off several cars, drawing angry honks and sending Kate—why use a seatbelt if you're immortal?—careening into me, right hand coming to rest on my crotch.

I shoved her away.

"Where the hell are we going?"

"We just turned around. We had been heading east on 42nd Street. Now we're going west," she said, as if she actually believed that she'd satisfactorily answered my question.

I told myself to stay calm and focused, ignore her bullshit and attempts to irritate. She was awfully cocky. Played right, this still could be an opportunity to get valuable information.

"You told me you couldn't have had any involvement in Walker's death because Hakan was aligned with the FSB and the Russians were working with Trump. I wonder if there isn't an alternative explanation—that Walker had uncovered something about Hakan that you wanted to stay covered."

"Interesting, like what?"

She leaned forward wide-eyed, a parody of sincere interest.

"Oh, and McKuen told me some terrible things about you and the disappearance of your partner—his frat brother. Then, strangely, he retracted them, almost as if someone had threatened him. Now he's dead. And Curtis, or to use your pet name for him, Muhammad-Ali Abdur-Rahkman—"

"You can't be implying that I'd want to put a stop to his plan to even out the demographic playing field."

Yes, maybe. I'll had to think about that.

"I'm saying you might not want me to spend too much time and energy trying to connect the dots," I said.

"Your involvement with Muhammad-Ali Abdur-Rahkman must've lit up the J. Edgar Hoover Building like Westminster on Guy Fawkes Night." Her cadence accelerated until she no longer sounded like an awkward liar but rather like a bipolar sufferer deep into her manic phase, which she might actually have been. "It's a national tragedy. If you can't trust the FBI, whom can you trust? In the old days, J. Edgar ran a tight ship, only blackmailing presidents, framing MLK and looking for commies in the country's linen closets. Now, one doesn't know whom to trust. It's gotten so bad that—and forgive me, but I don't know if I'm reading you right with the multiple layers of double messages you send out—but it sounds like you don't even trust me."

I put a hand on each of her shoulders and gripped hard.

She didn't resist.

"Listen very carefully Kate." I shot her a hard stare. She stared back, and my thumbs prickled. "I want nothing at all to do with whatever you're up to."

"Matt, you're not wearing a wire, are you?" Quizzical look, followed by a blazing smile. "You wouldn't do that. With every fiber of your being, you want The Nutsack-in-Chief dead and disgraced. You're just…that wry sense of humor of yours." Beguiling smile paired with a head shake. "None of us wants to make him a martyr, of course, but the sooner we're rid of him, the better off we'll all be. The dead don't tweet."

I felt like strangling her, but settled for shaking her… hard. She went limp, and I suddenly felt silly as well as angry.

"Come on, Matt. When the truth comes out about your role, your place in history will be set. Hmm, Wagyu Kobe Strip Steak, you should consider that for your last meal if things turn south. Pair it with a nice chianti, not so heavy as to overwhelm, just—"

"KATE, ENOUGH! Let me out of here!" I screamed, then took a series of deep breaths. I had to remain calm and think clearly.

"Lee Harvey Oswald, James Earl Ray, John Wilkes Booth." She screwed up her face. "You really could use a middle name."

"You're planning to frame—"

"Be reasonable, Matt. The genius behind the *mercy killing* has to be someone they can haul before the TV cameras in handcuffs. Or, if you happen to kill yourself, like your clients Jonathan Walker and Muhammad-Ali Abdur-Rahkman—"

"They didn't—"

"Don't interrupt." She slapped me on the wrist like an old-fashioned schoolmarm. "You're useful in part because there's an extensive record available of your involvement with terrorists, provocateurs and other malcontents, or at least there shortly will be, when my hacker-team completes its work."

"You're insane."

"Yes, that's yet another reason why I can't be seen as the one behind the plot. It's unsatisfying for the mastermind to be a crazy person." Her words ran together again as she'd gone into a hyper-manic-phase or pretended to. "Even worse, from a P.R. perspective, is the fact that I basically don't exist. That alone would turn the affair into a media circus. People, who knew me as Erinye, Freya, and many other equally absurd names, would be interviewed on cable news, but I'd be nowhere to be found. That would detract from the national cleansing and rededication to core values that the country needs. I considered other candidates, but none quite fit the bill as well as you. Zhukov and Muhammad-Ali Abdur-Rahkman are dead. Just as well. We don't want the blame to go to a Muslim, a foreigner or, for that matter, a drug lord like de Caldas. It has to be a good upstanding American. Not ideal that you're a Jew and a senior citizen, but we don't want someone straight out of central casting, now do we?"

"You do know that nothing you're saying makes a lick of sense?"

I buried my head in my hands. What was the point in responding to her bullshit screed?

"Did Lee Harvey Oswald make sense? Jack Ruby kind of did. Well, one step at a time."

"I don't believe anything you're saying, and I doubt you believe it," I said in the calm voice one would use with a crazy person. "I'd never have anything to do with a plot to—"

"Not intentionally, but one of the reasons I chose you is that you're so easy to frame. Most people think that, if you want a patsy, you should pick a feebleminded loser, but that's wrong, and anyway they all voted for Darth Hater. The best targets are the highly intelligent, who too greatly value their intelligence. They continue to cling to the belief that the world is rational and if they'd just think a little harder they'd be able figure out what's happening to them. By the time they finally realize that the absurd always trumps the rational, it's too late. It's like that parable about how, if you want to cook a frog, you don't drop him into boiling water but into cold water, then slowly turn up the heat. By the time he realizes what's happening, he's too enervated to hop out."

"I've been talking to the FBI," I said, even though I knew nothing I'd say would make a speck of difference.

"Eyes on the prize, Matt. We don't want the Bouffant Buffoon to be a martyr. So you need to off him in the most ignominious way possible. Something on the order of drowning him in Russian-whore-piss. Sounds impossible, but with the Secret Service playing a role analogous to the Praetorian Guard's in the death of Caligula… I'm sure when the time comes, you'll devise better. And not to worry, I'll be behind the scenes pulling the strings. You'll need to do little more than be in the right place at the right time, and even that I'll arrange for you. You won't even know it's happening."

I stammered with rage.

"Is something wrong?" she asked, sounding genuinely concerned. "Matt, you're perfect for the role. You hated him from the days you represented him. In my mind's eye, I see you manipulating him to get him to settle the cases you were handling for him, almost as if I was actually there by your side. Also, you're a highly respected lawyer with no history of mental illness or scent of scandal. Hmmm, now that I think of it, the Jew thing's a positive. We can spin it as retribution for the Cheeto-Dusted Bloviator's proto-Nazism."

A block before we reached the West Side Highway, the driver made another sudden U-turn, leading to another discordant symphony of honking horns and squealing tires.

"The FBI is on to you," I said, once my heartbeat returned to normal. I saw no point in commenting on the absurdity of driving back and forth on 42nd Street.

"Those clowns Anderson and Grae? Come on, Matt." Her irritating wrist flick highlighted that she was merely trying to push my buttons—and succeeding mightily. "They're not real FBI agents. They killed the real ones, ate their bodies and are masquerading as them. They're our tools."

A flash of lightning, followed a few seconds later by a crash of thunder.

"Kate, you're out of your mind. This is like listening to Sean Spicer on meth. Let me out of here. I don't believe anything you say."

"Understandable. This is war and in war the first casualty is the truth. It's impossible to know who or what to believe. You've chosen not to believe me. Weird, since I'm the only one who's been truthful from day one. Okay, when I said they ate the bodies, I was speaking metaphorically. But they have been looking well-fed lately, and there's only one food that has the precise mix of amino acids in human bodies."

"Whoever they are, I wouldn't be surprised if they're tailing us right now," I said, knowing it to be a transparent bluff.

"Neither would I." She cast a glance at the rear-view mirror. "Of course, I was dying to see you, but drawing them out is one of the primary purposes of this get-together."

"Enough horseshit! Why am I here? Certainly, not for you to tell me your plans to frame me. That's too much like a bad movie."

"My, aren't you the sharpest knife in the drawer? Not to mention the sharpest tool in the shed."

I tightened my fists and fumed, too angry to express a coherent thought. Not that it mattered.

For several agonizing minutes, Kate hummed *You Can't Always Get What You Want,* which ironically was one of the theme songs played at Trump's campaign rallies.

As we approached Grand Central Station, the sky opened up and rain came pouring down in sheets.

A couple of slow heavily trafficked blocks later, she tapped on the driver's shoulder, and he directed his attention to the mirror. She said something in sign language.

Our Toyota swerved, jumped the curb and almost ran over a pedestrian in the midst of an intimate relationship with her cellphone. Then the driver floored it.

The car fishtailed on the wet pavement, drenching a pregnant woman with a rooster-tail of filthy water, then spun around, in a controlled one-hundred-eighty degree skid. Coming out of its spin, the Toyota almost smashed into an NBC TV live news truck, complete with antenna and satellite transmitter, that happened to be parked at the side of the street.

Calm and focused, Kate slipped on a pair of latex gloves.

A siren and flashing red lights came from the car, a silver Ford, that had been behind us and now, after we'd turned around, appeared to be about to collide head-on with us.

Our driver spun the steering wheel and again floored it, sending us into a terrifying one-hundred-and-eighty-degree turn, some of it taken on two wheels. Inertia slammed me against the locked door, as we spun around again. So focused as to be seemingly immune to centrifugal force, Kate didn't move.

Swerving to avoid us, the Ford sideswiped a second parked news truck.

Kate rolled down her window.

Our Toyota slowed. Also slowing, the Ford came up alongside like a Nineteenth Century man-of-war preparing to deliver a rolling broadside.

Kate pulled a sawed-off shotgun from under the seat.

Grae rolled down her window.

"Don't!" I screamed.

I tried to grab the gun.

Kate fired.

At least one of their tires blew.

I grabbed again.

She elbowed me hard in the kidney. Ooof!

She fired again, and their windshield shattered.

Skidding into an uncontrolled three-sixty, the agents' car spun into oncoming traffic, colliding with at least two taxis.

Our driver slammed on the brakes. A taxi swerved around us and smashed into the FBI vehicle.

We drove on. I fought to control my heaving breath.

"Gee, I hope I was right about Grae and Anderson having killed the real agents," Kate said, normal conversational tone. "That pile-up looked awfully bad. Had to be done, though, they were on to us. We needed to draw them out into the open."

She threw the shotgun to me. Acting on instinct, I caught it with my right hand. She grabbed it back.

Oh fuck! My fingerprints. Too late I realized why I was there.

I reached for the shotgun.

Kate slammed the butt into my knee. Ouch! Then, finger on the trigger and a deadly look in her eyes, she pointed the gun at me. The two muzzle openings looked huge.

Our car snaked through traffic, fast but not reckless enough to call attention to itself. It turned up Madison Avenue and onto a side street, deserted in the storm, where it came to a stop.

The door locks clicked open.

"You better go," Kate said. "Too, bad about your prints all over the attempted murder weapon, but I'm sure with your talents, you'll come up with a good explanation. A piece of friendly advice, though, you might want to stay away from 'Kate made me do it'. It not only sounds infantile, but also it's preposterous. You're way too old to have an invisible friend, let alone a nemesis that only you see."

"Plenty of people at your soirées have—"

"All my different names, different descriptions." She gave me her most serious look. "Have you considered the insanity defense? No, that, requires the inability to distinguish right from wrong, something you've always devoted inordinate time and energy to trying to figure out. Also, wanting to destroy Putin's Puppet is a sign of preternatural sanity."

The driver pointed a pistol at me—just in case I was about to fight Kate for the shotgun?

"So to help you answer that *why me* question you keep asking," Kate said in her normal, non-hyper voice, while the driver trained his handgun on my forehead. "I was only talking to you this evening to kill time while we waited for the agents to appear, so I could kill them. Or rather, given that your prints are on the weapon and there's a record of your call to Uber, so *you* could. As for why I brought you in in the first place, I needed to tie up the Walker, Zhukov, McKuen, Curtis and de Caldas loose ends and you seemed a convenient bow. Hate to break it to you, but you're nothing but a way to connect them all. They needed lawyers, I knew about your Trump history, and, as I said, you're as good a dupe as any, better than most. The inordinate fees you received for such little work look awfully suspicious in retrospect. Too bad about the FBI agents—as you probably figured they're real—but, with them seriously injured, the Bureau will be all over you like a ton of bricks. You'll have a few days to get your affairs in order before they find the shotgun. We can't have them arresting you before we play our Trump card, can we?"

It took all my energy to climb out of the car.

"I'd say good luck," she said, "but let's face it, luck's never been your strong point. So go with God. I'm afraid we won't see each other again, but we'll always have the memories of the times we shared. And after all, what is life but a collection of memories, right?"

The car drove off, leaving me standing in the pouring rain.

Sirens and flashing red lights seemed to come from all directions but whizzed past me.

I took out my phone to call 911, but instead I slinked down into the nearest subway like a naked mole rat retreating into its burrow.

I arrived home soaking wet and shaking from fear and cold.

Lauren took one look at me and said, "Take off your clothes."

She ran a hot bath. Then helped me get undressed and handed me my bathrobe.

"Would you like a glass of whiskey?" she asked.

I shook my head.

I felt as if I had the flu *and* had fallen from a five-story window. Her concern told me that I looked as bad as I felt.

"You want to talk about it?"

I shook my head again.

That she didn't press me highlighted the extremity of my situation, not that it needed highlighting.

"Kate?" she asked.

I nodded.

"What can I do?"

I shook my head a third time.

"May I make you something to eat?"

"No thank you." My tremulous voice didn't sound like my own.

She helped me into the scalding bathtub. In other circumstances I'd have screamed and hopped out—like the frog Kate had compared me to. Instead, I stuck my head underwater and held my breath until I no longer could. The scalding water seemed the least I deserved.

"You need a lawyer, the police?"

"A rabbi."

She made a face as if I'd punched her in the stomach.

"Sorry," I whispered.

169

"It's okay," she said, too sympathetic for comfort. "What are you going to do after your bath?"

"Go into the living room and think until I come up with a way to stop Kate from framing me for the attempted murder of Federal agents."

She stared at me, hoping I was joking.

Her jaw dropped open in slow motion and her eyes went wide.

"I saw a bulletin on the news," she said. "Four people seriously injured, including two FBI agents rushed to the hospital. A few blocks from your office. Was that…"

I nodded.

Sure, with the news trucks on the scene, the story would break immediately. Part of Kate's plan probably.

She put her hand over her mouth. We'd moved beyond words.

I again immersed myself in the steaming water.

Most problems couldn't be solved by thinking about them, but I hoped mine—and the nation's—were exceptions to the rule.

XIV
The Vultures Come Home to Roost

I have tremendous respect for women and the many roles they serve that are vital to the fabric of our society and our economy.
Donald J. Trump, March 8, 2017

I put on flannel pajamas and a fleece bathrobe. To complete the old man look, I wrapped myself in a blanket. Lying on the living room couch in the dark, I reviewed the history of my interactions with Kate, or whatever her name was. Then I repeated the process, hoping I'd remember a useful fact that would lead to my devising an effective plan.

I didn't hear Lauren come into the living room, until she pulled a rocking chair up to the couch.

"What can I do to help?"

"Nothing I'm afraid."

"How's your thinking coming?"

"So far…well, it's a process."

"I sensed you didn't want me to ask about how Kate framed you."

"No, I have to—"

"Seems like you could use my help."

I hadn't wanted to scare her but not telling her what happened certainly wasn't going to help with that. So, after a deep sigh, I told her, not bothering to hold back on the grisly, absurd details.

She listened without comment, which I greatly appreciated.

"When I'd met her on the subway, I had the feeling that I knew Kate from a former life." I spoke slowly, trying to convey a calm confidence I didn't possess. "That feeling repeated itself, with varying degrees of intensity, at each of our run-ins after that. Perhaps, if I can recall where I knew her from—assuming it wasn't actually a former life—I'll be able to figure out her true identity." Lauren hadn't turned on the light, so I couldn't see her doubting or terrified facial expression.

"Which will accomplish what?" she asked, curious not critical.

"I'll tell the FBI, so they can find her, and maybe that'll get me off the hook."

"You sure they're even looking for her? Hard to believe that anyone in this day and age can be that hard to find, particularly for the FBI with all that facial recognition capability at their disposal."

"There's something weird going on here, something I'm missing," I said. "Trying to come up with Kate's identity at least makes me *feel* like I'm taking action, which is almost as good as actually taking action. Not nearly as good as taking productive action, but for now, productive action is beyond my reach."

"How can I help?" Bad sign that she didn't tell me I was full of shit or reiterate her advice that I retain counsel. I must've been really fucked. Well, I knew that already.

"Thanks, but for now, I need to think things through on my own. Get some sleep. Don't worry, I'll be okay," I lied. "I'm going to power up my computer and outline the history of my interactions with Kate. Perhaps typing will help stimulate my memory. Maybe when you read it, you'll have some thoughts."

She left for the bedroom. I immediately felt lonely, regretting her departure, even though I knew I had to do this alone.

I typed quickly and sloppily and went back to fill in events I'd left out, add new thoughts and correct the battalion of typos that had made my first draft look like a rejected effort by one of a theoretical infinite number of monkeys dragooned into the effort to type Hamlet. Then I revised it again, punching up the language and filling in bits of conversation. Although I'd made a persuasive case for Kate being a terrorist, I had come up with nothing that would help law enforcement find her. Assuming, that is, that they were actually trying to find her, one of the many crucial straws that I could only grasp at.

On the plus side, I succeeded in blowing through five hours without a major anxiety attack, Lauren was asleep—I hoped—and not as worried as she could be, and I was still a free man.

My fear-and-exhaustion-addled brain was becoming increasingly inefficient. I told myself, though, that fatigue would free it from the strictures of reason, enabling a revelatory breakthrough.

I again let my mind go where it wanted to. I was too wired to

172

fall asleep, but my mind didn't seem to want to go anywhere. So I spiffed up the history of my contacts with Kate, saved it to the cloud and sent a copy to my wills file, where it would be discovered upon my death. Perhaps my son would publish it, if the infamy of carrying my genes wouldn't force him to change his identity like how the children of Julius and Ethel Rosenberg became Robert and Julius Meeropol.

I sat with my eyes closed. Maybe sitting up, rather than laying down, was the key. I vowed not to sleep or eat until I not only remembered where I knew Kate from but also uncovered useful information that the FBI could use to locate her.

An unproductive hour later, I decided that my vow had been excessive. Fatigue overcoming agitation, I permitted myself to doze off for five-to-fifteen-minute stretches, on the theory that inspiration might come to me in a dream. The only dream I remembered, however, involved Trump punching me in the face, his tiny fist imbedding itself in my right eye. Ouch! Kate laughed her ass off. It floated into the air and got smaller and smaller until it disappeared like a child's balloon, then it reappeared, and I tripped on it.

"Matt, you okay?" Kate asked, sounding concerned for me and not at all worried about her butt.

No. It was Lauren

"Oh, hi, just a nightmare. Short nap."

"So?" she asked.

"Letting my mind go where it wanted hasn't been helpful. Perhaps I didn't know Kate from anywhere."

I handed her my laptop, and she read, while I continued to think, to no particular purpose.

"I never understood why she'd devoted such effort to you and sent you those lucrative matters," she said. "Perhaps that's the question you should be trying to answer."

"When I was getting out of the car tonight, she told me she'd used me to tie up loose ends. It just occurred to me that that was the only time I'd heard her mention Trump by name."

"What do you make of that?"

"Nothing."

"Try to connect the dots among Kate and Walker, de Caldas, Zhukov, McKuen, and the FBI agents."

"Too many dots—too few clear lines."

"Focus on particular events."

Reading quietly, she rocked back and forth. I was glad she was there.

Fatigue crept into my joints, causing a generalized ache.

"I need another short nap. Wake me in five," I said, part of me hoping she'd interpret that to mean five hours. "No. Actually, I need to re-review my interactions with Kate and the clients she sent me."

"Okay." She stood. "Please call if you think I can be helpful."

"Will do. Thanks for being here for me."

"Of course."

By 5 A.M., without having made the conscious decision to do so, I found myself aimlessly surfing the Internet, like Jason used to do in middle school to avoid homework. I told myself that mindlessness would free my consciousness, not that surfing the net and playing video games had done anything similar for him. Sunrise found me reviewing old *Penthouse* magazines online. If I'd thought about what I was doing, I'd have concluded that fatigue had freed my libido from the constraints usually imposed by my super-ego and that nothing productive could come from looking at pornography. Not thinking about it, however, was an essential part of the exercise.

I was so sleepy that…

The door sprang open with a loud, ominous screech. They were coming to arrest me.

"You'd screamed," Lauren said, running in from the bedroom. "Are you okay?"

"Yes, fine, just a nightmare. Fortuitous, as I can't afford to sleep."

Embarrassed by what I'd been looking at, but not as much as I should've been, I turned my laptop so she couldn't see the screen.

"What was it about?"

"I can't talk now," I said oxymoronically. "I'm on the verge of a major breakthrough."

Sunrise beginning, I could see that her facial expression combined incredulousness and frustration. She retreated into the bedroom without further comment.

I returned to my *Penthouse* work, telling myself that there must be a valid subconscious reason why my search had focused on this corner of the World Wide Web—something other than that my id liked looking at the pictures—and that epiphanies come when they're least expected. At least I was starting to understand the allure of alternative facts, or was that rationalizations? The *Penthouses* became almost as tedious as Trump's tweets. There's just so many spread legs one can look at without feeling like an unpaid gynecologist. *Breakthrough?* More like a *breakdown*. Yet a terrible inertia compelled me forward, or rather compelled me on, as it didn't feel as if I was moving forward, or in any other direction, just moving.

Exhausted, stressed and unable to think straight, all I wanted was to climb into bed and embrace failure like a pillow. Yet, I pressed on, refusing to give up until I hit upon a useful revelation or if that didn't happen, a more productive way to go about my task.

"Yes!" I shouted, without having intended to do so.

Lauren rushed out of the bedroom.

"What happened?"

I showed her the screen.

"Well, that is exciting."

"No that's…. The Penthouse Pet. That's Kate! Or rather Margarette, Trump's former receptionist, assistant and putative bed-mate."

"Really?"

"I hadn't been able to place her when I saw her on the subway and afterwards, in part because she'd changed her hair color, stopped wearing violet contacts and had had her attention-getting breast enhancements removed. She'd aged over a decade and gained maturity, guile and gravitas."

"But still—"

"Also, she'd learned how to project a mesmeric otherworldly aura."

Trump had bragged to me about using his pull to get her into *Penthouse*, but from the look of her in the spread, she hadn't needed any help. She looked almost as good as Melania had in her *British GQ* appearance showing her handcuffed to a briefcase, wearing only a diamond-encrusted choker and matching cuffs.

"When I'd left Trump's office for the last time, I'd mock congratulated Margarette on getting into the magazine, and she'd told me it was 'part of the job' and less disgusting than what Trump had her doing with her clothes on. Trump told me, 'She'd do anything for me, and I do mean *anything*.' He must've had her do some pretty repulsive things. No wonder she hated him."

"Makes some sense, but—"

"The magazine listed her name as Hilaria Bormann, possibly the only time when she'd used the same name twice. Mystery solved!"

"Great," she said without much enthusiasm. "Now what?"

"Maybe now that I've uncovered her motive, this extra piece of information will give the Bureau a means to locate her."

"I'm not sure that Trump having objectified her and used her for disgusting purposes is really a motive," she said. "If everyone he'd objectified and used for disgusting purposes were planning to assassinate him, Congress would have to reinstitute the draft to bring in a sufficient number of Secret Service agents to investigate."

The elation began to leak out of me like a punctured balloon. I was so tired. Maybe a nap, a bit to eat. Refreshed, I could take on the problem of finding a use for my discovery.

No. I needed to put in more thought. I sensed—hoped—that I was on the verge of an actual epiphany.

"Isn't she the one you'd told Emily about?" Lauren asked. "Why don't you send her the picture, let her investigate?"

"Not sure I have the time, and with all my communications being monitored...."

"You told her about Walker and McKuen and that you didn't know who'd thrown the party Walker had been at."

"In part, I'd hoped to tip-off Kate-slash-Margarette that I was on to her. I had the feeling that when Emily had called about McKuen, Kate had been her secret source."

"So call her."

"I'm almost certain that Kate had contacted her anonymously."

"I'll send the picture to her." She took my computer.

I sat in a rocking chair and rocked and thought.

On her return, Lauren said, "Here's the question—how was Kate-slash-Margarette able to operate in secret, without running afoul of law enforcement? Hundreds of people had attended her soirées or worked there as drivers and waiters. Didn't any of them know how to contact her? She must've left an electronic trail somewhere?"

"The FBI played for me recordings of conversations we'd had

at the soirée. Oh, and also our first telephone conversation where she'd posed as the involuntarily committed Hilaria."

"Then the FBI must have tons of other recordings of her that they could use to put together a clear picture of her activities."

I tented my fingers. Lauren waited.

"According to Grae her records had been wiped clean."

"How did she accomplish that?" Lauren asked.

Yes. That was the crucial question.

"The simplest explanation is that she's a witch endowed with supernatural powers. Except that witches endowed with supernatural powers don't exist."

"She must've had collaborators," Lauren said.

"More than collaborators, she must have had serious protection to have gotten away with what she had," I said. "It's almost as if she was some sort of government informer or agent gone underground."

"Go on."

I tried to think and sort of succeeded.

"Well, right-wingers accuse mega-wealthy progressives of furthering their ends by illegal means. Over drinks, James Kaplan once ranted to me about George Soros financing the murder of police in Baton Rouge."

"I assume you found that preposterous."

"Of course, but there are more than a few assholes out there with more money than sense, Exhibit A being Donald J. Trump himself."

We were both quiet for a while.

"The more I think about it," I said, "the less I'm able to make the unhinged-left-wing-billionaire hypothesis explanation work. Among other things, it doesn't account for the deaths of Zhukov and my former clients."

"What then?"

"Well, Kate had blamed Walker's death on a mole. Maybe an FSB mole killed him and Hakan as well as Zhukov, who according to Kate was a former Russian agent."

"But that doesn't explain McKuen's and Curtis' deaths," she said.

"Unless they were involved in activities I didn't know about, which is likely."

"Look at it from a different angle."

"You mean like perhaps she actually does have supernatural powers?"

I regretted my sarcastic tone as soon as the words left my mouth. Lauren was trying to help and indeed was being helpful. Wasn't her fault that I wasn't making as much progress as I needed to.

"Maybe most of what you believed about Kate had been the product of an overactive imagination fueled by your distaste for Trump," she said. "Perhaps her soirées had been harmless networking events and the deaths of the clients she'd referred had been coincidental."

"You don't believe that for a minute."

"I'm trying to get you to look at the situation with fresh eyes."

My eyes were so tired that I'd have needed several oil tankers full of Visine to refresh them.

We sat and thought some more.

"What if she's not out to destroy Trump but rather to protect him?" she asked.

"Hmmm. That would be contrary to everything she said and did, but it might explain her protection," I said. "Maybe Trump, or his people, had Zhukov killed because of the pee tape. Walker had just discovered a connection between Hakan and the Russians and the Turks—perilously close to the subject of the Flynn investigation and the companion one looking into collusion between the Trump campaign and the Russians."

"Curtis' plan to kill off Rust Belt whites and de Caldas' assistance in that scheme speak for themselves," she said. "What about McKuen?"

"That one's an outlier, but maybe he had information on Kate, via his frat brother, that she needed to cover up. Of course, he could also have been set upon by a gang of Trump-haters—unlikely, but these days, senseless violence is far from unthinkable."

"Sounds like you're on to something."

"Hmmm," I said.

"Well, that's interesting. Perhaps, though, you'd like to expound on that?"

"When Trump had told me that Margarette would do *anything* for him, maybe he wasn't talking about sex, and she was his dirty trickster from the beginning."

"Okay."

"If, through presidential connections, she'd wormed her way deep into the Secret Service or better yet the NSA, that might account for the absence of an electronic footprint. That she was supporting Trump and knocking off his enemies would go a long way toward explaining why she'd been using me."

"Keep going."

"Actually, she'd explained it. Her victims all had reason to retain lawyers. She wasn't going to use me to assassinate the President. She intended to use my supposed shooting of the FBI agents as a pretext for blaming me, thus, giving her a free hand to frame me for my clients' deaths, putting a lid on an investigation that might otherwise lead to her."

I didn't articulate the balance of that thought—under that scenario, I'd likely be killed resisting arrest or soon thereafter by a modern-day Jack Ruby.

"Perhaps Curtis hadn't killed himself but had been Jack Rubied," I said. "No more loose ends, everything tied in a nice neat mobius strip, tighter than the increasingly painful knot in my stomach."

"Can you prove any of that or at least put together a sufficiently credible story to interest the FBI?"

"What if I were to post last night's outline on Facebook? Perhaps some social media devotees would share my post and others would add their own information to it." Words started to flood from my mouth, until I sounded like Kate in her phony manic phase. "There have to be many people who'd attended her soirées, or served as drivers, musicians or waiters, and have concerns about what went on there. If a news outlet, even a disreputable one, picked up on it, others, including some more reputable ones, might follow. I don't know much about how social media works—such information is forbidden to us senior citizens—but that makes sense doesn't it?"

"You don't need the social media," Lauren said. "Emily would be delighted to help. Spiff up your outline and send it to her."

"Give me a half hour or so. I'll call when it's ready for you to look at."

Lauren left me to do my work.

I started putting my outline in the appropriate form to grab her attention, but within fifteen minutes abandoned the idea. If Emily were to publish an article in the *Huffington Post*, it would merely be one of a daily flow of Trump-related allegations, and hardly the most credible. At best a left-leaning congressman would call for an investigation. Barely a day went by when a congressman didn't call for an investigation into Trump. Those demands were stacked up like planes trying to land at LaGuardia in a pre-Thanksgiving blizzard.

In anticipation of such an article, Kate's hacker collaborators were undoubtedly already undermining my credibility by creating an extensive record of my supposed involvement with terrorists, provocateurs and other malcontents. That was one of the few things she'd told me in the car that I believed. Once she had that in place, she'd arrange for law enforcement to find the shotgun and with a minimal amount of investigation they'd uncover the fruits of her hackers' efforts. I'd be debunked as well as dead.

So while contacting Emily could be a last resort, I needed to come up with better.

Back to undirected thinking in the hope of an epiphany.

"I have a better idea," I called to Lauren in the bedroom. "I'll go over Kate's head."

"What does that mean?"

"I'll tell you in a few."

I called my right-wing law school friend, James Kaplan.

"Jesus, Matt, do you know what time it is?"

His angry, croaky voice communicated that he thought I'd give a shit about waking him.

"No, but if your watch is broken, I'll check for you," I said, cheery. "James, I need a huge favor, and lucky for me, you owe me big time."

"Oh, fuck. It's good you woke me. I'm about to be late for the dentist. I'll call you later."

He hung up.

I called back. He didn't take my call.

I texted him. Call me ASAP.

Nothing.

Sure, he didn't believe that global warming was man-made or thought that the Republicans would come up with better, cheaper health care, but how could he possibly have thought he could avoid me?

I told Lauren what I had in mind. She wasn't enthusiastic but had no better idea. So I showered and chugged hot coffee while I dressed. Having burned a layer of skin off my esophagus, I headed for the Chrysler Building.

XV
The Blood-Dimmed Tide at its Flood

Despite the constant negative press covfefe. Donald J. Trump,
May 31, 2017

The tallest building in the world for the eleven months, the
Chrysler Building represents a pinnacle of Art Deco design. That,
however, had nothing to do with why I was here. James Kaplan
would soon pass through the lobby on his way from Dr. Klineman's,
the dentist he'd recommended to me several years earlier when I'd
had a tooth-rearranging bicycle accident and mine was on vacation.

About ten minutes after I arrived, Kaplan appeared, walking fast
for someone in his late sixties with an artificial hip and over a
hundred pounds of excess fat. His ill-considered mustache, a recent
affectation, looked like a tiny mammal that had crawled there in
search of a warm place to die. His orange socks with black chevrons
contrasted with his conservative navy pinstriped suit and starched
white shirt but went well with his orange and black rep tic
emblazoned with tiger heads. The man had gone to Princeton, but
some would say it was time to get over an event that occurred more
than four and a half decades earlier.

"Hey, James, what a coincidence seeing you here." I flashed a
friendly smile. "May I walk you to your office?"

"Matt, you needn't stalk me. I told you I'd call you later."

"Later might be too late." I matched him step for step. "I need
a favor."

His squinched face communicated a disappointing lack of
enthusiasm.

"Not to worry. It'll be less painful than what Dr. Klineman just
put you through." Another smile. If only I could have conjured up
one as compelling as Kate's. "All I need is for you to set up a
meeting between me and Jared Kushner."

He gave me an incredulous look, then burst out laughing,

sending waves cascading through his jowls and stomach.

"For a minute there I thought you were serious," he said upon finally catching his breath.

"I'm serious as a dirty bomb in Times Square," I said. "Has to be today. The only hitch is that you can't tell him what it's really about. Best thing would be to tell him there's an emergency business matter. Set up a meeting or even lunch or drinks, and I'll show up."

He winced as if I'd stomped on his toes.

"The fate of the country depends on it," I said.

Under the force of my stare, his laugh died in his throat.

"Do you have any idea how many people want a meeting with Jared?" He turned toward me and took off his glasses, like Cronkite announcing Kennedy's assassination. "If I were to suggest that he meet with an over-the-hill, small-time litigator…"

Over-the-hill, small-time? I'll match my last five years' income against yours, you fat fuck.

He began walking, even faster than before. I still matched him step for step.

"That's one of the reasons why I told you not to tell him I'm involved."

Yet another grin. My facial muscles were getting an unaccustomed work-out.

"You do know that Jared is practically a one-man State Department. The guy just returned from Iraq and—"

"He looked cute in his flak jacket and chinos." My attempt at another smile failed. I felt as if I'd been struck with an attack of Bell's palsy, but all that had struck me was the lack of any reason to smile. "Much to everyone's surprise, he came back emptyhanded. I guess the world will have to wait another week or two for peace in the Middle East."

"Matt, are you okay?" He again stopped walking and stared at me as he would have if he'd actually given a shit about my wellbeing. "Your eyes are all spider-webbed, big bags under them. Your skin has a greenish tint. You really don't look—"

In light of my facial muscle rebellion, I went with a firmly set mouth and piercing eyes. "Jared will be eternally grateful to you for setting up this meeting. Okay, not eternally but he'll be beholden to you until you're too old and feeble to care. Maybe you'll even get to handle the bankruptcy proceeding for the Kushner real estate empire once foreign money flees after the impeachment."

He looked as if he'd swallowed a bar of soap.

"If you're trying to convince him to persuade his father-in-law—"

"I'm not."

He sighed: no one would believe the shit he's had to put up from me; one more miracle and a conversion to Roman Catholicism, and he'd be a lock for sainthood.

"Fine, I'll listen, but only out of respect for our long friendship. Give me the elevator pitch, because your chances of convincing me are about the same as us being hit my meteors while standing here."

"I can't tell you the details," I said. "You'll have to take it on faith."

"If you told me you'd then have to kill me?" he said, his idea of clever repartee.

"No, but plenty of others would, and you'd be far from their first or last victim."

A purplish crease appeared between his eyebrows.

"Your hyperbolic horseshit isn't helping your case."

"Come on James, you know I wouldn't be here if it wasn't a true emergency. Have I ever asked you for anything?"

"I don't keep score."

Like hell you don't.

"What if I were to tell you that there's a highly credible threat to assassinate Trump?"

I no longer believed that that was Kate's goal, but I couldn't totally dismiss the possibility, and it was the only explanation that could be compressed into an intelligible elevator pitch.

"I'd tell you to call the Secret Service, and so would Jared. He's not in the personal protection game."

"You heard about the crash on East 42nd Street last night, where four people were seriously injured, including two FBI agents?" I said, dropping my voice to a portentous whisper.

"Yes. So?"

"I didn't pull the trigger on the gun that blew out the agents' tires."

"Phew." He wiped imaginary sweat off his brow. The guy was an old friend, but that didn't preclude his being an asshole. "That's a relief."

"But my prints are on the shotgun."

"Matt, you sound delusional, not that it matters, Jared isn't going to give a crap about your problems, real or imagined. His plate is overflowing with the world's problems, not to mention some well-publicized real estate issues approaching their crises points."

"I've read that his family's flagship property is taking on water. Who'd have thought that paying twice what it was worth would turn out to be a problem and that the lenders actually expected to be paid back. He claims to not be engaged with the family business, but that one's his fuck-up." I reestablished and held eye contact. "That's one of your deals, right? You can get his attention by saying there's a crisis there. Totally credible from what I read."

"No way I'm doing that."

"He knows me, from long ago, we'd had a pleasant lunch. Not only did he value my advice but also he laughed at my jokes."

"So call him yourself. Tell him you've come up with some new achingly clever witticisms."

"My emails and phone aren't secure."

"You're sweating like a pig. You really need help."

"Exactly. That's why I came to you."

"I'm sorry, Matt. You're on your own on this one."

He picked up the pace to make the light before it changed.

"You remember that time, when, very much against my better judgment, I covered for you about your *tête*-à-*tête* with your top-heavy associate? What was her name? Oh, right, Tanya Robison."

"Long fucking time ago," he said, breathing hard from the exertion.

"Your firm passed her over for partnership well within the statute of limitations," I said in a pleasant conversational tone. "I heard she was looking for a lawyer to bring a sexual harassment/gender-based discrimination case against you and your firm."

"Bullshit."

"You ever tell Cindy"—his wife—"about your fling with Tanya, or disclose to the firm that you were *schtupping* her while she reported to you?"

He stopped so short that his belly continued on for at least an inch.

"You better not be suggesting—"

"Calm down, James. I'm just shooting the breeze to fill up the time, so you can come around on your own. You're going to set up a meeting with Jared for me to pop in on, mostly because of your patriotism and loyalty to one of your oldest friends, but also because I'll do whatever it takes to make it happen. Nothing personal, but you force me to choose between my duty to my country and my duty to you. It wouldn't be an easy choice, but in the end…"

We stared at each other.

Finally, he blinked.

"Jared's probably not even in town. As you know, if you bother to read the papers, he and Ivanka are spending most of their time in Washington."

"A short flight by commercial airline, less by private jet. Probably only cost the taxpayers, low six figures."

"Jared's my most valuable connection, even though he's delegated running the business to others." He started walking again. I again matched him step for step. "No way I'd let you interfere with that."

I fiddled with my phone.

"Wow. What are we talking dollar volume?"

He puffed out his chest so far that it matched his already extended gut.

"Last year low seven figures."

"Impressive."

"Damn straight. I really stepped in shit."

It took me a few seconds to realize that, in this context, stepping in shit was a good thing.

"Is that all Kushner family real estate business or does it include stuff for the Trump Organization and Kushner and Ivanka personally."

"That's just the real estate. The other is well into six figures in billings. And I mean *well* into six figures."

"So your firm has resolved all the conflict of interest and emolument clause issues and also those involving the foreign investment money pouring in in the hope of gaining influence?"

He snickered.

"Just between us"—he dropped his voice—"some of it's more than a bit iffy, but that's the President's counsel's problem. I wouldn't say he's a rubber stamp, but the President doesn't like it when someone says no to him or his immediate family members. And Jared's more enmeshed in the family's business than he'd like or than he lets on. With his kooky sister being the alternative, he has little choice. At least that's how he sees it."

"I guess with the Republicans in control of Congress, no one's going to look too hard into the conflicts of interest or for that matter the foreign money."

"The liberal media is always sniffing around, but Trump's done a great job of casting them as the enemy." He smiled. "Even you have to admire his ability to get away with shit that would have sunk any normal President."

"Jared, though, must be touchy about stuff like that hitting the press. Surely he doesn't think of the President's counsel as a yes-man, wouldn't want the world to know how much legal fees he's running up on his real estate business, his reliance on foreign money that's seeking to buy influence or the extent of his continued involvement in the business. I bet he'd be pissed if your comments came out publicly. I imagine your firm's management committee would look for someone to blame."

"I don't know where you're going with this." He glared at me.

"I did tell you, didn't I, that I'm recording this conversation for a piece on law firms' self-serving resolutions of conflict issues in the time of Trump that I'm co-authoring for *The Huffington Post* with my friend Emily? She's their top writer/editor."

I played back what I'd just recorded.

He reached for my phone, fast for an old fat man. I jumped back. Fast for an old slim one.

"You fuck! You piece of shit!"

"James, please, use your inside voice. That an educated, mature professional would so rapidly stoop to vulgarity. It's disheartening."

He reached again. I jumped again.

"Give me the fucking phone!"

"Relax, I'm one of your oldest friends. And need I remind you that you owe me big time?" I said, the soul or reason. "You know I wouldn't do anything to hurt or embarrass you, not unless I was desperate, and in that case, as one of my oldest friends, you surely wouldn't let it come to that."

He sucked in his gut and stood up straight, literally pulling himself together.

"I don't know what you'd do in your current unhinged state, but I do know I want nothing to do with it, particularly as you've just threatened me."

I sympathized with his position. I myself wasn't so sure of the decisions I'd made in my unhinged state. Was my belief that I had to do something and that this course of action was the best *something* I could come up with sufficiently compelling for James to risk his career over?

"Threatened you? I'm just giving you a heads-up. As your friend, I'm telling you that you can't conceive of the amount of bad publicity, and concomitant shit, that will pour down on you if your casual attitude toward conflicts of interests and foreign bribe money and your criticism of the President and his counsel is made public."

"You're really pissing me off!" he said, voice low but harsh. "If you were to go to the press about any of this, the shit flowing down on you would be so much deeper and smellier. My prints aren't on any weapon used to shoot FBI agents. Push me hard enough, and I'll give them a call. So get the fuck away from me. You just threatened the wrong person. This conversation's over."

"I'm really sorry, James. Please accept my apology."

He rested a fat avuncular hand on my shoulder.

"Go home, Matt. Get some sleep. I'll email you the name of a top-flight therapist. I recommend that you call her. You really sound like you've gone off the deep end."

He began walking, and I again fell into step alongside him.

"What I apologized for was my failure to communicate the situation clearly. Shit flowing down on me is irrelevant, since if I don't see Jared, I'll be dead. I've crossed people who are more unhinged than you think I am and far more dangerous."

"You sound delusional," he said, but his voice lacked conviction.

"Don't count on that. You can't afford to be wrong here, James." I fixed him with my most serious stare. "If I'm killed, the material I put on my laptop last night will be all over the Internet, including Tanya Robison, your conflicts of interest, the plot to kill Trump, your opportunity to foil the plot, all of it." If I had the time, I'd add this part to my outline, if only so that post-mortem I wouldn't be seen as a liar. "An attempt to assassinate the President, and everything even tangentially connected to it, will get colonoscopic attention. If that were to happen, you'd be removed like a minor polyp."

He stared back, until his nerve failed.

"You're one big fucking prick. You know that?"

"Lauren tells me that every night. But, not to worry. Set this meeting up, and you'll come through this a hero."

I put my hand over my heart.

He shook his head.

I held him in my stare, then released him, and we marched in silence until we reached the entrance to his office building.

"James, how many times have you told me that you owe me for covering for you with Cindy, which I did even though it turned my stomach. Also, sending you the client that made you a partner, and representing you in that case that could've gotten you disbarred."

"I did nothing wrong."

"But the case could've gone the other way. Point is, you've many times acknowledged your debt to me. Now, I'm collecting."

I held him in my stare.

He sighed.

"No promises," he said, "but I'll think about what you told me."

"I'm coming up with you. I'll wait in your office."

He turned toward me.

"Matt, tell me the truth, no bullshit. Is the President's life really in danger?"

Probably not, but I'm not sure, and others' lives are in danger.

He stepped toward the entrance, as if trying to outrun my response.

"James, have I ever lied to you or been the least bit dishonest about anything, anything at all?" Well, except maybe for the last few minutes.

Ever the gentleman, I jumped ahead and held the door for him. We entered his lobby.

"You're plenty devious, but you always have done it in an honest way, I'll give you that," he said. "But you just threatened me twice, and you do seem quite unhinged."

"You think I'd do that if it wasn't life and death?" I asked. "And you think I'd threaten without an intention to carry through if I had to?"

"You really are an asshole."

"Stop the presses. We've finally got some real news."

He grimaced and shook his head. What had he done in a former life to merit being here with this friend/lunatic seeking to drag him through unimaginable shit?

"Is there a rational reason why you can't go to the Secret Service."

"There's a chance they're in on it."

He rolled his eyes.

"And you came upon this information how?" he asked.

"Someone I knew from when I was representing Trump thought I hated him enough to make me an excellent fall guy," I said. "If the choice comes down to the country's best interests or mine, I'll take the fall."

He shot me an incredulous look.

I shrugged: so maybe I'm a schmuck, at least I'm a generally honest one.

"Why Jared?"

"Because I'm pretty sure he's not involved. He and I have met, and I made a solid impression on him, even if it was more than a decade ago. Also, unlike many of Trump's toadies, he's smart enough to listen, capable of standing up to his father-in-law and seems to have Trump's ear." And dumb enough to manipulate. "And, hey, why not give him a chance to redeem himself after the scandal of his conspiring with the Ruskies?"

The press touted Jared as the smart one in the family—a low bar—and, looking for someone around the President they could praise, had frequently referred to him as a good listener.

"I thought you were going to say, 'because he's a *lansman*'."

"After all these years, you still view things through Jew-colored glasses," I said. "Better, I suppose, than my shit-colored ones."

He sighed like my grandmother who'd spent her formative years in the Pale of Settlement and had never completely overcome her fear of pogroming Cossacks. She'd had but a single question in the face of every news story: *Is it good for the Jews*? If she were alive today she wouldn't need to ask. Trump wasn't good for anyone, except maybe the super-rich, the Chinese, the Russians and the Iranians, and even they would suffer from a trade war, a real war, global warming or an economic collapse fostered by his naive economic policies.

"Against my better judgment—"

"Thank you. You won't regret it."

"You sure of that?"

Not wanting to lie to him, I made a confident face and put my hand over my heart.

Probably not wanting to hear the truth, he appeared to accept this at face value.

XVI
Hope Sung in the Key of Lunacy

The FAKE MEDIA is working so hard trying to get me not to use Social Media. They hate that I can get the honest and unfiltered message out. Donald J. Trump, June 6, 2017

It turned out that James had a legitimate business reason to meet with Jared Kushner, even if he had to exaggerate the urgency with which the problem needed to be addressed: 666 Fifth Avenue, the family's flagship investment, was falling into the toilet. Although he'd been distancing himself from the family business, while he brought about peace in the Middle East and reorganized the Federal government, 666—coincidentally the sign of the devil—was his responsibility. Everyone who'd offered to fish the property out of the crapper had ties to hostile or semi-hostile foreign governments and desired an explicit *quid pro quo* of governmental favors. Jared was looking for James' assistance in structuring a transaction in a way that wouldn't lead to his testifying under oath before a special prosecutor.

As luck would have it, Jared happened to be in New York. He cancelled a 2 P.M. meeting with a potential lender on James' sound advice that pursuing the transaction could result in an unpleasant piece on the front page of the now-thriving *New York Times*. One would have thought that Jared would've learned something from the fallout from his clandestine meetings with Russian bankers/FSB agents. Apparently, though, the Trump family, as Talleyrand said of the briefly restored Bourbon dynasty, "had learned nothing and forgotten nothing."

In his telephone call with Jared, James's halting speech, needless gilding of the lily and frequent repetition would have raised a red flag, if Jared had been paying attention. So much for his reputation as a good listener, on which I'd hung so much hope.

By the time James hung up, a saddle of sweat had stained his white shirt, a vein was throbbing in his temple, and his breath was coming in short, hard bursts. If I'd thought of a tactful way to pose the question, I'd have inquired whether his firm had a defibrillator handy.

"You owe me big time," he said.

"The entire nation owes you a debt of gratitude."

"But I plan to collect from you."

"Fair enough." If I lived. Otherwise, his claim against my estate would be dubious and with Lauren as my executor he'd better have a damn good lawyer.

"You're sure this isn't going to queer my relationship with him?"

Well, no.

"Have I ever let you down?" I said.

"Past performance does not necessarily predict future results."

I obliged him with a laugh.

He laughed as well, and our laughter fed off each other, not because of anything funny but we needed a release. Someone closed his office door with a nasty bang, this is a law firm, can't have laughter around here, what would the clients' think?

Two cheap-business-suited, fit-looking young men of humorless military aspect entered the small conference room where James and I awaited The Anointed One. I sat at a round table with five chairs and James, having stopped pacing when they entered, stood behind a chair like a footman waiting to serve a British aristocrat. At taxpayer expense, they patted us down and scanned us with electronic sensors, stopping just short of giving us prostate exams. Apparently having determined that we weren't mortal threats, the Secret Service agents led Jared into the conference room. I wasn't sure that I'd have done the same in their place. Sweating profusely, irises shrunk to jiggling pinpricks, and legs twitching, James fit the profile of the paranoiac assassin. Presumably, though, it was departmental policy to give old, fat white guys a pass. One of the agents belatedly scooped up a pair of sharpened pencils from the table. A good move; if the meeting were to go poorly, James might use them to stab himself in the jugular, his spurting blood threatening to ruin Jared's bespoke suit.

Jared's gaze lit on me, then flitted to his lawyer.

"Who's this?" Jared asked, his surprisingly squeaky voice as hostile as if I were offering him a plate of two-day-old pork tartare with cream sauce while wearing a T-shirt depicting Putin anally violating Trump.

"Hey, Jared. Great to see you again." Grinning, I stood and extended my hand. "Maybe you don't remember, but I used to represent your father-in-law. Back then you and I had a very enjoyable lunch. You like me."

"If you say so," he said, arms at his side.

Sitting, I wasn't offended. The President had had a similarly icy reaction when Angela Merkel asked him to shake hands, and she was the leader of the free world. Perhaps germaphobia was a feature of the new White House protocol. The snub, however, had a deleterious effect on James, whose face had become tinged with blue, as if he required an immediate application of the Heimlich maneuver.

"I'm not going to ask you again." Jared fixed James with a wilting stare. "What the hell is he doing here?"

"He in-in-insisted," James stuttered. "Said it's a matter of life and death. I had to... I..."

"James, you had to know that I wouldn't appreciate this sort of ploy," Jared said, in a tone so icy that I expected frost to form on the windows or James to jump out of one.

James made a sound like a cross between tuba being run over by a garbage truck.

"Jared, you're lucky I'm here," I said in my most charming tone. "You need my help."

"James, as you should've realized, I don't have the patience for this," Jared said, avoiding eye contact with me and giving no indication that he'd heard me. I wondered if Ivanka accused him of being on the spectrum.

He turned toward the door. James fought for breath.

"Remember Margarette, your father-in-law's receptionist, occasional mistress and dirty trickster?" I asked, in an affable conversational tone.

"Not that way I don't," he said, finally including me as well as James in his field of vision.

"Come on, Jared, think. Picture me a dozen years younger. We discussed, your coming nuptials, Ivanka's disapproval of Melania's and Margarette's nude photo spreads, and how your dad was faring in prison." That got his full attention, liberating my friend from Jared's hostile stare. A calculated risk, as I knew referencing his father's incarceration wouldn't endear myself to Jared. If, however, James sustained a myocardial infarction or brain hemorrhage, that would have derailed my plans, so I had to draw Jared's attention away from him. "We joked about Chris Christie, the U.S. attorney who prosecuted your dad, *throwing his weight around and having more chins than the Hong Kong phonebook.*"

"Oh, I remember you now." Finally, I merited a hostile stare. "Donald hated you."

"That was after he loved me."

"James, I expected better from you."

Jared's tone having gone from denial to anger to depression, I hoped to bring him to the bargaining stage and ultimately to acceptance. A good negotiator must believe in his position and believe that he will emerge victorious.

James crumbled. I regretted not finding out about the defibrillator when I'd had the chance.

"Jared, please just give me three minutes," I said. "You're by far James' largest client and certainly his favorite, you and he having bonded over AIPAC, etc. You know he wouldn't have brought you here unless he was absolutely certain you needed to hear what I have to say."

"These days most everyone I meet has his hand out."

"Mine's extended in friendship, fulfillment of the duty of national service, and a desire to help you avoid a disaster that neither you nor anyone close to you has seen coming."

"Make it two minutes," he said, in a tone of *noblesse oblige*. He scowled at his watch, as if it were betraying him by not ticking off the seconds fast enough.

"Margarette referred four clients to me. Three are now dead, including Muhammad-Ali Abdur-Rahkman, the supposed opioid terrorist. The other is in prison charged with trafficking in opioids on a massive scale. I was in the car last night when Margarette caused the crash involving two FBI agents."

"I couldn't help you even if I wanted to, which I most assuredly do not."

He took two steps towards the table. Having been dragged here under false pretenses, he relished the opportunity to use the allotted time to heap more abuse on James and me.

"Then we're on the same page, as I don't want your help," I said.

"Good. We're done here. James, do we have to meet about our deal or was that just—"

"Jared, *you* need my help." I extended my hand toward an empty chair. He remained standing. "Margarette *appears* to be the mastermind of a plot to assassinate the President."

I couldn't fully discount the possibility, and I thought that was the best way to ease into the discussion.

"Do I look like the Secret Service? Call them, if there's anything to this supposed plot."

Skin having taken on a greenish tinge, James leaned against a wall. Even if we were both a decade younger, I wouldn't have time to make it up to him for what I'd put him through.

"Thing is the *appearance* is different from the reality," I said. "The assassination plot is a ploy to cover up for a campaign to smoke out and kill the President's enemies and those who are on to her plan."

"I've heard enough." Jared's eyebrows knitted in anger.

"Not yet you haven't," I said, my harsh tone taking him aback. "The only way she could have gotten away with what she has would be if she has serious protection. Flynn is out, so maybe that means Bannon or... Well, you know better than I."

He snorted but stood where he was. His eyes had opened wider at my mention of Bannon. Hmm. Maybe there was a rivalry there I could exploit.

"I don't suppose you have evidence to back up these claims." While his tone had lost none of its hostility, he'd let the two-minute deadline come and go without mention. Perhaps we'd entered the bargaining phase.

I pointed at my laptop.

He cast a belligerent glance at James and a put-upon one at me, but he sat in the chair to which I'd directed him.

I walked him through my outline, pointing out Kate's anti-Trump rhetoric, the people I'd met through her and what happened to them. I then directed his attention to my conclusion that she was working directly, or indirectly, for the President, with protection from on high.

"I see a lot of coincidences but no evidence of anything other than that you're a typical knee-jerk Donald-hater with an overactive imagination," he said, his tone indicated that he thought he'd delivered the ultimate insult.

He stood.

"This whole thing stinks of putrefying bodies," I said. "If you're unwilling to follow the stench, others will, and you'll lose the ability to control the situation."

He rolled his eyes.

"I'm perfectly happy to take that risk. Bring this whole stinky pile of so-called evidence to *The Huffington Post*, *The Times* or whatever other left-wing, so-called news source you prefer. Maybe you have enough to persuade them to do their usual biased investigation. In the unlikely event that they think there's something to it, maybe they'll publish one of their so-called exposés, and some nutsy congressional leftist, like that Maxine Waters, will yet again call for a special prosecutor. That will go nowhere, like all her other ridiculous fantasies." He pointed a manicured finger at me. "But, a word to the not-so-wise: you'll be looking at one heck of a libel suit. And if this turns out to be the shakedown or blackmail attempt it appears to be, you'll be prosecuted to the fullest extent of the law."

He sat. I suspected he might not even have made a conscious decision to do so.

"Going to the press is my fallback," I said. "That, though, would be bad for the country, and leave it even more deeply wounded and divided than it already is. If I thought my revelations would be enough to get your father-in-law impeached and convicted, I'd go public in a heartbeat. But the spineless Republican Congress won't impeach as long as he has a favorable rating with a substantial number of their constituents. Also, the investigation would have to turn up a direct tie to him, which might or might not exist. So my going public would only further divide the country without having a decisive effect."

"Your two minutes are up. We're done," he said. "If you decide to go public, you sure as hell better be judgment-proof."

"If I'm right, Margarette and her confederates will continue to smoke out, entrap and murder people with anti-Trump agendas. Each act will be harder to cover up. One major slip-up and the entire story will come out, like Athena emerging from Zeus' head in full

196

battle-dress, my disclosures to the press having laid the groundwork. I'm here hoping to head off more deaths."

"As I said, Mr. Bloom, you have a decision to make. Not my problem." In spite of his forceful words, Jared's voice, drained of affect, conveyed none of its former arrogance or confidence.

James took a loud deep breath and let it out slowly.

"If Margarette is working for someone close to Mr. Trump and has high-level protection," James said, "why did she try to kill the FBI agents? Why frame you?"

"I suspect the agents were getting too close to uncovering her scheme and refusing to go along with orders to back off. She tricked me into getting in the car with her, knowing the FBI agents were tracking my movements and hoping to get them out in the open, where they could be disposed of, with me taking the fall. Easy enough with my connection to three dead clients and a Mexican criminal and her having no electronic footprint and no governmental records evidencing her existence. In the car last night, she said, 'I'm basically a ghost. No one can find me. No two people even know me by the same name. You, though…'"

"You have a fertile imagination," Jared said.

This time I sensed that his dismissive tone was real. I was losing him.

"Thank you. You know who else has a fertile imagination?" I paused for a three-count. "Steve Bannon with his nutsy conviction that, for a new world order to rise, there must be a climactic conflict between Islam and the West."

I didn't know what to make of Jared's tilting his head and squinting. I hoped he was thinking about what I said—painful process for him.

"So, you're a Good Samaritan, sacrificing for the public good," he said, more sarcastic than necessary.

He remained seated.

"If I had my own interests in mind, I'd publicize my story and push for being sued and prosecuted. The increased visibility would make it more problematic to kill me, and the publicity would be the best thing that happened to my career since I fired your father-in-law as a client."

He stared at me like I had tarantulas nesting in my eye sockets.

I responded in kind. Assholes didn't intimidate me, and I put most everyone that disagreed with me into that category.

"By the way, if something were to happen to me, that would add a whole lot of credibility to what I've written and saved to the cloud in various places, with bots programmed to flood the social media on my demise."

I didn't know the difference between a bot and a bat, but that was neither here nor there.

The stare from my blue eyes held his dark brown ones.

"I hope you're not suggesting that I would—"

"No, but I'm in the sights of Margarette and her handlers, and significant effort went into setting me up as a fall guy."

He appeared to be studying me.

"Well, good luck with that," he said. "I'd say it was good seeing you again, but it wasn't."

"I asked you here in order to give you the chance to backchannel this and stop Margarette before more people die," I said. "It's possible Margarette isn't conspiring to kill off Trump's enemies. You, though, are in a better position to find that out than I am…if you're smart enough to make the effort."

I paused for a ten-count to give him a chance to jump in, although I sensed that he wouldn't.

He continued to hold eye contact. I had him…almost.

"I'm handing you an opportunity that you can exploit to further your own interests, while furthering the country's," I said. "This sort of opportunity taken at the flood, leads on to fortune. Omitted, all the voyage of your life will be bound in shallows and in miseries."

I mentally slapped myself for drifting into pedagogy. The Athena/Zeus reference had been more than enough, even if his father had bought his way into Harvard for $2.5 million—payable in $250,000 annual installments.

He neither responded nor turned his attention to James, who'd recovered somewhat. It seemed that the prospect of furthering his interests had captured Jared's attention—perhaps he and Bannon were locked in a Manichaean struggle for the President's heart and mind—and that had given James a slender reed of hope.

"My file, even without further investigation by you and your people, already contains enough to be quite useful to you," I said. "Margarette has to have had protection on high to have had the federal databases scrubbed of all references to her and for the deaths she caused to be swept under law enforcement's rug. If her protector isn't you or your father-in-law, then he's someone whose misguided actions have already harmed your-father-in law's interests—and your own—and will do increasing damage."

He bobbed his head, seemingly thinking.

Fearing even the slightest bit of subtlety was wasted on Jared, I said, "This *someone's* fall from grace would elevate you and those you're allied with."

"I ask again, what do you want for yourself?" Curiosity replaced hostility.

"I don't want anything. I can take care of myself or I can't." I shrugged. In the negotiating zone, I was as indifferent to my fate as I appeared to be. "In which case I'll face the consequences."

He nodded, indicating nothing more than that he'd heard me.

"Margarette and whomever she's reporting to need to be dealt with, with extreme prejudice," I said. "Maybe a quiet plea bargain that puts them away, without full public disclosure, or a fatal accident, like how Russians that displease Putin just happen to fall out of windows. Perhaps that ugly black spot on Bannon's face turns out to be a melanoma, and he needs to resign for medical reasons—assuming, that is, that Bannon is the ultimate baddy here. Even if he isn't, it might be in everyone's interests if he is persuaded to take the fall for the people he reports to. He could even be consigned to the basement, like a physically deformed madman locked away from view, scribbling on his whiteboard, barred from further contact with the press or meaningful contact with the President."

Jared tented his fingers.

He was thinking, and that, being something he wasn't so good at, would only lead to trouble for him. Perhaps, motivated by the information I shared, he'd pick a turf war with Bannon. Bannon would fight back. Leaks would begin to trickle out of the White House, then flow, then flood. Kate would likely be seen as an unaffordable luxury, perhaps even be terminated with extreme prejudice.

I warned myself that I shouldn't get cocky, I still had a ways to go with Jared.

A squiggly smile crawled onto James' face, then sought refuge under his moustache.

I thought I saw a nascent smile form on Jared's lips, but that might have been my optimistic projection.

"With some ambivalence, I decided it was best to give you the chance to deal with this privately and with finality," I said. "Now, all I can do is hope you'll do the right thing."

"And if I ignore what you've told me?" he asked, giving no indication of which direction he was leaning.

"If I don't hear from you—or get a clear indication from you—by this time tomorrow, I go public and trust that the truth will rise to the top of the fake news."

He frowned.

"Why are you dropping this turd in my lap?"

"To give you the opportunity to act in your self-interest." I still had his attention, but from the look on his face, I deduced that I hadn't answered his question to his satisfaction. "When we had lunch, you impressed me as a decent guy. I had a connection to you through James, and according to the news reports you've been a sane, intelligent and moderating influence on your father-in law. His stupidest tweets coming on Shabbat when you're not around."

"You shouldn't believe everything you read," he said.

"After a lifetime of litigating, I don't believe much, but here's one thing: in spite of the mountain of evidence to the contrary, I believe truth eventually triumphs over falsehood."

"Is he as weird as he seems?" Jared asked James.

"Weirder, but he has an infuriating habit of turning out to be right. Good instincts or good luck, no one knows which."

"Thank you for setting this up, James." I stood. "Jared, good to see you again. I trust you'll do the right thing."

I walked out.

Glancing behind me, I saw Jared's and James' jaws drop, my abrupt departure having taken them by surprise.

Twenty-three hours after our meeting, my phone lit up with a news report that, after a clash with Jared, Bannon had been demoted. Trump publicly dissed him, and he appeared to be on the way out.

Of course, he would fight back.

While Bannon was a far better strategic thinker than Jared, Jared was family, so that leveled the field. The process had begun. The backbiting and the drip, drip, drip of leaks would interfere with Trump's plan to aggrandize himself at the expense of the country and most particularly the people who voted for him. Assuming I'd read the situation correctly, the drips would eventually become a deluge that would undermine the whole shaky edifice. I hoped it would take less than four years.

If not, the nation deserved Trump. One problem with democracy was that the people generally got the leaders they deserved. But at least I'd done my part, or tried to.

Lauren hugged me when I got home and congratulated me, even though I couldn't miss her tone of doubt.

"What about Kate?" she asked.

"Probably We'll never know."

"And the FBI, when they find the shotgun?"

"I hope their investigation will be quashed."

"You got no assurance of that, though."

Before I saw him, I smelled the homeless man crouched on the sidewalk, his back against the side of my office building. His sign said, "I bet you $1 you'll read this sign."

I gave him a dollar and a smile.

He handed me a ringing phone.

"It's for you," he said.

He stood shook off his smelly rags, wig and false beard and walked away, leaving behind a jar of one-dollar bills.

As my curiosity wrestled with my good sense, I neither pressed the green button nor tossed away the phone. It kept ringing. Fighting dirty, of course, curiosity gave good sense a knee to the groin, followed by a kidney chop and a vicious kick to the chin. With good sense down and out, I pushed the button.

"Congratulations! Great work! I knew you could do it," said a familiar, if unfamiliarly ebullient, voice. "You stopped the conspiracy dead in its tracks just before it was about to get really ugly,"

"You didn't need me," I said. "You could've just walked away."

"I had professional responsibilities, like you with Trump, when you couldn't just dump him because of your ethical duty to put your client's interest ahead of your own. So you had to hang in there and favorably settle his cases."

"I didn't realize that professional teases had such a strict code of conduct."

201

What was wrong with me that I so easily fall into repartee with a murderous psychopath?

"It's worse for us, there's no governing body like a bar association. All we have is our reputations, which depend on us keeping our word with our employers."

A cop gave me a casual glance. I shuddered with guilt-born concern, but without breaking stride, he strode over to a sidewalk hotdog stand.

"What about your obligation to humanity?" As soon as my question left my mouth, I realized how lame it sounded.

"Humanity? Hmm. Let me think about that," she said. "Seems I helped. There are one-point-four billion people in China, four times the U.S. population. They all, to some degree, benefit from Trump's diplomatic blunders, particularly his abandonment of the Trans Pacific Partnership and the consequent strengthening of China's hand in Asia. His pulling out of the Paris Climate Accords has stimulated the European and Chinese alternative energy businesses, helping those counties' economies and, thus, their populace."

"How about the four murders and the injuries in the 42nd Street shooting?" For whatever reason, I was curious about her mental processes.

"While perhaps justified, I can do without your self-righteousness. Curtis, whom I single-handedly smoked out, had an entire cell that we quietly rolled up. Had he gotten the chance to distribute the pills de Caldas was sending to him, the consequences would've been horrendous."

"Does that rationalization make it easier for you to sleep at night?" Stupid question to ask a sociopath.

"If I hadn't been around, it would've been worse. Certainly more clumsily handled." Her ebullience having bubbled away, she sounded exhausted.

"So, you were working for Trump?"

"Not directly. He can't be trusted to keep his mouth shut, can't focus long enough to make and stick to a plan, and he'd have probably wanted us to Putinize the media and worse."

"Who then?"

"Guess."

"Bannon, or his alt-fight friends, allied with Trump's Russian and Chinese lenders, or to be more precise, the spymasters they report to," I said after a moment's thought. "I suspect they all have vested interests in keeping Trump in power, manipulatable useful idiot that he is."

"See, you're even smarter than you think you are," she said. "Through the U.S. contingent, I got an official government position, and a classification of *Deep Undercover*—licensed to kill, like 007—making me off limits to law enforcement."

"I didn't know there was such a thing."

"There isn't. Ask anyone of us. We'll all tell you the same thing. We have no electronic footprint and complete deniability." I practically heard her smile and felt a slight burn in my retinas from its brilliance. "Grae and Anderson were going off the reservation, pursuing an investigation that could've gotten unpleasant for those in charge. Something had to be done, before they stumbled on an organization that didn't exist. But if it makes you feel any better, they're both out of the hospital."

"My role was to tie up the Walker, Zhukov, McKuen, Curtis and de Caldas loose ends?"

"That's what I told my superiors, but mostly I wanted you to expose what we were doing before things spiraled out of control."

"Seems things had done that from day one, certainly by the time Walker and Hakan were murdered."

"Purpose of this call wasn't to justify my actions. People have done far worse than me in the service of their governments."

"Sounds like you were servicing three governments."

"Three times as good, right?" I pictured her enchanting smile and felt sick to my stomach.

"So what was the purpose of this call? Just tell me in a few words. I need to get home and take a hot bath in Lysol."

"To congratulate and thank you, as I have, and to tell you that you're off the hook with the FBI," she said. "Just so you know, your meeting with The Boy Wonder pumped him up to take on President Bannon, thereby making the White House yet more dysfunctional. The AmeriKlan Idol knows all about the Trump family's collusive frolics with the Ruskies, and his Breitbart days taught him how best to leak such information and make it look like the leaks came from others. Who knows, maybe he'll end up back at Breitbart taking potshots from the alt-right at the Trump *globalists*."

"Good to know," I said, and in spite of my sarcastic tone, it was.

"The idea is to keep Trump in power but pathetically ineffectual."

"They're doing great then," I said, "but I still don't understand what was in it for you. Why did you do it?"

"Money, excitement. It happened in steps. I hardly noticed. I'd had a bit of a drug problem, dropped out of college, got a job with Trump as his receptionist, which led to side jobs like helping bring in illegal workers. Once we got the *Penthouse* thing behind us, I slowly transformed into the only woman around him whom he didn't treat like just another piece of ass. That was flattering. One thing led to another, and when he began thinking seriously about running, he farmed me out to the campaign dirty tricksters. By the time I realized what they expected me to do, I was in too deep."

"The frog in the pot of slowly heating water?"

"I hope we'll get the chance to work together again. On the same side this time. You're a little green, but you have good instincts."

"You're kidding."

"Of course, Lauren would have to give you permission."

"Well, great talking to you as always," I said, and in case she hadn't picked up on my level of disgust, added, "I'm going to throw the phone down a sewer grate."

"First, wipe it down, then crush it with your heel."

Some weeks later, a news story came out, under Emily Bovant's byline, about a former Penthouse Pet turned undercover Secret Service agent who was killed in a late-night head-on crash with a gasoline truck on I-95. According to the story, she'd been awarded several citations—in secret ceremonies, due to the nature of her work—for thwarting assassination plots. Although she'd been burned beyond recognition in the crash, Kate looked hot in the photo that accompanied the article. Lauren, said she looked like a slut and professed not to understand why I'd found her attractive.

I asked Emily about her sources.

"Matt, you know I can't disclose that," she said, punctuating her statement with a most irritating wink.